12/14

FC   scan

D0958078

Buffalo Boy and Geronimo

a novel
by
JAMES JANKO

Curbstone Press

First Edition: 2006

printed in Canada on acid-free paper by Best Book / Transcontinental
Cover design: Les Kanturek

Portions of this book have appeared in different form in *The Sun* and
The Massachusetts Review. The author thanks their editors.

The quotation from "Beyond Love" by Octavio Paz, *Early Poems
1935-1955*, translated by Muriel Rukeyser, is reprinted by permission
of New Directions Publishing Corp.
China Men by Maxine Hong Kingston is published by Random House.

This book was published with the support
of the Connecticut Commission on Culture
and Tourism, the National Endowment for
the Arts, and donations from many
individuals. We are very grateful for this
support.

NATIONAL
ENDOWMENT
FOR THE ARTS

Connecticut Commission
on Culture & Tourism

Library of Congress Cataloging-in-Publication Data

Janko, James, 1949-
  Buffalo Boy and Geronimo / by James Janko.— 1st ed.
    p. cm.
  ISBN 1-931896-19-4 (pbk. : alk. paper)
  1. Vietnamese Conflict, 1961-1975—Fiction. I. Title.
  PS3610.A5697B84 2006
  813'.6—dc22
                                      2005030285

published by
CURBSTONE PRESS   321 Jackson St. Willimantic, CT 06226
     phone: 860-423-5110   e-mail: info@curbstone.org
                    www.curbstone.org

For Maxine and my parents,

for Chanpidor,

for Scoby and Vicki and Jeremiah,

and in memory of

Robert Ray Boeskool

Outside the night breathes, it expands,
full of great hot leaves,
of mirrors of combat:
fruits, talons, eyes, foliage,
backs that glisten,
bodies that push their way through other bodies.

Octavio Paz

Men build bridges and streets when there is already an amazing gold electric ring connecting every living being as surely as if we held hands, flippers and paws, feelers and wings.

Maxine Hong Kingston
From China Men

When a water buffalo dies, we do not eat it. We bury it in the field where it worked, where we ourselves will one day be buried.

Vietnamese peasant
Cu Chi countryside

May all beings be free of suffering.
May all beings be free.

The Vietnamese call the Vietnam War the American War.

They spell the name of their country with two words—Viet Nam.

They call the Ho Chi Minh Trail the Truong Son Trail.

They call the Milky Way the Silver River.

Buffalo Boy and Geronimo

1
Buffalo Boy

In my next life I will be the sun, I will light the fields.
I will eat java birds, rice birds, before they steal our harvest.
I will be the green of the rice, the yellow of sunlight.
I will have the strength of a bull buffalo, the body of a mountain.
I will carry a rice field and a pretty village girl on my spine.

His boldest song had to be sung in whispers. Nguyen Luu
Hai sang to his buffalo and to the sun on planted fields, the
light of trees, but he did not sing to his family. At age
fourteen, Hai lived with his mother and twin sister in a village
near Cu Chi. Had Ma Xuan heard him singing of heavenly
light as his light, of buffalo strength as his strength, of a
mountain's body as his body, she would have interrupted.
"Why waste your time making noise? You think you're
special?" She would have reminded him of the danger of
pride, the sin that separates an individual from his ancestors,
his family, his elders, his village, the ten thousand helpers
who guide his life.

So his Sun Song was not for human ears. He whispered
it to sky and trees, sunlit fields, and to Great Joy, his bull
buffalo, the largest in the village. The animal never
complained when Hai rode on his back. After the boy and his
family worked in the fields in the morning, Hai would hoist
himself on Great Joy and suddenly be taller than most houses
in the village. The boy liked to brag to the animal about how
tall he had grown. He would scratch the beast's ears and
whisper, "Taller than our village, tall as the young bamboo.
Tree-tall, sky-tall. Taller than an American soldier. Tall as
my bull buffalo and the blowing wind."

He would slap the beast's right flank and sing out, *"Di! Di!"* As Great Joy began his lumbering stride, Hai felt beneath him the power of a moving mountain. The buffalo's curved spine had a mountain shape, and he could carry a boy or ten boys, could drag a plow over ripe earth, could haul a cart heavy with rice from one village to another. He would snort and breathe loudly, and Hai would imitate, snuffle the air into his belly. Nostrils flared, the boy took buffalo breaths, Great Joy breaths. Nose in the wind, eyes shifting, shoulders raised and rounded, he rode across the fields.

He wondered if Great Joy smelled what he smelled. The moisture of a tree near the river. Or a stone in the sun, a ripening field, a white flower, a fish, a muddy shoreline. For Great Joy, did rice grass have a fresh sourness, a smell of longing? Did a fish smell salty and cool? Did a white flower smell of sunlight and rain? Did a river have a night smell, a smell of darkness? Hai wondered if the animal knew more of these intimacies than he would ever know, if the smells—indescribable—were richer and more complicated than those funneled through human nostrils. Once, petting the buffalo along the ridge over its snout, he whispered, "Tell me your secrets, tell me." The buffalo snorted, shook his great head, and licked Hai's fingers. The boy sniffed two hands that smelled of salt and heat and rain.

The animal sheltered him each night. In the sandbagged pen near the family home, Hai curled beside Great Joy, and on nights when the sky roared with wind and fire, his mother and sister also took refuge beside the animal. Sometimes when sleep came, if it came, Luu Hai dreamed of birds that scarred the earth, of green rice fields turned to flames, of trees and huts burned, ravaged, of gaping holes in the ground large enough to bury all the buffalo. But sometimes he dreamed that he and his father rode Great Joy, that his father had returned with powerful arms to swat the birds from the sky, that the buffalo used the fury of hooves to stomp fire into ashes. In dreams, Hai would see his father alive, arms and legs whole, no shrapnel or belly wounds, each part of him in place: eyes, teeth, arms, legs, the wholeness of a body. The boy would wake, reach for his father's arms, and curl into the round warmth of the buffalo. Great Joy took care of him, comforted him, harbored him. And each morning, though often hungry himself, Hai left offerings of food at his father's grave.

Soldiers came and went, came and went, eyes like hammers. They would search the huts of the village, poke their rifles through thatch roofs, pound their eyes in every direction. Their uniforms were identical, their faces nearly the same, except for one who seemed to admire Hai and his buffalo. On the shore of the Sai Gon River, the boy once saw a soldier separate from the others. As his American platoon searched the village, he stood in a small cove and skipped stones in the river. After playing, he squatted, a brown-faced man, his elbows on his knees, his rifle propped against a log, and smiled at Hai and Great Joy. The boy flickered a smile—pure reflex—then scolded himself. This brown-faced demon had a rifle, he too was an invader. He might wish to kill the buffalo, taste its meat, strengthen his body. Hai petted Great Joy and advised him, "Don't trust this man; don't trust his brothers." Most Americans had a frenzied, hungry look as if they could devour every living thing and instantly crave more.

One morning in late April, the heat stifling, monsoon clouds on the horizon, the foreigners burned two huts and left. An hour later, stooped between his mother and sister, transplanting *ma* rice—bright green—in a watery field, Hai heard a sound overhead, a distant buzzing and then a roar, and then the sun fell from heaven. He had tethered Great Joy to a coconut palm thirty meters away. Hai saw a gold light splinter the palm. He heard the buffalo's cry, the thunder of disbelief. The boy ran forward and saw a hoof not attached to a leg, a length of bone in tall grass. The beast crumpled on his side, eyes vague, head tilted at a crooked angle. Hai heard the cries of his sister, his own cries, but the buffalo had stopped thundering. He touched the animal's throat and whispered, "Wait, hold on. Someone will know what to do. Someone will help you." Hoof, bone, flesh—maybe someone would piece them back together. Blood gushed from the spine and flanks, but the belly was still rounded, still whole. Hai placed a handful of rice grass in the open mouth that wouldn't move, wouldn't chew. Before it was too late, he lowered both hands to the animal's belly and took comfort in the warmth.

In the late afternoon, Hai dug a hole at the edge of the rice field. Quoc Nam, his cousin, and Qui, his friend, helped him widen it and deepen it, and they harnessed the carcass to Nam's buffalo and Qui's buffalo, and the buffalo survivors dragged Great Joy over the field into his grave.

The next morning, Hai found fresh meat in the shallows of the Sai Gon River. A great bird, an osprey, had drowned, and clutched in its talons a carp the length of Hai's leg. Newly dead, the yellow-brown eyes of the bird were iridescent. It must have dove fiercely, sunk its claws into flesh, and plummeted in darkness. Hai imagined the thrashing of wings, the desperate plunge of the fish. At first, the carp must have swum toward deep water, and later, as it was dying, it rose in the grip of the bird in an upswell of currents. Hai found the bodies in the cove where Great Joy had often drank and bathed. With effort, he unhooked the claws and separated the fish and bird. He extended one osprey wing, then the other, and marked where the edges of feathers touched earth. Hai could have lain down on the wings, for they were longer than his body. He hid the carp in tall grass and carried home the osprey. He rested, drank a ladle of water, and returned for the fish that lay heavier in his arms.

Midday. His mother and his sister Nhi were taking strips of salted fish meat and bird meat from a barrel and hanging them on a bamboo rack in the heat of the sun. Hai, squatting beside them, said, "Two gifts. One from the sky and one from water."

"We can give some away," said his mother. "Your Aunt Hoa and Aunt Lan need meat. They need it as much as we do."

Hai hesitated. "Can we give a little to Miss Thien's family? She has no mother or father, only her grandma."

"We'll see."

"Just a few slices," he said, "to dry on her fish rack. She and her grandma would be very happy if we offered them some meat."

Three days after Great Joy's burial, Hai and Nhi and their mother, Ma Xuan, began the first weeding of the rice field. The task would be less arduous than usual since much of the field had been destroyed by bombing. Several paddy dikes were damaged, and in some places the irrigation water had bled back to the river. Squatting near his mother, Hai glanced at the adjacent field where Miss Thien worked beside her grandma. The girl was his age, fourteen, nearly fifteen, and in Hai's eyes she was lovely. He recalled the morning in the fields when he almost touched her hand in passing. Her breath came fast, her shoulders stiffened, and maybe this meant she liked him. He had called her name, but she turned away and said nothing. She was like most girls of the village: secretive, cautious, too shy to flirt with boys.

Now he swayed as he plucked weeds from the paddy. How did a girl change her body, change the shape of her chest? How did Le Minh Thien spread her hips wider over the earth, and deepen the print of her feet on rice fields and shorelines? Maybe soon the girl would grow wings, lift herself in the air, and soar above the fighter bombers, the *may bay sau rom* that light the earth with fires. He looked up and saw a bird in the far sky, maybe an osprey. As he watched it circling, drifting higher, he asked himself why his own body changed slowly. Luu Hai wished he were wider, stronger, twice the size of an American soldier. At night, often without warning, his middle part thickened and grew hard, but every other part stayed skinny. Now he glanced at the sun and envied its beauty, its bulk. With the help of rain it turned rice stalks bright green in fields cratered by bombs, illuminated the last leaves of skeletal trees, and no matter what happened on the earth that received its warmth, it traveled the sky each morning and afternoon, a force as magnificent and opposite as the new darkness of a girl's body. The sun could not be stopped, nor the stars, nor the darkness of a girl.

Hai plucked another weed and pictured Thien's walk: her hips that swayed, threw shadows; her body as graceful as a moving river. Whether she walked in moist fields, stooped and pulled weeds, or gathered water at dawn, shouldered buckets on a pole, her body remained fluid. *Water girl*, he thought, *rice girl. Girl of the bua ruong, the best soil. Village girl, grass girl. Girl of the changing body.* Hai shaded his eyes and looked toward the Sai Gon River. Something carried the water, formed waves, and it seemed that Thien, in her growing body, was carried by something larger than the currents of a river. *"Cac,"* he whispered, *"day duong"* (oceans). Fish-like, Thien could plummet in water, but with sharp eyes, osprey eyes, he could watch her body changing. Maybe she would swallow some darkness, change the shape inside her, and if it were necessary, if she could find no other way to survive, she would grow wings out of water. She would lift herself in the air, fly far above fire, and those on earth would see a dark bird in heaven. Strong wings were better than hands, feet, hooves, claws, fins. The winged ones had to be careful only when they touched down on the earth for food.

The boy ate his lunch, rice balls wrapped in banana leaves. He let the rice moisten on his tongue before he began chewing. Hai thought of how happy he would be if tonight his mother let him bring Thien offerings of fish meat and bird meat. He imagined telling the girl that he caught the carp with a giant worm, that he snared the osprey with a net after it lighted on bushes. But Thien, aware of how much he liked her, would probably know he was telling stories. Maybe the boy would speak truthfully, tell her what he now told his mother and sister who ate beside him: "Great Joy helped me find the food, who else?" He paused, reflected, and said, "And maybe the osprey helped me a little; all my life I've had eyes sharp as a bird's."

Before sundown, when it was still safe to move through the village, he came to Thien's house with strips of salted carp and osprey. He hoped to hand her the white plate that held the offerings, but Ba Ly, Thien's grandma, came to the door, accepted the meat, and thanked him. "Lucky gifts," said the boy. "I found a bird and fish in the river." He stepped forward and smiled. "They were dead," said Hai, "but they clung to each other and washed up near the shoreline." He couldn't see Thien from the doorway, but he imagined her listening and watching from the hut's shadows. "A few minutes after sunrise," he said, "I spotted them floating. I waded in and lifted them in my arms—many kilos." He spread his arms, turned his palms skyward. "Wings wide as a man is long," he said, "or longer." He grimaced. "So I used all my strength to carry them home"—no need to tell them he carried one at a time—"the fat fish and the long bird."

Something sweet, maybe mangos, mixed with the fleshy smell of carp and osprey.

"These strips of meat need to dry more," he said. "They're not ready to eat."

"I know."

"We can be grateful for my buffalo," said Hai, but he was not sure how to elaborate. It occurred to him that those outside his family circle might not understand that a slaughtered animal had guided him to this bounty. "I was lucky," he said, "but I also had some help."

Ba Ly, puzzled, said, "Yes, your mother's a saint, be sure to thank her." She bowed slightly and left Luu Hai standing outside the door.

Maybe to impress Thien he would need to bring her a live fish from the Sai Gon River. He already had poles, bamboo sticks, hooks fashioned from sewing needles, but he needed to make fishing line from green worms—*sau cuoc*. The next morning, after visiting the graves of his father and his buffalo, he found several worms on a low branch of a *sau* tree. He plucked the fattest ones, each worm about the size of a rich man's thumb, and lay them in a wooden box. His father had once shown him how to peel the flesh with a knife, then use his fingers to unravel the intestines. The inner parts of each *sau cuoc*, approximately three meters in length, could be transformed into fishing line strong as nylon. Hai, his father's knife in one hand, lifted the fattest worm from the box. He glanced behind him at the rice fields, the wedges of green, the bamboo forest north of the village. His father's grave was nearby, and the buffalo's, and the sun would warm their bones, their spirits. Maybe *cha* could somehow witness his son's newfound skill: making fishing line from worms. Hai had to catch fish, not merely to impress Thien, but to compensate for three seasons of poor harvests, ravaged paddies. Head bowed, he peeled the flesh of the worm and imagined his father's approval. "Don't grow soft," *cha* would say, "or the family ends up starving." Hai worked quickly and stripped the flesh of each worm. Now he could unravel the intestines and soak them in vinegar until they had the hardness and suppleness of nylon. Struggling with nausea, the boy did what was required. Come morning, if he was still alive, he could fasten the ends of the intestines, dig up earthworms for bait, and cast a line into the deep waters beyond where he had found the osprey and the carp.

That night he could not sleep. He tried to pretend he lay near his buffalo, but there was no *bua ruong* smell, no smell of paddy earth, and no belly and hooves that smelled of river mud and fishes. He lay on a mat between rice bins, separated from the rest of the hut by a bamboo curtain. If there was shooting, or if the sky became loud with planes, he would hurry to his mother and sister and guide them into the tunnel he and his father had carved beneath the cookstove. They would huddle there, or he would lead them through a side tunnel and into the now vacant buffalo pen fortified with sandbags. For Hai, nights of silence were often worse. Only shooting or bombs allowed him to join his family, and while he waited for morning there was no buffalo for warmth, no father on a nearby mat, no one in this hut or this village to offer the comfort of their body. He wished he were young enough to share his mother's bed. A few years ago, she and his sister Nhi wouldn't have minded if he lay between them.

Now his mother would shoo him away. "Go on," she would whisper. "You have your own place to sleep."

Shortly before dawn, Hai asked himself if his family should look for another home. Since the good rice was mostly gone, since they now ate chicken rice, *tam* rice, maybe they should pack their belongings and search for another village. Although his mother had told him the worst tragedy was to leave one's home, to leave the fields, abandon ancestral graves, Hai could not imagine his family or his village surviving much longer. He wished his elders could advise him, provide direction, but his village was mostly fatherless. The old men, Ong Quan and Ong Truong, made important decisions after consulting with Viet Cong cadre. The young men, the fathers, had vanished into Viet Cong or Republican ranks, or were lost to bombings and shootings, or were taken away by various factions (American, Republican, Viet Cong) to unnamed places their families could not locate. Hai, now among the oldest boys of the village, carried the responsibility of an elder. He sympathized with the Viet Cong, often helped set booby traps and dig tunnels, but he had no desire to live his daylight hours underground, only to emerge at night to harass whatever enemy force camped near the village. Hai knew he would soon have no choice but to be a soldier. He could join the Republicans, support the invaders, or he could live in the tunnels north of the river, a half-buried soldier with the Viet Cong.

He slept briefly and dreamed. He showed Thien his fishing line, told her how he made it from worms, and she followed him along a riverside trail to the cove where he tossed his line toward deep water. The river roiled with fish: carp and cod, a few catfish; one of the carp was the length of the girl's body. Hai tended his line and waited. Nothing happened, no bites. Soon Thien lay on the shore, asleep, but she woke when a great fish took his line and pulled him toward water. The girl stood and shouted, "Let go of the pole! Let go!" Hai, smiling, waded out waist-deep in the river, then chest-deep, and worked the fish until it was too exhausted to fight him. After several minutes of struggle, he dragged his catch to the shore and stopped its frantic flopping with a blow to the skull. For the girl he revealed his sun-strength, his power to pull a great fish from an untamed river. He was happy momentarily, but then he shuddered. The fish, once beautiful, was dead. Thien lay on the shore, asleep again. Hai heard his father's voice: "Catch another one, a bigger one. Stop pitying the world before the world starves you." Hai re-baited his hook, cast toward a deeper hole, and waited. The boy admired the fish darting and circling, the dark waters swelled with currents, the muscles of the river. No bites now, no struggle. Nothing had to die. Again he heard his father's voice: "Watch your line, stay alert." Hai fought the urge to lie down on the shore and curl his stick-shaped body into the gracefulness of Thien.

He woke at first light, dug up earthworms near the river, and went fishing. He fished all morning, caught nothing, and moped his way back to the rice field.

"Be patient," said his mother. "You can't hurry the river. Maybe tomorrow you will catch a fish."

After lunch he began repairing a dike, and it was then that he saw a bird over the river, another osprey. Maybe it was hungry for fish, or maybe it longed for its mate, the drowned osprey. The bird appeared more majestic than sad, however, and Hai envied the wings that gave flight, the keen eyes that could observe the river and earth from here to the horizon. If Americans crossed distant fields, the osprey would see movement and light, the dark silhouettes on bright grass, the spokes of sun on barrels of rifles. And it would see the bomb-torn paddies, the fringes of forests and hedgerows, and in one glance the oversized wings that soared toward the sun, or the helicopters that skated low and fast over the Sai Gon River. Hai wished that the osprey could send warnings, or that he too could fly. He imagined himself rising on wings, flying in a swift arc over the village to signal the approach of helicopters or planes. If soldiers came on foot, he would light in a field, gouge his talons in earth, and each family would retreat to a hut or a tunnel, and bring with them any object that might be viewed with suspicion. Butcher knives, tools, even sacks of rice would be placed in difficult-to-find caches. Once the enemy departed, Hai would touch down on the rice paddy nearest the village, fan his wings, strut and cackle. The villagers would emerge from hiding, thank him for his warnings, and prepare a feast from whatever food they could salvage. If their provisions of meat had already been used, Hai would catch fish in the river. Carp and cod, large and small, a variety of fish food. He would watch the river carefully, patiently, and avoid sinking his talons into a fish too great to carry upward through the sky.

The osprey flew away, but another—or maybe the same

one—appeared the following morning. Hai set down his shovel, stopped repairing a dike, and stood still as the bird traced a spiral thirty-five meters over the Sai Gon River. He wondered if Thien, from her family's rice field, had spotted the fisherbird. Hai lifted his arms and cackled. The osprey spiraled a long time, and then it seemed to halt momentarily, float effortlessly, before it folded its wings and plummeted toward water. Hai watched it split the light of the river's face, a dark blur that rose with a fish, silver and small, bright as jewelry. He heard a soft snapping sound, the breaking apart of fish bones. The osprey soared to a treetop nest a short distance downriver. Hai watched the rise and fall of the beak, the ripples of flesh torn from the fish, most likely a cod. He wondered if Miss Thien liked fresh fish fried in coconut oil and sprinkled with salt.

The next morning Hai caught a fish at sunrise. A carp, nearly three kilos, that he dragged through the shallows and onto the muddy shoreline. Flopping and twitching, the fish threw water sparks, drops of light. The boy struck the skull with the knotted edge of a stick. Soon the fish stilled and quieted, mouth agape, body sunlit. "Lord Buddha," Hai prayed, "forgive me." He looped a thin coil of rope through a gill, hoisted the fish, and saw it was nearly the length of his arm.

With his catch, he walked to the paddy where Thien and her grandma were weeding. He lifted the fish in both arms, said, "Lucky day," and they stared at him.

"A nice one," said Ba Ly. "Where'd you catch him?"

Hai motioned with his head. "There," he said, "where I saw an osprey catch a fish." He smiled, straightened his shoulders. "*Khong sao*," he said. "If you want to know where the fish are, you have to watch the great birds."

He swung the stringer over his right shoulder so that the fish hung down his back, silver and sunlit. He turned away, trusting Thien would watch him as he sauntered toward the village. She would see the ease with which he carried the fish, the surprising strength of his shoulders, the fish scales as bright as the sparks of his body. He glanced over his shoulder, but Thien's face was hidden beneath her sun hat. *One day you'll look up,* he thought, *one day you'll see me.* He walked faster and felt the coolness of the fish down the length of his spine.

In the late morning, he hurried to the jackfruit tree near Thien's house. He looped the stringer on his left wrist, and the fish dangled and swayed as he shinnied up the trunk to a wide limb. Perched, Hai unwound the rope, lay the fish on its side, and waited for Thien. At midday, she ate her lunch in the shade of the jackfruit. Hai's sister Nhi often joined her, and other village girls, but Thien was always first to arrive. Today, before she began eating, Hai would leap from the tree and clutch as with talons the fish he had caught for her. He would approximate the great birds who flew from heaven to thrust their talons into the giants who moved through water. He would make wing sounds, wind sounds, swooping sounds to inspire fear and admiration. Maybe his sky-strength would frighten her more than the changes of her body frightened him. For Miss Thien he would fly, touch down on earth, and display for her this prize fish, this carp the width of his thigh.

As she came toward him in tree shade, he leaned out on his branch, clutched his fish with talons, and plummeted down. He made wing sounds, wind sounds, and cried out in a voice more bird-like than human. Hai fell to the earth beside her, lifted his catch, and heard her say, *"Anh dang lam gi?"* (What are you doing?) He whistled, gripped the fish with his claws, but Thien had no other comment. The girl walked to her family's hut and disappeared through a doorway. He waited for her to come to the side window and wave to him. After a long minute the window remained dark, shaded, so Hai bowed to the hut, her family's nest, and hurried off before his sister and the other girls arrived.

2
Tiger Medic

For whoever would listen, most often himself, Conchola told ten thousand tales. He claimed stardom as a high school running back, a punt return specialist, a high-dive artist, and a Mexican-American Casanova. "*El Rey del Mundo*," he would say, "King of Kings, with a football or whatever." Truth: Conchola played second-string halfback his freshman year. Restless, he dropped out of school, chased after neighborhood girls who didn't want him (mainly white), ignored those who did (mainly brown), and worked as a security guard at a Beech Nut Baby Food factory until he was drafted. The war might relieve some suffering. No more baby food job. No more chasing unattainable girls. No more days and nights when nothing interesting could happen. Less than an hour after receiving his draft notice, he imagined himself a hero. One day soon he might lead a parade, walk down a street amid swirls of confetti and flowers, Sergeant Antonio Lucio Conchola, the most decorated soldier of the Viet Nam War.

For his mother (Catholic, pious, devout), he had his forearms tattooed with rosary beads the night prior to his induction. "*Tontería*," she said. "You cut your skin with needles. Don't call this praying." She lit candles to the Virgin of Guadalupe and made him pray with her. Bored, Conchola felt the ache of his knees on bare wood. He saw his mother's lips moving, so maybe the Virgin read lips, untangled meanings hidden in a mother's throat. Conchola read: "*Cúrase a mi hijo de la agitación, el tormento.*" Yes, cure me of torment, thought Conchola. *With the help of all the saints in heaven.* His mother's lips moved more urgently, but he

14

could still decipher a few words, a prayer of affirmation: "*Dígalo a él la verdad, nada más.* He is no less worthy than the morning sun."

But the morning sun had escaped him. He couldn't find it in his blood, his voice. He couldn't see it reflected in the eyes or face of any man he knew. He requested training as a machine-gunner on a helicopter, but the army made him a medic. He volunteered to be a combat medic, a line medic, and after three months in Viet Nam he had only proven that wounds scared him. Confused, he longed for combat, significant experience, and he longed for release. He ached with desire and fear when he heard his battalion would enter Cambodia, lead the Cambodian invasion. He lacked confidence in his medical skills, his ability to apply hemostats, start IVs. He feared that the sight of a fatal wound (say disembowelment or decapitation) would embarrass him, cause him to vomit or faint.

In his head he wrote a postcard to his Mama:

Cambodia, I've been ready for this how many years? Suerte, *Mama. Luck. A cat with nine lives.* Tu entiendes? *Papa got greased in Korea, but no one's made a bullet fast enough for Antonio Lucio. I'm* fuerte, *slippery. Invisible. So don't worry, Mama. All right? Maybe this is the one time in my life I can make you proud.*

Tu hijo, *Antonio Lucio*

On the night of April 29, 1970, his platoon lay in wait four kilometers from the border. The jungle vibrated, the sky howled. Cobras, F-4 fighter jets, Willie Peter, napalm, artillery—and Conchola didn't know what else—took turn setting fires. From his foxhole, he heard tree limbs splitting and falling, heard high-pitched cries—maybe monkeys, maybe birds—whatever was burning. He noticed a few stars, dim light over walls of fire. The night sky seemed insignificant, candlelight over conflagrations. Feverish, Conchola imagined the girls he loved would love him if they pressed their knees to this earth, these eruptions and tremors, or if they stood before orange flames that leapfrogged over trees, that blew a halo of light over the horizon. *Tree scorch*, he thought, *animal scorch. Bone mountain.* The flames were radiant, sublime. Darkness became light as suns burst forth from jungle. In his foxhole Conchola tried to believe that the girls knew him now, that they loved him, and could see his likeness in any light, any fire. In the fever of his body he was the sun, the stars, the explosions of trees, the blood of animals. If his girlfriends were asleep, they were dreaming of firelight. And if they lay awake, they were holding their breasts and trembling. Conchola giggled until Billie Jasper, in the next foxhole, said, "Yeah, pull the plug, man. Can it." Conchola quieted, but kept watching the rise and fall of firelight. The flaming trees sounded like insects, a whir of wings, mouths. Fleshy things split open by fires. *Tormento. Agitación. A kind of beauty.* Yet late at night when Conchola gazed out on a quieter jungle he saw a vast unexplored darkness beyond the light of fires.

Only so much could be done to prepare for battle. In the shadows that ran deep as the earth you could never kill everything that could kill you. Gooks dug holes, animals burrowed. They hunkered down, quiet as ashes. You could bomb the stones, the mist, set fire to trees, but ashes contained seeds, heartbeats. *How do you kill the seeds?* thought Conchola. *Or the shadows beneath them?* At best you could scorch a few gooks, turn gook jungles into vapor and smoke, but still there were shadows. You burned the earth and back she came—wing, tooth, fang—a raging of shadows. After each fire something crawled out from beneath the ash—an insect. Soon swarms of them moved amid skeletal trees, wounded animals, gooks—all devotedly against you. The embers of their bodies were unsafe, their ashes deadly. *Gook roulette*, thought Conchola, *each chamber a round of darkness coming for your heart.*

At first light, he remembered a boy near Cu Chi who had befriended an animal. A water buffalo, a mud-wallower. A filthy beast who plowed the fields and cooled itself in a slow-moving river. The beast and the boy had seemed to commune. A month ago, on a riverbank pocked with craters, Conchola heard grunts, whispers, soft snorts as the boy petted the bony ridge over the snout of his buffalo. Now Conchola, in his foxhole near PFC Jasper, shivered with a thought: *That was love, cariño. Something powerful.* He suspected gooks and animals shared the same tongue. Maybe a child, a VC, knew the language of water buffalo, monkey, snake, bird because animals protected gooks and vice versa. Conchola remembered the buffalo slobbered on the boy's hands. Instead of backing away, the boy sniffed his fingertips as though to savor the various scents of a garden. Maybe beasts and gooks shared secret smells and sounds, and were difficult to kill because the earth was their keeper. Maybe they could speak and commune with stones, rivers, trees—whatever listened and responded. Conchola feared their language offered protection, solace, while his own language was lies—*mentiras*. He began to imitate animal sounds, gook sounds (groans, grunts, snorts), until PFC Jasper said, "You trying to piss me off? Want me to quiet you?"

Conchola said, "Just covering my ass, baby. Incantations." He gave a few last sounds and quieted. Crouched, he glanced at the jungle, the darkness and firelight, and feared all that was born of ash.

By mid-morning they were hacking machetes through foliage. Cambodia. Three or four whacks for each step. Through a jungle mostly alive. Smoldering here and there, but mostly virgin, pristine, layered in shadows. A medic could slip back, walk near the end of the file, but Conchola followed Billie Jasper, the point man. He asked the Virgin of Guadalupe for courage. He asked that he not panic with the first shot, that he remain calm amid chaos, that he leave Cambodia with medals. He wished he were a common rifleman rather than a medic. The sight of blood, or mere thought of it, tensed the pit of his belly, tightened his sphincter. He realized his prayers were unlikely to be heard. He began to pray that his mother pray for him because the Virgin, if she existed, might hear those who believed, those who were holy. Conchola tried to force his sentiments into a heart and mind ten thousand miles away. With luck, *La Señora* would express his precise wishes: "May my son withstand the sight of carnage—*matanza*. May he be fearless, tireless, and return to me with medals." Conchola whispered mother prayers as he swung his machete. He tried to envision the circuit of the prayer, the invisible wiring that arced from the fear in his belly to the heart of his mother. "May she pray for me always," he thought. "And may the Virgin of Guadalupe listen. May she hear my every breath."

Discouraged, he remembered the Virgin was also known as the Dark Madonna. If she understood all that arose from shadows, she might listen more keenly to the prayers of gooks, trees, *animalitos*. The jungle enveloped him, enveloped the platoon, and the jungle was a prayer of darkness. The point man stepped forward and disappeared in foliage. "Billie," said Conchola, "wait up, man. Hey!" The medic crashed through brush until he saw Billie on his knees, his right fist held high to signal the platoon to halt.

"Can you make less noise?" Billie whispered. "Can you shut the fuck up?"

Conchola nodded.

"I smell somethin'," said Billie, "somethin' wounded." He pointed to dark red smears that edged a small leaf.

The platoon gathered. The lieutenant touched the leaf, sniffed his hands, and said, "Blood trail." *Gook or animal?* thought Conchola. *Tree blood or plant blood? Does it matter?* PFC Jasper brushed a finger against the leaf. Conchola reached tentatively, said, "Could be anything," but didn't touch it. The platoon moved on in search of blood. They found patches of it on the exposed root of a tree, the edge of a fern leaf, a dark spot on the earth that smelled of blood and urine. The jungle was unnaturally still. Conchola heard no insects or birds, only the cumbersome movements of boots, machetes, rifles. He wondered if the lieutenant could pinpoint their location on a map. Most likely they were lost, following a blood trail in a jungle too remote to be charted. *Stupid*, thought Conchola, *we're wandering in shadows.* The best strategy would be to call in an air strike, illuminate the darkness. But the lieutenant couldn't request air support while lost, unable to report the platoon's location. Canopies of trees, vines, creepers—nothing familiar. Maybe with the coming of night they would be too submerged to see the light of a single star.

They trudged across swale of grass where something had lain. They forded a stream and found traces of blood on leaves, stones, severed tree limbs. They stopped when Jasper, on point, saw a large pugmark pressed in the earth. There was a humming in the trees, soft wind, and Conchola heard breathing. The beast did not roar. Conchola trained his ears to the susurrus of trees, wind, throat, water. The tiger lay in the shade near the stream. Jasper, instead of firing, had dropped his rifle and stretched flat on his belly. The beast made thick, sucking sounds in its throat. Its chest and abdomen vibrated, swelled, and its mouth gaped open. Conchola saw a throat wound, a chest wound, and un-clicked the safety of his rifle. He dropped to one knee and aimed. He sighted the open mouth, then the light of the eyes (too much glare), then the black stripe that arced downward—V-shaped—between the throat wound and chest wound. Conchola couldn't steady his aim. He edged closer, dropped to his belly, and heard Jasper say, "Shoot the fucker and get it over." Conchola fired wildly at darkness. Head down, he switched to automatic and kept firing until he noticed his left hand and forearm were bleeding. *I'm wounded*, he thought, and then he said it aloud: "Wounded!" It seemed the tiger had vanished in the shadows beyond the stream.

Conchola lay still. The beast must have moved with such speed that he hadn't seen it lash with its claws, carve its initials, disappear in jungle. The claw marks cut through tattoos of rosary beads and graced the outer sides of his hand and forearm. A smell lingered (meaty, sour), and when did smells ever lie? The tiger had clawed him. The King of the Jungle had come close enough to take one quick swipe and retreat. *He touched me*, thought Conchola, *one time. He disappeared when I blinked.*

Joseph Garms, the medic from third platoon, crawled up with his aid bag. "Everybody all right?"

Conchola raised his left arm and said, "Clawed me, fucker clawed me."

"The tiger?" said Garms. "Would've eaten you alive. You wouldn't have a mouth to tell stories."

Conchola, shaking his head, saw soft light in the branches of trees. "*Heridas de fiera,*" he said. "Tiger wounds. Honest." He probed his wounds with his fingers, tried to widen them for scarring. He refused to let Garms bandage his arm. As he glanced back and forth—wounds to trees, soft light, blood and light—the air was ringing. "Jesus," he said, "clawed by a tiger. Fast as lightning."

"Yeah," said Garms, "maybe in a dream. In real life you scraped your arm on a branch. Nothing mysterious."

Misterioso, thought Conchola, *misterio puro. You envious fucker, you'll never have any decent wounds.*

The platoon found more blood trails. At midday, Conchola knelt beside a stream and noticed blood-smeared leaves and grass. The blood was dry, mostly dark, but brightened some when moistened with water. Conchola dabbed the leaves and grass until his fingertips were bloody. He touched his cheeks, his chin, rouged himself with tiger blood. PFC Jasper said, "War paint, huh?" but Conchola ignored him. Jasper said,

"The tiger's dead, or half dead. Not much charm left." Just in case, though, for whatever protection it offered, Jasper touched the stained earth, sniffed his hands, rubbed his cheeks and forehead. "Smells bad," he said, "mangy. I doubt he's still alive."

That night, in jungle, under giant trees, they shared the same foxhole. The earth—cool, moist, smooth—was not entirely shadow. Conchola touched earthen walls smudged with color. Grains of light, soil light. *Tierra de Madre*. No moonlight or starlight reached this earth. In his hands, in the curve of his throat, the cavity of his chest, he absorbed soft colors (shades of gray, brown, yellow, gold), traces of light and long shadows. *Luz*, he thought, *sombra. Spark and shadow.* He turned and pressed his back to the earth. He still wanted medals, his fear was not gone, but he had the beginnings of faith—the light of the soil, the glow of a body. His fingers traced his wounds as he prayed that the tiger survive the war. He prayed to the Dark Madonna that his own wounds were tiger wounds, that he had not devised them out of need, desperation. Crouched near Billie Jasper, shivering a little, he confessed to past lies. "Bench-warmer," he whispered, "second-string. I never played much football in high school. And I chased after the wrong girls, eyes blue as the sky. I wouldn't go after anyone who loved me." Later, in a voice barely audible, he admitted he was never a high-dive artist, couldn't swim, feared water, and his only job before the war was as a security guard at a baby food factory—Beech Nut. "I was sad," he said, "*triste*. A kid just marking time."

Jasper, startled, said, "You're tellin' the truth, man. Gospel. But don't switch gears and tell me that tiger clawed you."

Conchola sniffed his wounds, licked them. "Swear to sweet Jesus, swear to my Mama. Paw-to-paw combat. What else is there to say?"

Jasper, after a pause, admitted he panicked when he saw

the beast. "Couldn't believe it," he said, "a tiger. I fell to the ground and shivered." Confession is contagious. Jasper revealed a childhood of small crimes, petty thievery. He whispered into the night as Conchola went back to licking his wounds, honoring the tiger in private. *Ojos de luz* (eyes of light), *sangre* (blood), *rayos* (stripes), *garras bendecidas* (claws that blessed). The eyes had exploded in suns, furies of light. They lit the trees, cast a light as unfathomable as the light within the earth, or the light of a seed, a vein, a body. *Primordial*, thought Conchola, *primitivo. How else to describe it?* Again he probed his wounds, again he licked them. The blood was partly his, partly the tiger's. For now it didn't matter much what anyone else believed.

At dawn, he was still contemplating wounds. He had deepened and torn open the scratches, and had carefully smeared the blood of the wounds on the tattoos of the rosary. His arm was slightly mutilated. PFC Garms tried to apply a bandage, but Conchola, a less experienced medic, said, "I'll care for my own wounds, nothing requires a bandage."

"Come on," said Garms. "You're a medic, not an idiot."

"*Claro*," said Conchola, "*no soy idiota.* Last thing I need is another medic's help."

The light in the trees had diminished. The grayish light that now filtered through the jungle canopy was of a different quality than the light that had graced him. The light of dawn could be fathomed, comprehended. A distant sun rose over the world, penetrated the crowns of trees, and was deflected by a mass of foliage. The result—gray light, poor visibility, a sea of shadows. Conchola feared the tiger had died. Maybe soon they would find the corpse, the eyes rolled back, flies lapping blood, a small mountain of putrefaction. Conchola noticed his wounds were slightly infected. Tiger claws were feral, unclean. Infection was a natural process. He studied his arm and convinced himself the tiger had struck. The medic couldn't have cut himself simply by passing through jungle, brushing against vines, fronds, branches. He clucked his tongue and nodded when he remembered his mother's faith. Maybe truth could never be reduced to a factual account of occurrences (he had not seen the tiger's claws), but could be hinted at through the light that bloomed in trees, the ringing in the air, the power of a wound, the mercy of a body. His mother had faith that what needed to happen in this world eventually would happen. Peace even. Happiness. Good health. Whatever. He wondered if she prayed to Saint Francis, the animal-charmer, or if the Virgin of Guadalupe, the Dark Madonna, loved animals as much as Francis. It seemed the Virgin would be an animal-lover, a lover of light in tree shade, of air that rang clearer than every church bell. Head bowed, Conchola prayed that what needed to happen to him had happened. "Please, Guadalupe," he said, "if I die, I die happy." Tiger wounds. Claws. Scarring. Pure sound and light amid broken trees.

3
Giant

Calling "Soldiers, Americans!" Luu Hai sprinted across the rice fields. His mother's voice trailed after him ("Slow down, slow down"), a reminder that the enemy often left in a bloody heap any man, woman, or child who moved swiftly across the landscape. Hai slowed to an amble, circulated among peasants, and halted at the edge of the field where Thien and her grandma were weeding. "Soldiers," he said, "didn't you hear me?" He motioned with his arms. "From the top of the banyan tree I spotted them moving toward the village." He pointed to his lookout tree north of the fields. "They'll be here in ten minutes," he said, "maybe less. They seem to be checking the road for mines."

Ba Ly, Thien's grandma, vowed daily to protect her granddaughter. Upon hearing Luu Hai's warning, she led the girl back to the village to prepare for the arrival of Americans. In their hut, she retrieved Thien's grayish pants from a basket and smeared the crotch with *nuoc mam*, a strong-smelling fish sauce. Dark brown, the stain could be mistaken for menstrual blood and might discourage the randiness of soldiers. No girl in the village had been assaulted, but stories of abuse—some of them too obscene to imagine—had circulated from outlying regions. Ba Ly gave her granddaughter the stained pants and said, "Put these on. Hurry. Sometimes you move as slowly as a cow."

In silence, Thien removed her black pants and put on the pants that might protect her. Moments later, head bowed, she squatted near her grandma and began tearing up leaves of cabbage for soup. They used their hands, no paring tools or knives; nothing suspicious. Ba Ly called it Good Luck Soup,

Long Life Soup. They would boil the cabbage, add a generous splash of *nuoc mam*, and maybe the smell of their cooking would help keep the enemy at bay.

Behind the stove, Ba Ly peered through a slit in a bamboo wall. The Americans, weighted down with packs, passed within thirty meters of the hut, turned and tramped noisily across the rice fields, and disappeared into the hedgerows to the east.

"Stay put," she said to Thien. "They might be watching us from behind bushes."

The girl began taking off her pants.

"Keep them on," said Ba Ly. "You do everything the wrong way. Hurry when you need to go slow, go slow when you need to hurry." Ba Ly spat and wiped her mouth. "A cow is too fast now. Sometimes it is wise to move like a snail."

An hour later, the earth quiet except for insects and birds, Ba Ly allowed her granddaughter to change her pants and follow her to the fields.

Hai approached them and waved. He hurried to the paddy where they were weeding, squatted beside Thien, and nearly touched her elbow. "Do you need any help?" he said.
The girl turned away from him.

"Thank you," said Ba Ly. "We don't need help, but you're kind to offer."

Thien, silent, kept weeding.

"Did you see the fish I caught yesterday?" said Hai. "The giant carp?"

"You showed us," said Ba Ly. "Very lucky."

"I know how to fish," said Hai. "I can make the hooks, the fishing line. Green worms."

She nodded.

"I can bring you and Thien fresh meat," he said. "We're sure to have extra."

"Wait and see."

"No, the fish is huge," said Hai. "Fat as my leg. I'll bring you and Thien a strip of fresh meat."

After the boy left, Thien said to her grandma: "I don't want to marry him."

"Yes," said Ba Ly, "you keep telling me. But you will not be the one to decide."

Thien felt something brush her left ankle in the shallow water of the paddy. She flicked her hand at what could have been a leech, a slender snake, a freshwater crab. Still weeding, she thought of her parents, killed by Americans, and her older sisters, Mai and Yen, killed by South Vietnamese mortars. At least her sisters no longer bled between their legs. She prayed they no longer suffered, no longer felt the burden of eyes, tongues, and mouths that hungered for their bodies. Neither Hai nor any village boy could guess that six months earlier Thien first began to bleed. She showed Ba Ly her stained clothes, and she listened to her grandma tell her of *mau co toi*, the blood of sin. When Ba answered her question ("No, boys don't bleed this way"), it somehow made sense. The other sex bled mainly from bullets, bombs, knives, fragments of metal. Her dead sisters had bled in both ways, but now their bleeding was finished. They died of head wounds, chest wounds, but at least could be properly buried because their bodies remained intact. Three days ago, Thien had tended her sisters' graves at the one-year anniversary of their deaths. Maybe now, if Mai and Yen were lucky, they were akin to air and light, a softness that bore no wounds.

The next day, she and her friend Nhi ate their lunch in the shade of the jackfruit tree. Pointing to the branch from which Hai had leaped with his fish, Thien said, "I could smell it when I left the fields. He should have cleaned the fish hours earlier, but he jumped from the tree holding it up and whistling." She popped a roasted jackfruit seed in her mouth. "Crazy," she said, "your brother's crazy. He reached out and tried to give me the fish, his fingers curled like claws." She cracked the seed with her teeth. "Discourage him," she said. "Maybe when the war is over I will be ready to be a wife."

"By then you'll be old," said Nhi. "No one will want you."

"Maybe so."

"Hair white as clouds," said Nhi. "You must let someone marry you while you are young."

Nhi spoke of village boys: the handsome, the homely. The ones least likely to hit a girl, a spouse. The ones who were polite, well-mannered. And the ones who might yell at you and hit you for not having enough food to serve to guests. "Nam's my favorite," said Nhi, "but he's my cousin; our mothers won't let us marry. What if I marry someone mean?"

Thien touched her shoulder to quiet her. On the road at the south edge of town, a shape rose, billowed, drew silently forward. For a moment Thien thought it was a tank, a crew of Americans. But a tank would roar, rip holes in the road, and the peasants would have heard it long before anyone saw it. Maybe a spirit, a thing covered with mist, had sailed down on the road north of the village. Cloud-colored, edges humped and rounded, it followed the curved path as if it were a human traveler with human boundaries. The grayish mass thickened, a cloud gathering rain, and then it halted. An appendage rose from the great bulk, shaped itself into a tentacle, and reached for a branch of a tall bamboo. Thien's mouth clamped shut, then yawned wide. "*Con voi*," she said, "*con voi*," (elephant). She abandoned Nhi, who hid herself behind the trunk of the jackfruit. Deaf to Nhi's warnings ("Careful, careful!"), Thien dashed barefoot toward the road. The leviathan, swaying, was about one hundred paces away.

Silvery gray, with splotches of pink on its ears and trunk, the elephant dwarfed every water buffalo in every field. On its neck sat an elder, a figure so slight Thien at first mistook him for a child. Up close, she saw white hair on a saggy chin, loose skin beneath eyes as wrinkled as the skin of the elephant. After greeting him as she'd been taught to greet every elderly man, *"Xin chao, Ong"* (Hello, Grandfather), she asked if he was hungry.

The man said, "I've eaten, thank you. And as you can see my companion rarely does anything else."

The elephant grazed bamboo leaves. Thien noticed its whitish toenails, a tuft of silver hair at the tip of its tail. Maybe the old man could move safely over the earth, go wherever he pleased, because the Americans had respect for the beast, its pale color similar to their own, the enormity of its body. Maybe American soldiers studied and admired its quietness because they could move neither themselves nor their machinery without pummeling the earth, alerting the heavens. Thien wondered if the elephant man had somehow layered the animal's feet with cushions. Each footfall, not much louder than hers, made a faint, rubbery sound. Thien edged close enough to sample the smells on the animal's body: water, river mud, road dust, bamboo leaves, and something acrid—maybe bark. She skirted around the moving elephant to verify that it was a cow, a female. Smooth between the hind legs, the ovals of flesh merging in a fold.

"Does she have babies?" said Thien.

"She had one," said the man, "but it's gone now. She's been childless many years."

The girl pictured a small elephant resting in the shade of her mother's body. Maybe the mother had used her trunk to offer her calf fresh leaves and twigs, or maybe she had nursed her from the wrinkled breasts sagging between her forelegs. The calf was most likely killed by an explosion, a burst of metal and fire, but Thien forced these thoughts from her mind. She pictured the baby elephant alive, twitching its tail. Thien stepped closer to the mother, the giant who could protect any child. She tried to convince herself that the beast, her body as great as a mountain, had been spared the misery of loss.

Peasant boys left the fields and gathered near the road. Luu Hai, standing near Thien, said, "White elephant," but in

her mind she corrected him: *Cloud-colored. Pink. Ashen.* Old
women and children emerged from huts. Most of the adults
had seen baby elephants in the markets of Tay Ninh and Cu
Chi, but no one had seen an adult elephant three times the
size of a bull buffalo. The beast raised her trunk and sniffed
the air. Thien wondered if she smelled water, the nearby river.
"Here," she said, "this way," and she led elephant and rider
along a path bordering the south edge of the fields.

Ba Ly called, "Ong, keep the animal from our paddies."

"Grandma," he answered, "that's what I'm doing. Your
rice fields will survive."

The old man's bare feet tickled the beast behind her ears.
Thien, walking close by, asked questions ("What's the
elephant's name? Will she have more babies?"), but he
ignored her. His attention focused, he kept touching the
elephant's ears with his feet, apparently to guide her, prevent
her from entering the fields. The beast, her trunk raised,
seemed to be smelling things—rice grass, weeds, yellow
flowers—but she stayed in the center of the path. Three water
buffalo stood still and gaped. The bull grunted a threat, but
did not lower his head, stomp his hooves, or advance toward
the giant who loomed above the fields.

In loose procession, the villagers trailed the elephant
toward the shoreline. Luu Hai darted past Thien and touched
the animal's tail. When the beast furled her trunk, suckled
the air, the girl breathed deeply through her nostrils. Near
the shore the elephant accelerated until her master, massaging
her ears with his feet, whispered, "Stop, stop." The animal
took two more strides and halted. "Good," he said, "now
kneel." His feet slid downward along the creases of her ears.
"Slow and easy," he said. "Down, down, down."

Thien noticed provisions, two packages tied to the rope
netting on the animal's back. The elephant knelt, back legs
first, then stretched forward on her belly. The old man untied
the packages, lowered a rope ladder down the animal's side,
and began his descent. Halfway down he handed Hai his food

supply, his rice cakes and roasted corn, bananas and mangos, a few oranges. He handed his other package to Thien: white clothing, shirt and trousers, the proper garments for a funeral. The girl knew many traveled long distances, took great risks, to honor their dead. "A funeral?" she said, but he turned away. "Third-day ceremony," he whispered. "For my grandson I will be on time."

He stepped stiffly onto solid ground, unfastened a strap around the animal's girth, and freed her of constraints. Trunk raised, the elephant ambled to a cove of the Sai Gon River. Flapping her ears and snorting, she entered the shallows. She sucked water into her trunk, raised the tip of her trunk to her mouth, rocked back, guzzled. Thien watched the beast gorge herself, eleven trunkfuls, eleven long drinks, before she began to shower. She waved her trunk and sprayed her back with water. She sprayed her sides, and then her trunk curled in a hook shape, straight above, and brown water rushed down over the dome of her skull. Luu Hai and his cousin Nam and his friend Qui called, "*O hay! O hay!*" The beast raised her right foreleg, let it fall with a splash, and repeated the action until the shallows became a mud hole. She billowed, swayed, knelt down, rolled on her side, and thick waves combed out across the cove. Immersed in a watery mire, she lolled about with the languor of a queen.

Luu Hai, yelping, bolted from Thien's side and ran up and down the riverbank. *Show off*, thought Thien. *What are you trying to prove?*

The elephant wallowed to the shore and sunk her trunk in the moist earth. She slurped mud, waved her ashen trunk, let it unfurl, and sprayed herself the color of rain clouds. Village boys, buffalo boys, shouted their joy. The elephant was much like their buffalo: a water creature, a mud creature; a creature who invited the soil onto her body. Hai and his cousin Nam ventured within five meters of the beast. Thien, more silent, came within three, and squatted to muddy her hands and forearms. She restrained the wish to wallow in river mud, plunge herself in a mud hole. She looked above the elephant's back at the nearby coconut palms, the sunlit crowns. She felt at home near the mud-spattered animal, the river, the trees, and could have been happier only if the elephant had showered her with mud.

The beast raised her trunk and let out a trumpeting scream. Hai and Nam jumped back, their bodies swift as eels. Thien, mouth open, inched closer. The animal's voice, the reverberation, filled the girl's lungs.

Ba Ly asked, "Where's your village?" and the man gestured to the north: "Ben Cat."

"The soldiers didn't stop you? Check your belongings?"

"They did as they pleased. Stopped us, searched us. Had the elephant do tricks every other kilometer."

"It does tricks?" said Thien.

"Picks up a log," he said. "Drops it at my feet. Raises her trunk, stands on her hind legs. The usual."

"Can the animal do buffalo work?" said Luu Hai. "Fieldwork?"

"No, forest-work. She can lift a hundred-kilo log, haul it from a forest." He glanced at the beast. "Now there's not much left, a few scrubby trees. Today all she has to do is carry me and herself down the road to Cu Chi."

"Too far," said Thien. "You won't arrive by nightfall."

"Nine kilometers," he said. "A few hours."

"The road's dangerous," said Ba Ly. "You could stay with us and leave for Cu Chi in the morning."

"The road will still be dangerous."

"Less so than at dusk," she said. "And you'll be rested."

The old man shrugged.

"Can you keep the animal out of our fields?" said Ba Ly. "Can you promise Ong Quan and Ong Truong there will be no damage to our rice?"

He appraised the beast, then nodded. "At night I shackle her near something she can forage," he said. "She might eat a few bushes while I'm asleep."

Thien leaned toward her grandma, whispered something, and then invited the elephant man to their hut for a bowl of cabbage soup.

That night the elephant began eating the jackfruit tree. Thien heard its branches bend and break, heard the elephant's teeth tearing at twigs, leaves, strips of bark. She lay with Ba Ly on a mat in the rear of the hut. The elephant man snored, suckled the air, but she was comforted by the ebb and flow of his breathing. Earlier, Thien's grandma had arranged the man's bedding. A floor mat between the ancestral shrine and the rice bin that contained the scant remains of their best rice— *Nang Thom*. This had been the father-side of the house, but tonight it was occupied by a grandfather, an elephant-keeper, whose snoring was nearly as raucous as the tearing and breaking of branches. Ba Ly dozed and woke, dozed and woke, and finally collapsed in an exhausted sleep. When her breathing steadied Thien inched away from her, rose quietly, walked past the ancestral shrine and the snoring grandfather, and out into night.

The elephant, now motionless, could have been a hill or a small mountain; a roundness rising behind a tree, a dome balanced upon pillars, four supports rooted in a valley. But Thien did not smell the stones of a hill or mountain. She smelled river earth, bed and shoreline. She smelled nearby waters that reeked of what swam through them (carp, cod, eel, crab), and what bathed in them (elephant and buffalo). She had never before appreciated sour smells. Jasmine for her, lotus for her. But in something sour, a smell the opposite of flowers, maybe there was safety. If Thien's own body smelled of river earth, Ba Ly would not stain her clothing. And if Thien could cast her shadow wide, compress the earth with each footfall, the most ignorant soldier would understand she was dangerous. *A giant*, she thought, *a smelly giant*. She would scare off not only the Americans, the day ghosts, but Luu Hai and all the boys.

The elephant snaked her trunk over a wide branch. The beast leaned back, pulled, and the branch broke from the tree like kindling. The elephant ate the forest. A browsing beast, she filled herself with leaves, twigs, bark, and in her body, in wide valleys, there had to be seeds, roots, gnawed limbs, the makings of trees. She loved the earth, too, in trunkfuls. Earlier, on the riverbank, Thien had watched the elephant suck mud into her trunk and shower her spine and belly. Now the girl came closer and whispered, "You're strong, you eat everything. Our buffalo just chew the grass."

Flapping her ears, the beast looked at Thien. She sniffed the girl's neck with her trunk, then turned and stripped leaves from the fallen branch. Thien looked up the wall of the elephant's body to the crown of the jackfruit, white stars between branches. She said, "*Dung lo*" (Don't worry), and lifted both hands to the elephant's body. She rubbed the back of the left foreleg, the side of the belly, the tip of the trunk. She touched the soil, the river mud pasted over belly wrinkles, leg wrinkles, the leathery texture of the skin. As the elephant bent closer to the earth, Thien stroked the flap of her left ear, a rubbery slab the shape of a giant leaf. The girl said, "You're a forest, a thousand trees." She massaged the ear, the outer side first, and now the underside that lay against the neck, the skin as thin and smooth as human skin, the veins warm and branched like trees. Thien whispered to the beast, "*An, song lau hon*" (Eat, survive). Later she said with the sternness of an elder: "Don't take too much for granted; you should toughen the skin at the back of your ears."

4
Stream Animals

On the second day in Cambodia, near the stream where Antonio Lucio had confronted a tiger, the platoon found a well-camouflaged tunnel, three sacks of rice, the spent shells of an AK-47, and a fresh blood trail. Conchola dipped his hands in the stream. Maybe the blood that led to the shore was tiger blood, *sangre de fiera*. Or maybe it fell from a mere human, or from the wounds of a lesser animal—a wild pig, a dog, a monkey. He dabbed moist fingers on spots of blood and rouged his left forearm. The medic had wounds here, claw marks, evidence of combat. He traced a finger over the damage as he scribbled in his mind a letter to his mother in San Jose:

Mama, we're alone in Tiger Country, Indian Country. A new shade of darkness. Do you know a tiger can lunge so fast you don't see the claws that cut you? Rapidísimo, Mama. The speed of a prayer is faster than a bullet. I looked down at my arm and saw some blood. The tiger was bleeding too, from throat wounds and chest wounds, and now I wish I had helped him. He must have been wounded two nights ago during heavy bombing. Our planes razed the earth, scorched the jungle into flames. A million fires, Mama, a million dead bodies that I could feel but couldn't see—snake bodies, gook bodies, monkey bodies, perros, *and whatever else once lived here. They didn't kill* mi maestro, *though, who crept with his wounds and his suffering into the deep jungle where we caught up with him yesterday morning. Jasper, this black kid from Carolina, saw him first, and I crawled up thinking,* Dios mío, Dios mío, *how do I kill a tiger? I shot up jungle walls,* tiroteo, *but the tiger lives. Never will I see anything more*

34

true than eyes of fury, rabia pura, *red wounds simple as fire, and the blood that fell from his body. Beauty and rage, the fury of eyes—nothing else is true here.* Un milagro, *Mama, one miracle. Maybe there's something inside him none of us can kill.*

You remember that spring morning, El Cinco de Mayo, when Uncle Mundo gave me a cat the color of fire? Mundo said, "Careful, he's a Tomcat, he'll claw you." I gave him tío's *name, Mundo (World), but he wouldn't answer to Spanish or English or anything human. He was wild, ran away from me that first night. Remember? Maybe he's still out there, Mama, a cat with nine lives, wandering alone through some lost woods.*

Mama, don't work too hard for those white people in San Jose. Too much lavando, limpiando, *washing clothes, caring for babies. Mama, I have a confession, something I never told you. The only girls I ever liked were white and pretty. Sara Peters, Jennie Doyle, Mary Safranski. I can't say why it is they don't seem so sweet anymore. If you see them, you can tell them what happened to me in Cambodia. Nobody should worry, though, no se preocupa. I'm feeling better than I've ever felt in my life.*

Love you, all my cariño, *Antonio Lucio*

P.S. Some of the muchachos *are ignorant enough to doubt the tiger clawed me. They call me names like Tiger Medic, Cat Man, but not with much respect.*

In the late afternoon the platoon was fired upon by snipers. When the first American casualty of the Cambodian invasion called, "I'm hit, I'm hit!" Conchola grabbed his aid bag. The foliage beside the stream was nearly impassable. The medic, with his bandages and IV fluids and morphine, snaked through dense bushes and vines and allowed the voice ("Meow, I'm hit!") to guide him. He found PFC Mullaney curled in a nest of reeds, caressing the side of his left hand

and clamping a thumb over the bloodied stump of his little finger. Conchola lifted the hand, applied a pressure dressing, and said, "Beautiful, baby. On your way home, back to the world. And I mean *mundo*, baby. *World*. US of A. Capital of easy living." Whether the wound was the loss of a limb or a pinkie, Conchola comforted the casualty with similar chatter. Of the tasks he performed none came easier than fabricating stories, exaggerating, spinning lies (Mullaney would rejoin the platoon in a week) to counteract episodes of shock.

The sniper fire lasted seconds, but the response exceeded an hour. Billie Jasper tossed grenades at leafy shadows. Warren, the M-60 machine-gunner, sprayed bursts of fire through foliage. No one had seen the snipers or could accurately estimate their location. At random, responding because silence seemed suicidal, the platoon fired at trees, leaves, vines, flowers. Lieutenant Bateson got on the radio and ordered an air strike. Minutes later fighter jets roared overhead, swooped low and fast, and dumped most of their ordnance in or near the stream. Bombs burst through trees, carved craters and gorges, spouted geysers of mud, geysers of water. Belly to earth, Conchola heard thumping sounds, wood-splitting sounds, the air that rang with metal, the wind of trees as they swayed and fell, the shriek of an animal—maybe a wild dog, maybe a monkey. He saw Warren shoot white flowers that hung from a liana, saw blossoms spin and swoop down, blend with shadows. Conchola cringed when he heard a large animal scrambling through brush, moaning. "Cease fire!" he called. "Cease fire!" The strength and heat of longing surged through his throat and chest.

After the bombing, after Mullaney had been medevacked, the platoon reconnoitered the shore and found dead and wounded frogs, fish, crabs, turtles. The dead fish were mostly minnow-sized, but one—a whiskered thing—was wide as a tree trunk.

"Catfish," said Jasper. "Poor fucker got blown from the water."

Shards of metal had cut deep gashes through its belly; its eyes—protuberant, bloody—were bloated with pressure.

"Gook whale," said Warren. "KIA."

"Supper," said Jasper, "half-gutted already. Another knife slash and he be ready. Just skewer him on a stick."

Lieutenant Bateson came up and appraised the damage. A beached crab moved on three legs, a few minnows flopped, a small turtle leaked blood and slime as it inched toward water. "All right, gather 'em," said the lieutenant, "the dead and wounded. Before the gooks have a picnic." Via radio, he informed command the platoon would be held up a few minutes to destroy a cache of food, a significant surplus. "Fresh fish," he said, "crabs, turtles. Enough to fill a barrel." He ordered a squad to get out their entrenching tools, carve a deep hole, gather the animals, arrange them in a pile, and blow them away with C-4 explosives. Jasper, pointing, said, "But sir, that catfish. I could roast the fat fucker and have him ready for eating."

Bateson glanced at his watch. "No time," he said, "save your appetite. We'll move out, north-northeast, in ten minutes flat."

Conchola sat on the trunk of a fallen tree. He watched Jasper and three other *muchachos* carve a wide hole in soil the color of rust. Whispering complaints, moaning and groaning about the smell and the slime, the boys gathered frogs and fish, crabs and turtles. Jasper bent down to curl his fingers through the gills of the catfish. He took a deep breath, lifted, and said, "You sorry mother, you won't even feed us." Straining, he carried the fish to the hole, let go, and it fell in with a slapping sound, a moist thud. "You one sorry mother," said Jasper. "Can't even roast you on a stick."

Warren, the M-60 gunner, picked up a wounded crab the size of his hand. A lightning pattern traversed the split-open shell, but the animal was alive, its eight legs testing the air, probing. The boy said, "Hey, Tiger Medic, you ready? This one needs some assistance."

Conchola got to his feet.

"The shell needs some stitches," said Warren, "or some wiring. And the body needs some cat blood, jungle juice. Lace it with tiger blood and it'll be the first crab in the world that roars."

"Fuck you."

Warren nodded. He lay the animal on the ground and crouched over it, protective. "See the shell?" he said. "Such nice markings?"

"Leave it be," said Conchola.

"Our insignia," said Warren. "Tropical lightning. Twenty-Fifth Infantry Division. Amazing."

Someone said, "Yeah, toss the fucker in the hole, Sam."

"No way," said Warren. "This crabby's no typical gook. Look at the patch sewn on your sleeve. Tropical lightning."

"Yeah, but the crab's a spy," said someone. "Grease 'im".

Warren picked up the crab. "A gook spy? This pretty little fucker?"

"Put him down," said Conchola.

"But he deserves a trial," said Warren. "Is he wearing our insignia because he's with us? Or is he camouflaging his allegiance?"

The lieutenant, without glancing up from the map spread over his knees, said, "Kiddies, enough horse play."

"Crab play," said Warren. "Enough crab play."

"Warren—"

"I'm with you, sir, I swear I am. But you should look-see at this little crab, sir. A lick of lightning on its shell same as the patch on your sleeve."

The lieutenant, waving an arm, said, "Knock it off and secure the crab in the hole."

Warren nodded. He gripped the stems of the pincers, spread his arms, and tore the appendages from the body. The stunned animal flopped to the shore and quivered. Conchola saw the front legs curl toward the wounds, the stumps of the pincers. "Jewelry," said Warren, "jungle gems," and held the pincers near his ear lobes. Conchola heard a sound similar to a rush of steam released from a small compartment. The exhale of a crab? The strain of lungs? A small scream? He edged past Warren and lifted the crab in his hands. The flesh under the shell vibrated, pulsed; the stumps were bleeding. Conchola said, "*Nos vamos, hermano, uno, dos, tres*." And hurled the animal in the stream.

"Way to go," said Warren. "Just threw the snipes a picnic."

"*Chíngate, pendejo*."

"Yeah, talk spic if you want, but that's a high crime. Aiding and abetting the enemy."

Conchola turned his back to him.

"Lieutenant," said Warren, "Conchola just threw the gooks a snack. Juicy little crab, sir."

The lieutenant, still studying his map, said, "God bless it, boys. How many times I tell you to get the job done? ASAP."

"We're trying," said Warren. "But Meow Man threw a crab in the stream. Aiding and abetting the enemy."

The lieutenant folded his map. "Well, retrieve the damn thing, if your IQs will allow it." He stood. "Conchola, wade your ass out there, grab the crab and whatever else you see, and secure all of it in the hole."

Conchola didn't know how to swim. He had no intention of retrieving and securing anything, but he removed his helmet and boots, rolled up his pant legs, and entered the water. A pair of red-striped minnows darted away from his shins. The wounded crab worked its legs, all eight of them, and began to plummet. Conchola knew without its pincers it would die of trauma or starvation, but at least it would perish in the stream rather than be blown to ash by soldiers. Warren said, "Okay, numbnuts, catch the crab," but Cat Man pretended not to hear. The medic assessed the depth of the stream, maybe six feet at its middle. Ashamed, he remembered a TV program that showed a tiger crossing a wide river, navigating powerful currents with seemingly little effort. The narrator claimed that tigers, unlike most cats, took naturally to water, and in the heat of the day often submerged themselves in rivers. Warren said, "Hey, dick-lick, where's the crab? What the fuck you doing?" Conchola released his breath and sank down until only his head was showing. He heard the staccato call of a bird, an answering call, and a skittering sound in a nearby treetop. The currents tickled his throat, soothed him. He leaned back, inhaled, let go of his breath, and went under. He felt the rush of water on his body, the pressures on his belly and chest, the smooth flow over the inner sides of his forearms. He sank deeper, shut his eyes, covered his ears, and the world quieted. He could barely hear Warren heckling him: "Here, kitty. Here, kitty-kitty." The medic planted his feet, dug in, and resisted the outward pull of currents. Rising for air, he opened his eyes to frayed light, a spiral of blue framed by trees.

He breathed in and called, "Lost the crab, sir. Somehow lost sight of him."

"Never tried," said Warren. "Didn't do shit. Floating around in water."

"Skip it," said the lieutenant, "saddle up. Can't kill everything in the jungle."

Conchola, smiling, swaggered to the shore.

"You miserable dink," said Warren. "You let it go, didn't you?"

"*Tal vez.*"

"Meow-man, you got some weird ancestry. Mixed the spic with the meow and the crab and the gook, mixed all this bad shit together."

"Careful."

"Yeah, meow, meow, meow," said Warren. "Can't be too careful." He seemed to be searching his mind for a better insult when Conchola shrieked, lunged, and sliced Warren's right cheek with his nails.

Warren tried to tackle him, but got only one leg. Conchola swatted the boy's head, scratched the back of his neck, and spun free when Warren reached for his gonads. Warren said, "Real nice. That your only trick, Meow Man? Scratch and run?"

Conchola, smiling, said, "*Lo siento, pendejo*. Better wipe the blood on your cheek before it ruins your makeup."

"Yeah, fuck you," said Warren. "Take one step forward and I'll kill you."

Conchola giggled.

"I mean it, Meow Man, come on. Let's see what happens when a kitty-cat has to fight."

The lieutenant stepped in and slapped each boy's chest with the back of his hand. "Goddamn it, troops, how old are you? Twelve? Seven? Four?"

"Maybe he's three," said Conchola.

"Infant mother-fucker," said Warren. "Cat shit baby—"

"Zip it," said the lieutenant. "Keep it zipped. I hear another peep from either of you, I'll tie you to a tree and leave you to the gooks."

Except for the crab in the stream, the animal bodies were piled in the hole, and the lieutenant ordered PFC Warren to add the sacks of rice they'd found earlier near the entrance of a tunnel. After Jasper and another *muchacho* rigged the explosives, the platoon took cover. Conchola peeked from behind a tree as the earth erupted. Aflame, the fragments of animals rose in a maelstrom of dust. Microscopic now, they were bits of this and that, particles of mist, blood, ember. Ashes to ashes, nothing larger than a mote.

He wondered if the wounded animals felt a last burst of pain. Did the barest fragments of a thing shelter nerves and feelings, or did sensation require larger shapes: limbs, paws, fins, pincers? Involuntarily, he considered his own body, his limbs still strong and intact, his joints movable, fluid. He could not bear the thought of someone tearing an appendage from his body. Nor the thought of tiger wounds, shrapnel wounds, splinters of metal lodged in his throat and chest, no anesthesia. At night, as he slept, Warren might now harm him if the Vietnamese didn't. Blow off a limb with his machine gun, for instance. Or whisper, "Meow, meow," and slice up his throat and chest, withhold the mercy of dying. Maybe it would be better to be lost in an explosion, blown apart cell-by-cell so that pain might be lessened, made bearable, by infinite division. Conchola wondered how a body could escape pain. Did pain disappear when flesh disappeared? Or did it continue in the earth and air, in the heat of ember and ash, or in the presence of ghosts—*fantasmas*? If his own body were irrecoverable, shredded, nothing left to send to Mama, would he still suffer? By now the animal dust, invisible, had begun to settle in the shade of trees, and maybe new spirits moved among shadows. Conchola looked around and sensed beings taking note of him, watching. Maybe the tiger was across the stream, or maybe the nearby spirits already had eyes keener than cat eyes. It was impossible to know the watchers, or to know what would happen to himself or anyone. "*Tigrito*," he whispered, "*maestro, ayúdame*. Help me to endure, survive. Help me to bear all wounds, all suffering." He glanced at the sky and prayed in silence. "*Virgen de Guadalupe, bendígame.* Maybe you can protect me as if I were your son."

That night he imagined his body sprinkled above trees. Dust of stars, dim light. A substance too ephemeral for suffering. He wondered if he'd done a disservice to the crab by letting it drift away in the remnants of a body. He wondered if the tiger, his *maestro*, would eat it, and might have waited downstream to paw wounded animals from the water. With tooth and claw, a tiger should have no trouble separating the shell from the flesh, devouring the remains of a crab. And would the crab still suffer when it became part of the larger animal? Or would it be unconscious, oblivious, abandoning its suffering to whatever breathed, whatever pumped blood and moved muscle, whatever carried over the broken land a skeleton of bones?

"*Tigrito*," he prayed, "*fiera*. Bless you."

5
Buffalo Tunnel

At sunrise, the children gathered on the south side of the village. As the elephant, hump-backed, cloud-colored, ambled by, Thien thought, *Wait, let me ride you. Lift me with your trunk, set me down on your spine. Take me with you.* Mounted on the beast, the elephant man steered her, calmed her, regulated her speed by tapping his feet on the under sides of her ears. Thien and Hai ran ahead until they were close enough to touch her. The animal, still smeared with mud, river earth, smelled faintly of fishes. Thien offered her fresh-clipped bamboo leaves which she lifted with the tip of her trunk and hurriedly stoked her mouth.

Thien spoke to the elephant man: "When are you coming back? How many days?"

"Three," he said, "or four. Unless I'm needed longer."

"Be careful," she said. "When you come back, you and the elephant can stay with my grandma and me."

"We'll see."

"You're welcome," said Thien. "There's enough room for both of you."

He smiled down on her.

"Your animal ate part of our jackfruit tree, but our tree's still healthy."

"Strong tree," he said.

"I kept watch," said Thien. "She didn't lay down to rest till the early morning."

The man hesitated. "You watched from your window, yes? You didn't go outside, did you?"

Thien found things to look at.

"Don't leave your house at night," said the man. "Unless you enter a tunnel for protection."

She nodded.

"No need to worry about this animal," he said. "You'd do better to worry about your grandma and yourself."

On the outskirts of the village, he insisted that the children join their elders in the rice fields. "Enough," he said. "You'll see me and this elephant in three or four days. We'll be back this way."

"But the road's dangerous," said Thien. "Sometimes the shells and bombs don't explode when they fall. They sink down in the earth where it's difficult to see them."

"I know about this."

"You could stay one more night," said Thien, "and leave for Cu Chi in the morning."

The man shook his head.

"We were shelled two nights ago," said Hai. "The road hasn't been cleared yet."

"We'll be careful."

"I can help," said Thien. "I can look for holes in the earth. Signs of bombs."

"That's my job," he said. "Your job is to help your grandma in the fields."

Thien began to plead, but he interrupted. "Stand back," he said, "all of you. I give no one permission to come with me to Cu Chi."

Thien, head bowed, joined the other children. Lips firm, eyes moist, she held back her tears as the elephant and the elephant man disappeared down a dusty road.

On a dark night, on his mat between rice bins, Luu Hai sang quietly:

> *Miss Thien loves the elephant,*
> *loves him more than any buffalo.*
> *The elephant loves what a buffalo loves—river mud.*

Rain cloud.
Storm cloud.
Flowing river.
The elephant and the buffalo
swim to the sea.

He sang his song three times, then curled on his side, one hand on his chest, the other on his forehead. He remembered Thien slathering her hands and forearms with mud. After she watched the elephant bathe in river mud, she could not resist rubbing the wet soil onto her body. The names he called her in secret (Water Girl, Grass Girl, Girl of the *Bua Ruong,* the best soil) described her better than her given name—Thien. Maybe she would never long for him, wish to marry him, but he still loved her. The mud she plastered on her arms was the color of rich, dark clouds.

He contemplated possibilities. If he were to wallow in river mud, squirm and roll and blow water from his mouth, would the Girl of the *Bua Ruong* believe in him? Maybe first thing in the morning he would jump in the elephant hole, lather himself with mud, and imitate the deep-throated scream of the cloud-colored elephant. He remembered, though, he failed to impress Miss Thien on the day he became an osprey. He'd leaped from her jackfruit tree, his throat alive with wing sounds and wind sounds, but when he showed her his wild fish clutched as with talons, she said, "*Anh dang lam gi?*" (What are you doing?) If Thien couldn't see him as an osprey, a great bird with fierce talons, how could she see him as an elephant the size of three buffalo? Until today, Hai had never seen an animal larger than Great Joy. Now he pictured himself walking with the buffalo, scurrying up on the animal's spine, and looking out over the rooftops of the village. Inside himself, Hai was as large as Great Joy, or larger, but Thien had no eyes for him. To her he was *con trai om*, skinny boy, buffalo boy. Maybe she would never know he was at least as large as the animal he loved.

At midnight, still awake, he could not endure the loneliness of his bed. His heart made wing sounds, soft flutterings, but they did not call to mind the strength of the osprey. He thought of rice birds, pests, the java sparrows that demanded their share of each diminishing harvest. Inside his chest there were wings, subtle sounds of feather and wind, but no flight of mercy. He prayed to the Buddha that his mother and his sister Nhi be protected, that Thien and the elephant be protected, that the spirits of Great Joy and his father be calm and peaceful. He prayed that his own loneliness end soon. He could not imagine Thien letting him touch her, but he could imagine touching Great Joy, the strength of the animal's spine, the broad shoulders, the softness of the throat, the bony ridge over the nostrils. The cloud-colored elephant, nearly white, was beautiful, but no creature on earth had greater dignity than a bull buffalo. Mounted on Great Joy, Hai could look out over fields, over village rooftops, and the body of the beast seemed to fit perfectly in *his* body. Each time Thien saw him riding she could have noticed his buffalo strength, his sun strength, his sky strength. Maybe the Girl of the *Bua Ruong* had seen so many buffalo and buffalo boys that they no longer caught her eye.

He dozed off and woke with an idea. The tunnel behind the cookstove led to the entrance of Great Joy's now vacant buffalo pen. There, at a juncture, one could rise to light or descend to the main tunnel that ran north and south under the village. Going south, the tunnel passed beneath Thai's house and Duc's house, snaked back and forth under the main road, and ended near the fringe of bamboo between Thien's house and Nam's house. Near the tunnel opening, Nam kept his buffalo in a pen, and he wouldn't mind if Hai spent some time with her. Although the buffalo was smaller and less powerful than Great Joy, the two had worked together in the fields, and they came from the same mother. The pen was within thirty meters of Thien's house, the house on the southernmost side of the village. At night it was dangerous to walk over the land, but if Hai could navigate the tunnel, crawl through high grass to the pen, he could touch the animal, pet her, and maybe peer through the wooden slats at the jackfruit tree, the tall bamboo, and the dark frame of the house in which Thien and her grandma slept.

Hai lifted a bamboo mat and slid down into the tunnel behind the cookstove. In darkness he felt his way to the juncture near Great Joy's pen. He inched forward, turned left, and the passage widened as it merged with the main tunnel. For a time he lay still and listened to the night. Small things sliced through soil—maybe moles, worms, burrowing insects. Hai smelled fresh root growth, but the strongest smell was of fungi, decay. He prayed that a bomb would not bury him in this passage. Once, several families had sheltered here only to be suffocated by the weight of the earth when explosions collapsed the tunnel. The tunnel was dug deeper, fortified, but many villagers still did not use it. Hai took a deep breath, tapped the earth for luck, and then burrowed through the dark.

He reached the opening near Nam's buffalo pen in less than a minute. He wormed his way into the grass, raised his head, peered in every direction. He saw round, dark mounds—Nam's house and Thien's house—and the dark wedge lower to the ground, the pen of Nam's buffalo. A thin cloud filtered the light of the quarter moon. The jackfruit tree and the bamboo, outlined in black, cast faint shadows. Soft light covered the land. The Silver River, the stars blurred as in one current, arced from one side of the sky to the other. Hai knew a small group of American soldiers sometimes set up camp on the outskirts of the village. If they spotted him or heard him, they would open fire, call an air strike. If they captured him they would interrogate, rough him up, torture him, force him to admit he had helped set booby traps and dig tunnels in and around the village. Hai sniffed the air for the scent of his enemy. Detecting nothing human, he guessed the Americans were dug in along the main road south of Thien's house, more than a kilometer from the tunnel. In recent months, they had avoided the village at night, for many had died here. Their caution might allow Hai to visit Nam's buffalo when he wished.

Stretched flat, he slithered toward the pen. He smelled hay, buffalo dung, and the grass yielded its night scent. He wondered if Miss Thien lay awake, if she could hear him moving through the dark. Amid the grass there were scattered stones, uneven shards the size of thumbs, knees, elbows. *Earth bones*, thought Hai, *field bones*. A surface root had cut through the soil and curved to the shape and firmness of a rib.

Hai heard the animal rumble. He lifted a stick from a slot, swung open her gate, and slipped inside. She lowed, began to rise, then lay back on her bed of straw. She knew Hai by the smell of his body. She slobbered, lolled her tongue as he petted her throat, her ears, the thick bone that slanted up from her nostrils. Above her was a tin roof, pitch black, but to her sides there were lights, chinks of starlight that sifted through where the wooden slats were not flush. Hai walked around her, leaned forward, and traced his hands over the hump of her spine. In comparison with Great Joy the animal was delicate, but he could feel her dignity, her pride, this long ridge of bone the shape of a mountain. She let him lower his hands over mud-caked flanks, sparse hair. He lay beside her, a hand on her left foreleg, and soon they were asleep.

6
Scent of the Tiger

Conchola, crouched near the point-man, Billie Jasper, saw a strand of wire camouflaged by foliage. "Trap," he said, "hold still. You see it?" Billie strained his eyes, but couldn't see beyond shadows. "Blow you away," said Conchola. "A few more steps and we'd be picking you from the trees."

Lieutenant Bateson crawled forward and said, "What's the hold up?"

"Trap," said Conchola. "One-five-five round."

The lieutenant squinted at clumps of reeds, bamboo. Nothing specific.

"*Derecho*," said Conchola. "A few steps ahead, sir." He leaned forward and pointed. "One loop of wire's tied round that bamboo. You see?"

"Where?"

"Right there, sir. And the other end's rigged to a shell down in that clump of reeds."

The lieutenant inched forward on his belly.

"Best blow the thing," said Jasper.

"You see it?"

"Not yet, sir."

"One-five-five round," said Conchola. "I'd bet money."

"Money?" said Bateson. "You in Las Vegas? Is this Vegas?"

"No, sir."

"Then drop the bullshit. If you're dreaming this up, Conchola, you'll find your testicles hung from the highest tree."

He ordered PFC Jasper and PFC Warren to use a large block of C-4 to clear away the bamboo, the reeds, the muck, and whatever else the Tiger Medic was seeing. "Careful," he whispered. "In case something's really out there."

"The Cat's got eyes," said Warren. "Wants to impress you."

"Zip it," said Bateson.

"Cat eyes, sees the shade. Eyes of a tiger."

"You deaf, Warren?"

"I doubt anything's out there, sir. That's all I'm saying."

"You'll do as you're told. Period."

Warren saluted. "Roger-dodger, sir. I suppose there's no harm in making a little dust."

The lieutenant radioed command that they were about to neutralize an enemy booby trap or suspected booby trap. Minutes later, the det-cord and explosives in place, the platoon at a safe distance, Warren called, "Fire in the hole," pressed the firing device, and the earth mushroomed. Showers of metal burst through nests of reeds and bamboo, hurled them through the air, trimmed the fringes of surrounding trees. Conchola heard wings beating the hot air, rising. Something chattered and wailed—maybe a monkey in the crown of a nearby tree.

Conchola nudged Jasper. "One-five-five round. What I tell you?"

"Kitty luck," said Warren. "Blind guess."

"No, sharp eyes," said Jasper. "Tiger-in-training."

Conchola grinned.

"Keep it up we might make it home," said Jasper. "You'll come to my wedding."

Warren snickered.

"Eight months away I'm a married man. No bullshit."

"Right," said Warren.

"Yeah, you ain't invited, but Cat Man is. Come meet the prettiest girl in the world, Lucinda Sayers."

"Lucinda?" said Warren.

Jasper lifted the cross on his necklace, brushed it to his

lips. "Miss Sayers to you," he said. "The luckiest, prettiest girl in the Carolinas and the world."

Lieutenant Bateson radioed command to report their success: "Detonated and destroyed a one-five-five shell. Booby trap, trip-wire variety. Could've done major damage." He spoke as though he himself had spotted the wire thin as a thread, the shell hidden in reeds, the trap—in his words—"ready to blow half my platoon to heaven." He accepted brief praise, claimed he was lucky. After signing off, he said to his men: "Okay, saddle up, stay alert. Keep your eyes peeled for wires and shells and gooks."

They made slow progress. Along the Cambodian stream the morning light barely penetrated the tiers of trees, the clumps of reeds and bamboo, the walls of undergrowth that had to be hacked with machetes. Since they found no blood trails, animal or human, Conchola hoped the tiger's wounds had closed and begun healing. He tried to convince himself he would never have seen the trip-wire or the one-five-five shell if the tiger had perished. *Ojos listos*, he thought. *Saw the trap with the eyes of the animal.* As he followed Jasper, the point man, he occasionally glanced down to admire the scratches on his left forearm. Here the beast had struck, lashed a lightning-quick paw, inscribed wounds that were essential. Swinging his machete, the medic noted the slight throbbing in his arm, the pressure behind his eyes, the subtle tingling in his breastbone. *Fiera*, he thought. *You too are alive, tingling, circling, nursing your wounds, waiting.* Conchola halted briefly to sniff his scratches, lick them. The wounds hurt a little, throbbed and stung, but gave solace to the tongue.

At night, after several hours of steady rainfall, the platoon bivouacked near the stream. Conchola and Jasper, again sharing a foxhole, crouched in water that had risen above their ankles. Leeches attached to calves and inner thighs.

Insects and worms in the flooded hole used legs as ladders of escape, and torsos became new earth, feeding grounds, islands of refuge. Jasper whispered, "Got somethin' botherin' my back, man. Slap me."

He turned so Conchola could slap him.

"Lower. Mid-back. Harder."

Conchola whacked him twice, open-handed.

"Aw, baby, whatever was wounding me is sorry."

Conchola wiped his hands on his pant legs.

"Creepy crawler," said Jasper. "Felt like it had fangs."

The platoon had set up their ambush in the foliage near the stream. The killing zone, the targeted area, was a rectangular wedge of reeds and tall grass traversed by animal trails that widened near the shoreline. The lieutenant received a radio call that an enemy force—thirty to forty North Vietnamese—were moving in their direction. He requested support (gunships, artillery, air strikes), but was told to wait for the enemy to pass within the semi-circle of four American platoons that would block possible escape routes. The lieutenant ordered his men to remain in their holes. Water or no water, they were not to crawl out and spread plastic ponchos on the ground. Nor were they allowed to rise and stretch their legs, shake off the bugs, make unnecessary noises. "One-hundred percent alert," he said, "no excuses. If you have any gripes, you can keep them to yourself."

Conchola feared the tiger, like himself, had become a feeding ground. He listened to subtle noises in the soil. The migration of insects, the small hissing sounds, the busy movement of legs, the scratching and clawing as creatures burrowed up through the sodden earth. All things struggled to breathe, to eat, to not be eaten. Conchola brushed insects from his neck. He and Jasper slapped each other's back until the lieutenant whispered, "Hush it up now, quiet." Motionless, Conchola monitored countless points of prickling, itching, biting. It seemed the world had slipped inside his skin: insect legs, claws, feelers, mouths, beaks, pincers. He prayed the tiger never suffered this way. He pictured the beast in a cave, a shelter, and for a brief time the image soothed him: the tiger at ease, the graceful curl of the body, the long breaths that sank down into the heart of the belly. *Tranquilo*, thought Conchola, *cómodo*, but he doubted himself. The words passed through him as empty as dreams.

He strained his eyes and tried to see shapes. There were glimmers of light, variations of gray and dark gray, but he couldn't make out the full form of a plant, a tree, a cloud, a body. He doubted that anything nearby could escape pain. Maybe in the air far up, in shadows above clouds, something rested. A pocket of cool air, a softness too distant to be breathed, absorbed, swallowed by a body. Whatever mingles with flesh—a frail breath, hunger—brings suffering. *So you escape*, he thought, *se va lejos, and leave your body. If you eat nothing, if nothing eats you, the earth has no memory of your presence. You die, lose yourself, stop breathing, and the flesh that once held your suffering falls apart like rain.*

Later, when the frogs sang loud enough that the lieutenant, on the far side of the perimeter, wouldn't hear a conversation, Conchola said, "Maybe the tiger's in a cave somewhere. Resting or sleeping."

"Sipping a bowl of milk," said Jasper.

"Warm and dry," said Conchola. "He knows every tree, every stone, every bush. If there's a cave he'll find it."

"Over the rainbow."

"He's all right now. He's better off than we are."

Something close by scraped at bark, skittered up a tree.

"That him?" said Jasper. "Your tiger?"

Conchola shook his head. "A squirrel maybe, or else a monkey." He leaned forward and cupped his hands over Jasper's right ear. "Tigers rarely climb trees. *Bien raro*."

He felt the slight twitch of Jasper's head, a gesture of doubt.

"Swear to my Mama," said Conchola. "A tiger might leap

and catch a monkey asleep on a low branch, but he won't chase it up a tree. Ever."

"Yeah, all right. Beautiful."

"Saw it back home on TV. Seems a century ago."

"Or more."

"Just telling you how it is. A tiger rarely climbs trees. He's too big for the branches."

"Fine."

"You have a one-in-a-million chance to see or hear a tiger in a tree."

Conchola felt his cupped hands dip and rise, Jasper's nod. "Enough," said Billie. "Wanna get your hands off my ear now?"

"Sorry."

"So what's in this nearby tree? Maybe these little sounds in the dark come from tree-climbing gooks."

Conchola slapped his right thigh where something was crawling. "Not a chance. No gooks tonight."

"Oh?"

"They know where we're at. They know where the other platoons are. They know they're outnumbered."

"Could be."

"*Bien claro*. Couldn't be otherwise."

"We'll see."

"The gooks keep their distance unless they have the advantage. Most nights all we have to do is survive ten million bugs."

In the wee hours, the jungle mostly quiet, Conchola smelled something other than rain and sweat, a thick, gamy smell that spread itself through foliage. There was no movement in the trees. No belching of frogs. No nameless legion of critters that skittered through marsh grass. *Milagro*, thought Conchola. A beast of some four-hundred pounds had left his cave and crept in silence through streamside reeds and grass. He listened for the sound of paws, breathing, the brush of the body on foliage, but only the smell gave evidence of the animal's presence. *Amargo*. The bitter smell of earth, urine, blood. The musty smell of wet fur, moss, fishmeat. Maybe the tiger had crossed the stream in the rain. Maybe on his way he caught a fish, ate it, and now he smelled of its flesh, salty and sour, *fresco*, cooled by fishblood. For a moment Conchola didn't notice the swarms of insects housed by his body. He inhaled and smelled the tiger and other smells: frogs, snails, the inside of a moist tree, a nearby sapling that had fallen. *Olor del Mundo*, he thought, *Scent of the World. A tree that holds water.* He inhaled deeply and stood straight up in his water-drenched hole.

"Billie," he whispered. "You smell it?"

"Smell what?"

"*Nada*," he said. "Just smells like a broken tree."

The rain abated shortly before dawn. Conchola, still standing, monitored breezes that sifted through marsh grass. He called, "Hold your fire!" when he heard the click of safeties, bolts, M-16s. It seemed the tiger was moving in an arc, coming nearer, and the ebb and flow of wind marked the rhythm of his breathing. For a few moments there was no sound. Then again the beast moved, retreated it seemed, as the wind blew more softly through marsh grass. The medic smelled traces of fish, snail, blood, tree moss. "Nothin' out there," he said. "Nothin' dangerous." But a split second later every gun but Conchola's opened fire.

The snap of M-16s along the perimeter. Conchola called, "Cease fire, cease fire!" but only Jasper stopped shooting. A burst of flares spread an unreal light over the earth—purple and green, blue and yellow. Conchola crawled from the foxhole and waved both arms. "All clear! All clear! Nothing out here." PFC Warren faced the stream and worked his machine gun left to right. He turned, adjusted his aim, and fired at Conchola. "Jump!" said Jasper. "Jump!" The medic dove in beside Billie and pressed his hands to the earth.

At first light Lieutenant Bateson ordered a cease-fire. Via radio, he gave a situation report: "No friendly casualties... enemy soldiers in retreat...fifteen to twenty enemy killed or wounded...body count to be verified later." He asked that Cobra gunships stand by, and artillery batteries, and a squad of bombers. "Situation secure at present," he said. "But there could be well-fortified enemy placements dug in along the stream."

Then he walked to Conchola's hole and said, "What the hell you think you're doing?"

"Sir?"

"I'll decide when the shooting starts and stops. Is that clear?"

"*Bien claro*, sir."

"And dispense with the Spanish. I order you to never again holler, 'All clear, all clear,' when you can't see two feet in front of you."

"But I knew what was there, sir. An animal."

"Private, you can forget your damn tiger."

"Maybe not."

"Conchola—"

"Sorry, sir. We have a zero body count. I can promise you."

"You can promise me nothing. You can drag your sorry ass out there with Jasper's squad and see what you find."

They found a fold in the marsh grass where something had lain. A little blood in the grass, a dark smear from a fresh wound, a circumference the size of a quarter. Conchola inhaled the scent of blood, rain, dank fur, marsh grass. He touched the blood with the thumb of his left hand, tasted. *Fiera*, he thought, *tigrito*. The King of the Jungle must have belly-crawled to the shore, edged into the water, and crossed to the other side.

The lieutenant came up, followed by another squad. Conchola pointed to the fold in the marsh grass and led the lieutenant to the bank of the stream where he found a fresh paw print. "See?" said Conchola. "Same animal as before, sir."

The lieutenant rubbed the bridge of his nose.

Warren said, "Okay, a tiger, big deal. But there was some gooks out here, at least a platoon. They was camped here with the tiger."

"Zero chance," said Conchola.

"Hush it up," said Bateson. "I don't need an analysis, a statistical overview."

"*Pues*—"

"And drop the Spanish," he said. "Keep your eyes peeled. The enemy can't be far away."

Conchola stood tall, pawed his crotch, and walked off toward the slow-moving stream. In the first light of day the water—gray and brown, dark green—gave a quiet glow, more tranquil, thought Conchola, than the stained-glass windows of a church.

Later he said to Jasper: "I wasn't worried much. They don't know how hard he is to kill."

7
Elephant

Brindled, cloud-colored, the beast entered the village and turned onto the muddy path that divided the rice fields and led to the shore of the Sai Gon River. Thien, hunched over weeds and rice grass, leaped to her feet, lost her hat, and called, "*Con voi, con voi*" (elephant). Her grandma took the trowel the girl dropped in the weeds and set it on the nearest bund. "And the elephant man?" said Ba Ly. "Did you forget him?" The old woman had prayed for the safety of the animal and her master every morning and evening since they went away.

Thien leaped onto a bund and began running toward the elephant. Her grandma called after her, "Walk! Walk or keep still! What have I told you?" Pretending not to hear, Thien sprinted. When Ba Ly called again the girl froze, her heart quick as a rabbit's. She waited for the elephant and the elephant man to pass her way.

Astride the beast, the man appeared as tiny as a doll, a miniature figure of a grandpa. "*Ong,*" said Thien, "can I ride her? Just once?"

The elephant man shook his head.

"Remember?" said Thien. "Remember you stayed with my grandma and me? Remember your elephant ate part of our jackfruit tree?"

His fingers combed the sparse hair on his chin.

"You can stay again," said the girl, "as long as you wish. Whether or not you let me ride her."

He tilted his head, thinking. "Well, are you strong? Can you hold on? Keep from falling?"

Her eyes flared. "I'm strong. I work the fields here."

He chuckled.

"I can hold on," she said. "I'm sure I can."

"We'll see."

"Honest," she said. "I'll sit still and quiet and do whatever you say."

The elephant folded her back legs, swayed forward, and lowered her belly to the earth. Over her side her master slung a net, a crisscross of ropes that Thien used as a ladder. Within seconds, the girl lighted on the beast's spine, gripped the elephant man's shoulders, and balanced in a low crouch. Bare feet immersed in the elephant, she stood as easily as in the watery soil of paddies. Thien could have let go, risen to her full height, stretched free her arms, but the elephant man gave instructions. "Sit down," he said, "hold onto me. Lean forward." The skin of her thighs tingled. Sitting, hugging the man's chest with one arm, bracing the other on the dome of the beast's spine, she touched webs of wrinkles, dry mud, white hair, a thick cushiony texture in which the tips of her fingers vanished. She felt herself rising, swaying, as the elephant pushed herself up and began walking. It was as though a great chunk of earth had formed a body, rolled over, crested. The beast snaked high her trunk, quickened her pace. Maybe she was spurred forward by important smells: the water and fish of the Sai Gon River one-hundred meters away.

Buffalo boys darted along the pathway. Luu Hai, alternately skipping and leaping, said, "Miss Thien, lucky Thien," and waved to her. The girl looked down at dark eyes, conical hats, a few arms that groped upward. Hai was gesturing, saying something, but she ignored him. From the spine of the elephant, she saw things in a different way. The river seemed smaller, curled more tightly over the land, and the light of ripples and waves resembled whorls of snake skin. The shallow lakes of the paddies made rectangular mirrors of blue sky, white sky. Silver. There were buffalo in green fields, women in black work clothes, and beyond the fields a grove of bamboo and coconut palms on the outskirts of the village. Thien, her mouth a small circle, called, "Awooo, awooo!" It seemed only the banyan tree, Luu Hai's lookout tree, rose above her. The boy began shouting, trying to get her attention, but she barely listened. She heard *toi* (which means me, or I, which she heard twice), *con trau* (buffalo), *con chim* (bird) and *mat troi* (sun). Thien grazed her knuckles over a vertebrae the size of a human skull. The animal carried her, this weight of a girl, maybe no more noticeable than an insect on the shoulder of a human. Luu Hai waved his arms, bellowed, but soon Thien heard nothing. The girl swayed as the ambling elephant lifted two right legs, then two left legs, and carried her and her master to the muddy shore.

The animal knelt and Thien clambered down the rope ladder. The old man lowered himself down the side of the beast, undid the strap circling her girth, and removed the rope netting. He squatted over the small packages still strapped to the net, his clothing and supply of food. He sighed pleasurably as the elephant tumbled forward and shocked the river with waves.

Hai, glancing from Thien to the elephant, said, "Beautiful, almost like a buffalo. Great Joy."

She did not look at him.

"But he's bigger than Great Joy," Hai admitted. "His body has different colors."

"*Her* body," said Thien. "She's not a bull."

"Oh?"

"She's female. She's a mother. She once had a child."

Hai nodded.

"She's three times larger than any buffalo. She's probably the strongest animal alive."

The elephant repeatedly dipped her trunk in the river, suckled brown water, funneled it down her maw. Satiated, she rolled on her side, splashed, and then waddled toward deeper water. Anxious, Thien asked the elephant man if the beast could swim. "Ong, does she know the river? Can she stay afloat if the water's over her head?"

"I wouldn't worry yourself."

"But the river's deep in the middle. I've never touched bottom."

"Nor will she," he said. "She's a swimmer, not a diver. "He squinted into the glare and pointed. "But whose bananas on the far shore? Whose banana plant?"

"I don't know."

"She can smell the fruit. If the wind's right, she can smell a banana plant two-hundred meters away."

Thien could tell by the angle of the animal's trunk, the prow-like surge of her shoulders, that her feet no longer touched bottom. No riverbed beneath her, the elephant snorkeled the air, churned the water, and a wide wake, muddy and brown, swirled behind her. "Be careful," called Thien, and waded out waist-deep into the river. "The currents," she muttered. "The currents are very strong."

The animal made whooshing sounds, whistling sounds, gargled snorts. Hai and other buffalo boys mimicked her, and then Hai and his cousin Nam leaped in the river. Kicking his feet, paddling with one arm, Hai held his other arm over the water as though it were a trunk. He wanted to swim in the wake of the elephant, but she had put too much distance between them. Hai rolled onto his back and spouted a stream of water into the air. "Thien," he said, "Miss Thien." But not so loud that she would hear.

The girl waded farther out until Ba Ly called to her. Thien retreated, stood knee-deep in water, and kept her vigil. Near the far shore the elephant's shoulders emerged, then the dome of her spine, her flanks, as streams of water poured from her body. She coughed, raised her trunk, trumpeted, and Thien felt a warm pulsation through the pit of her belly. Hai and Nam, still swimming, gasped and screamed, their voices insignificant to the girl. More buffalo boys jumped in the river, each holding an arm over his head to imitate the trunk of the elephant. Whooping, snorting, the boys made soft, trumpeting sounds. They and Miss Thien looked toward the far shore as the elephant walked out of the river and ambled toward a feast.

She swung high her trunk and pulled a stalk to the ground. She tore off a bunch of green bananas, lifted them to her mouth, and devoured them. After stripping the stalk of fruit, she began eating a banana leaf the size of a sampan. Her sunlit body, silvery white, ash-colored, was magnificent. *I rode her*, thought Thien. *I rode on her back! An elephant!* Buffalo boys splashed and swam and hollered. Luu Hai and a few others made chewing sounds, snuffling sounds, elephant sounds. Thien ignored their pitiful imitations. She squatted in the shallows and watched the leviathan until Ba Ly called for her to return to the fields.

Crouched in the tunnel opening near Nam's buffalo pen, Hai heard the elephant foraging in the stand of bamboo between Nam's house and Thien's house. Tearing sounds, chewing sounds. And now and then a soft thump, the sound of something being swallowed. Hai crawled from the hole and saw above him a tall darkness like the crown of a great tree. He breathed in the smells of water, river mud, the smells that reminded him of a buffalo. An owl gave a startled cry and flew toward the east.

He remembered Thien riding the elephant, her eyes wild and beautiful, her mouth half-open in a smile of pleasure. She had sat behind the elephant's master, held onto him, and she made a sound—*Awooo-awooo*—that spread over the fields and the river. Then, as now, Hai experienced a confusion of feelings: jealousy and joy, anger and appreciation. Why was he down on the ground while she paraded like a queen, oblivious to the peasant boy who loved her? She had risen to such a height one could say she moved through the sky on the spine of a giant. She called, "Awooo, awooo," but her song was not for Hai. Thien offered herself only to the elephant and the light of the sky through which she and the master rode.

Hai crawled to within five meters of the beast and saw chains on her hind legs. The animal could inch forward or rear back, but could not stride off through the village and into the rice fields. For a few moments his eyes locked on Thien's house, the humped darkness like a bush. Birds twittered in the jackfruit tree, and he noticed the branch he had leaped from—clutching a fish as with talons—was among those that were missing. During her last stay, the elephant had eaten approximately one-eighth of a fifteen-meter tree. Maybe tonight Thien's grandma had asked the elephant man to shackle his animal near the bamboo so the jackfruit would not perish. Now the beast seemed aware of Hai's presence, but did not hesitate in her eating. Bamboo leaves, tender twigs, shoots—they widened her body. Hai watched her and thought: *Thien loves you, not me, but she might love both of us.* He paused, listened to the animal eating, then continued his inner monologue. *Tell Miss Thien I'm an elephant's cousin, a buffalo—Great Joy. And you can also say I'm a wild bird, an osprey. A fisherbird.* He rolled his shoulders. *Strong talons,* he thought, *giant wings. Twice as large as the white bird with pink legs that pecks tiny bugs from the creases of a buffalo's hide.*

As though an agreement had been made, Hai nodded to the animal, then crawled to Nam's buffalo pen and opened the gate. The cow was skittish, shaking her head from side-to-side, tamping her hooves, snorting. "Go to sleep," said Hai. "The elephant's Miss Thien's friend, she won't hurt you." With both hands he massaged the bony ridge over the snout of the buffalo. He worked his fingers into the soft crevices behind her ears, the elasticity of her throat, her left shoulder. "Relax," said Hai, "we're safe here." He was able to coax her to fold her legs and lie down on her bed. He basked in the smell of grass, straw, buffalo dung, the warm, fishy smell that rose from the river. He petted the animal until her breathing slowed and deepened. On the straw mound on which she lay, her head angled to one side, there was also room for him.

Late at night he woke to whispers. At first he thought he was mumbling in his sleep, comforting the animal, but then he woke fully and heard a voice outside his body. "Too soft," said a girl, "too thin. Skin needs to be tougher. Your ears are soft as mine are." The buffalo, also awake, did not snort or move about, but lay still, semi-alert, eyes open. Hai comforted her a few moments, petted her throat and shoulders. Then he knelt, leaned forward, and peered through a chink of light that passed between wooden slats.

He saw five things: the moon, waxing and bright, a small figure, the elephant silver and tall, the nearby grass, the wall of bamboo. The figure stretched and touched the side of the animal's right foreleg. As the elephant lowered her head, curled her trunk under a fallen branch, the figure touched her right ear and said, "Still too soft. Really." Hai recognized Thien's voice, Thien's body. The small bowl of her waist, the wider shadow beneath, pure black and closer to earth—hips. Thien whispered something he couldn't hear. She scratched the animal's right ear, the inner side, and then spoke loudly enough for the boy to eavesdrop. "Eat and grow strong, thicken the skin. And where you are not strong you will learn to be lucky." She patted the elephant's trunk. "If tonight they come with bombs, no family in the village has a tunnel wide enough to hold you." She hesitated. "There are things even you can't do," she said. "You can't catch a bomb with your trunk, keep it from falling and exploding. You will survive because you're lucky, that's all. When planes fly through the sky, when they try to kill everything and everyone, you will find a way to escape."

If he were her older brother, he would rush from the buffalo pen to warn her: *Calm down, what are you doing? You come out in the night to pet an elephant. Your whispers grow noisy. You have no elephant pen, nothing to conceal you.* Now she moved to the other side of the animal, her legs and hips still visible between the legs of the giant. She mumbled something, coughed, and he heard her hands tapping the side of the elephant's body. Hai understood her need for comfort. He himself had crawled through one hundred meters of darkness to reach the pen of Nam's buffalo. Maybe Thien felt safe now, relaxed, and would be able to sleep after visiting the elephant. The girl bent down, round and dark, in the shade of the animal's body. Had he loved her less, understood her less, he would have come forward, revealed himself, ruined the silence between them, and tried to touch her with his hands.

Long before the sky paled, Thien left the elephant, bent down in the grass, and crawled thirty meters to her home. After watching that she was safely inside, Luu Hai returned to Nam's buffalo and the buffalo bed and slept off and on till dawn.

8
Make Tracks, Spread Wings

Something moved in the marsh grass. Maybe a wild boar, a small pig, grubbing for roots and tubers. Maybe a squirrel burying or uncovering a fruit, a seed. Or a young cat razing its claws on the earth, sharpening its weapons. Near the stream the grass bent slightly, parted, closed. Conchola, in his foxhole with Billie Jasper, whispered, "Small animal. Harmless. Nothing to write your Mama. No bigger than a hound."

Moments later three soldiers on his right opened fire. The air burst with popping sounds—flares, grenades. Then the bark of Warren's machine gun, the detonation of Claymore mines, the snap of M-16s, the rain of metal. Bullets plunged through trees on the far side of the stream. The limbs, laid open, made bird sounds, high shrieks. And there were deafening pings, whirs, echoes as bullets hit stone and exploded. PFC Warren worked his machine gun in steady bursts. More mines exploded, more grenades. The grass, lit with flares, turned orange and blue, then violet and yellow. Conchola saw the crouched form of an animal near the stream. It had a short neck crested with bristles, a round head that suddenly shuddered and jerked, a compact body that slumped forward. Conchola said to Jasper, "A pig, man. Wild pig. Dead now." The jungle darkened when flares floated down within canopies of trees. The platoon, minus the point man and medic, fired for several more minutes at the slain animal, the grass, the stones, the stream, the darkness of the other shore.

Visibility was too poor for the lieutenant to immediately request an air strike. He asked for the support of artillery, but was told the area in which the platoon had bivouacked was five kilometers beyond the range of the nearest firebase. The voice that came over the radio broke with static. "Wait thirty to forty minutes...first light...Could send air strike...Advise." "Affirmative," said the lieutenant, "air strike. Soon as possible. Send everything you got."

Conchola, half out of his hole, monitoring the radio transmission, learned the area to be bombed was across the stream, west-northwest of their position. According to Lieutenant Bateson, the main enemy force, in retreat now, had forded the stream, escaped westward, plunged deeper into jungle. The platoon rested their weapons, but there was a ringing in the air, a shrill whistle. Conchola had a premonition the tiger had moved outward through tall grass and into the trees on the far side of the stream.

He smelled pig blood, bowels and bladder. There was a rustling sound, something moving through the grass. "Hear it?" he whispered. "How it's circling?"

Billie Jasper crouched low in their foxhole.

"*Tigrito*," said Conchola. "On the other side of the stream. *Watchando*."

"Poor fucker."

"No, the animal has at least ninety-nine-million lives. More lives than we have bombs."

"Whatever."

"A magician," said Conchola. "For a split second you might see him near the stream, orange and black, but you blink your eyes and where is he?"

"I don't know."

"Vanished, baby. *Desaparecido*." Conchola shrugged, clucked his tongue. "A magician," he said. "Because to survive a single night he has to blend with all this dark."

He kept whispering, telling tiger tales, because he was frightened. Surviving an air strike was sheer luck. The earth erupted in flames, rings of fire. Animals that wandered alone—tigers, bull boars, bull elephants—and those that moved in flocks or herds had no defense whatever. Only in Conchola's imagination could a tiger, *his* tiger, lash a paw through the sky, tip war planes into nose-over-tail dives, raise his head over tiered canopies to watch distant explosions lovely as red flowers. There was an impossible divide between what should happen and what would happen. At first light the jungle would be bombed. No paw or fang or beak was capable of resistance. Conchola wondered where in this darkness the tiger waited. Maybe he watched the platoon from the tree line on the far side of the stream, unaware of squadrons of planes moving in his direction. Conchola felt a sharp tingling at the base of his spine. What if he gambled his life, helped his *maestro*? What if he abandoned his hole, walked through marsh grass to the stream, crossed over to the other side? Conchola couldn't swim, but maybe he could drift with currents, jerk his arms and legs, angle his body in the appropriate direction. If he floated to the far shore, he could flush the tiger from the killing zone before first light. He could enter the jungle and flush other creatures—monkeys, pigs, birds—things hidden in shadows. He remembered the first day in Cambodia when he saw the tiger near the stream. The long body, orange and black, the throat wound and chest wound, the light of the eyes, the fury—the one truth in his life he had fully witnessed. *Un soldado*, he believed he must shoot it, kill it, but he fired blindly at shadows. Now he thanked Jesus for bullets gone awry, bullets made harmless. The tiger, the escape artist, had vanished in silence into the darkness of trees.

He removed his helmet, his boots, and leaned his rifle against the wall of the foxhole. He nudged Billie Jasper and whispered, "I'll be back in a minute. Don't let these fuckers shoot me."

"Huh?"

"Montezuma's revenge," he lied. "I'll fill this hole with shit if I don't drag my ass out there."

"Just hold it."

"Yeah, would if I could. You ever feel like a greased pig ready to blow?"

"*Gee*-sus."

"Sir," said Conchola. "Lieutenant Bateson, sir. I have to go out and relieve myself."

"Concho—"

"Ay-yay, sir. Nothing to worry about. I'll be bent over in the marsh grass a minute or two."

"Don't move."

"Impossible, sir. I'm moving all over."

"Fuck up."

"No choice, sir. Montezuma's revenge. I'll crawl back to my hole soon as I'm relieved."

He lifted himself from the foxhole and into the grass. Lieutenant Bateson called, "Get your ass back here," but Conchola bent low and began walking.

Warren said, "Meow Man's up to his ears in his own shit. Not too surprising, sir."

Bateson said, "Okay, drop your drawers, drop your load. Get your ass back to your hole."

There was some whispering among the *muchachos* as Conchola, hunched over, stumbled to the shore. He squatted, groaned, sank down on all fours, and slipped into the water. He heard a jumble of voices: "Yeah, bad manners, sir, shitting in a stream." "Never trust a Mexican, man. I mean really." The medic worked his elbows, crabbed them front and back, pushed with his legs, merged with currents. The stream buoyed him and carried him. He felt its authority in his body. Electrical. Swift. Decisive. His stocking feet nudged bottom. He pushed off, kicked, jerked his arms, began to paddle. Someone popped flares, silver and blue. Conchola ducked, released his breath, and drifted underwater. Face down, he entered a vein in the stream, a current riffled with fins, claws, pincers. He could sense the animals flaring away, fishes and crabs rising and falling, making room for his body. The current turned him on his left side and carried him around a sharp bend, an oxbow. He rose for air and saw flare lights, pale blue, over the jungle canopy some thirty meters upstream.

He paddled his way to the opposite shoreline. Another flare, an umbrella of green light too distant to disturb him. He heard something scrabble in the soft soil of the shore, maybe a crab burrowing for safety. Billie Jasper called, "Okay, man, that's enough. Can't play Jesus for a tiger." Conchola crawled through high grass and into a tree line. He heard obscenities, fuck yous, Warren's voice and the lieutenant's voice. Now Billie Jasper called louder, "Seriously, man, don't leave me alone. I might not make it." Conchola, behind the trunk of a wide tree, lay still and waited. Another flare went off—soft purple—but failed to reveal his position. He belly-crawled deeper into the jungle until the voices of soldiers quieted. He couldn't make out distinct words now, only the tone—bewildered, angry. He estimated he had less then twenty minutes before the sky would rain with bombs.

He stood and began walking. "*Váyanse,*" he said. "Make tracks, spread wings. *Váyanse.*" He heard ticking sounds in trees, the rasp of claws. Something skittered, a small animal in the cover of high branches. "*Vete,*" he said, "*adios,*" and the creature whistled. Safely away from the platoon, Conchola began stomping and calling, stumbling against low-hanging vines, fronds, branches. Despite the probability that he himself would be bombed, he felt invincible, robust. He bumped against a tree, shivered the trunk, and birds— wings soughing and sweeping—departed. He opened his maw, attempted a roar, but the emerging sound was unworthy of a tiger. He tried again, louder, and inspired a short burst from Warren's machine gun. "Geronimo!" said Conchola. "*Oye!*" The jungle dark sung fire. Birds flew.

Speeding up, swinging his arms energetically, he kept repeating his warning: "*Váyanse.* Make tracks, spread wings. *Vayan.*" Away from the stream, less undergrowth impeded his progress. He discerned shapes, the silhouettes of bushes, saplings, tree trunks. For a moment he paused and sensed the alertness of trees, the alertness of his body. Around each object it seemed something vibrated, a bright sound that moved from tree to tree, ringing and resounding. Conchola raised his arms and said, *"Váyanse,* away from here. You'll be crispy critters." He heard a braying sound, deep and mournful. A caterwaul, an ululation. In his stocking feet he stomped the earth, waved his arms over his head, and said, *"Váyanse, ahorita.* All of you." Roaring, he kicked trees, wrestled trees, heard winged ones flying. "Geronimo!" he said, "Geronimo! Can't be killed by a bullet or bomb."

He smelled traces of urine and blood, traces of brine, and the air was ringing. He had an odd thought: *If Mama could see me, if the girls back home could see me. A lone human before dawn,* bien marcado, oscuro, *scarred by a tiger.* Conchola kept moving, calling out, warning as many beasts and birds as possible. He told himself to forget Mama and the girls back home; they were far away, unimportant, and would never understand what he was doing. Nonetheless, he occasionally stood tall for them, squared his shoulders, restrained giggles, imagined witnesses to his bravery. But mainly he spoke to the animal world, his voice now and then rising to the intensity of a roar: *"Váyanse, váyanse,* get out of here before you're dead."

9
Feast Day

Village women bathing, washing their hair, washing their babies, nursing, washing pigs, lathering them down, washing fruits, vegetables, baskets of rice on the shores and shallows of the Sai Gon River.

Luu Hai and his cousin Nam sat in the shade of a coconut palm. Twenty meters away Nam's buffalo sank slowly in a mud hole, a white bird perched on the island of her spine.

Eleven village boys played *Choi Choi Lon* on the riverbank. Huy Duong, Hai's cousin, drew a straight line in the mud. One-by-one, the boys crouched, positioned themselves behind the line, and hurled a rubber thong at a silver can.

Huy Duong struck the target. He made a bright sound, "Aiee, aiee!", as he raced down the riverbank. Hai heard the sun in his cousin's voice. He heard the slap of Duong's feet, small drums on the wet earth.

In the late morning, the elephant and the elephant man and Thien and Luu Hai and other village children waded in the cove where Great Joy once drank and bathed. The elephant man lathered the beast, scrubbed her sides with a brush, and Thien splashed her clean. The animal snorkeled mud into her trunk and showered her spine moments later. "That's her way," said the elephant man. "She needs a new coat of mud to shield her from insects and sun."

Ma Xuan and Nhi watered the pepper patch in back of their home. No enemy soldiers had entered the village in more than a week. The people who lived here began to remember their land ribbed with rivers, their gardens crested with banyans and palms.

Beneath Luu Hai's lookout post, a banyan tree, villagers gathered. Each family brought food for the cadre, the Viet Cong who had emerged from tunnels. Small baskets brimmed with fresh mango and pineapple, grilled corn, rice balls wrapped in banana leaves, pork buns, boiled jackfruit seeds, salted fish and pickled ginger. Cadre Duc, a senior official from the north, and Ong Quan and Ong Troung, the oldest men of the village, were offered the tastiest dish—eel poached in coriander. Duc had called for a rare midday meeting to announce that the Americans, the day ghosts normally operating in the area, were "now losing the war in another country. In Cambodia," he said, "they are bumbling about looking for a headquarters we moved several months earlier. They've found a few weapons, a few sacks of chicken rice, a few medical supplies no longer essential." He chopsticked eel and coriander into his mouth. "For the most part they're lost, wandering in circles. Sometimes the most intelligent strategy is to allow the enemy to defeat himself."

He was never the bearer of bad news. The people mostly ate *tam* rice, chicken rice, and this feast was a rare occasion. Once the Americans returned, many days might pass before the villagers could gather in daylight to share their best food, the scant remains of it. Cadre Duc himself, in the past six months, had eaten mainly chicken rice, and had spent most of his days in tunnels, sleeping or planning. At night—when the Americans were hunkered down, afraid to move—he emerged with his comrades from tunnels and spider holes to see what wounds he could inflict.

After he finished his meal, he and his wife, Cadre Minh, thanked the villagers for their ongoing efforts. Duc, standing on a dais, a wooden slab about one meter high, said, "It is our honor and duty to lead you. For five years now, my wife and my daughter and I have had the good fortune to live in or near this village, and we have come to recognize it as the backbone of our country." He smiled broadly. "Comrades, this village is a thousand villages, or ten thousand, each one working tirelessly to break the will of the invaders." He glanced from face to face. "I have nothing but praise for your commitment, your courage. In the past year, each able-bodied villager has dug at least one meter of tunnel per day. Each family has set aside the best available food for a Viet Cong soldier, and today—look around—a feast for the deserving!" He wagged his fingers over his head. "Sai Gon's puppet soldiers, where are they? The Vietnamese pulled by American strings, where are they?" He swept a hand as if shooing flies. "They know better than to enter this village, they have learned by dying. In summary, comrades, the enemies of Viet Nam are in disarray."

Duc raised both hands to silence the applause. "Today there is one more thing to consider," he said. "In a nine-kilometer circumference around the village, we now have thirty-three mines and booby traps. Day ghosts die here, and will continue to die until they lose the war and return to their country. As mentioned, they are now stumbling around in Cambodia. Wandering around child-like, following each other's tail—these are the Americans. Helicopters will soon rescue them from the jungles, bring them back to Cu Chi, the main base of the 25th Infantry. They will return, and before they leave Viet Nam forever, they will again patrol this village and attempt to destroy your homes, your fields, your animals—even the graves of your ancestors. As you have seen countless times, they thrive on destruction, nothing else. But they themselves will be the victims in the end."

He paused, searched out faces, then leaned forward. "Are we prepared to fight them?"

In unison: "Yes!"

"Will we win? Will we defeat the Americans? Will we humiliate them?"

"Yes, comrade!"

"Then listen," he said, "catch my words. This is what comes next."

Duc asked that each villager lend greater support to the effort of transforming unexploded enemy bombs and shells into mines and booby traps. "Our goal is specific," he said. "We will plant ten new devices to greet the day ghosts on their return."

Thien, barely listening, kept watch on the elephant. She and Nhi rested in the fringe of the banyan's shade and watched the animal graze a small clump of banana plants twenty meters away. The elephant man, who sat with Ong Quan and Ong Truong, had chained the elephant's hind legs to prevent her from wandering off through adjacent rice fields. Lathered with mud, eyes nearly closed, the beast appeared half-asleep as she devoured yellow fruit, banana leaves, long green stalks. "She's always hungry," said Thien. "She eats everything. Maybe if one of the ghosts came too close with his rifle, she'd snatch it with her trunk, tear it away, and swallow it up bullets and all."

Nhi, disinterested, said, "I wish my skin were light as Tuyen's."

"It is," said Thien. "Or nearly as light."

"I don't think so."

"You're prettier. Tuyen just thinks she's pretty."

"I wish this were true."

"She wears a scarf over her face. That's why our faces are darker."

"We should wear scarves."

"Too hot," said Thien. "I don't know how she can stand working in the fields with a scarf on her face and long gloves on her arms."

Tuyen, Cadre Duc's daughter, was nearly as light as a day ghost. Thien pictured her in the fields, her pale face, brown scarf, brown gloves. "She's cute," said Thien, "but not beautiful."

"*Gorgeous*," said Nhi. "Everyone but you and my brother thinks she's prettier than a Sai Gon girl. My cousin Nam wants to marry her, he already asked his mother. He says Tuyen's face is the most beautiful he has seen."

Thien shook her head. "They'll have ghost babies. Their babies will look like Americans."

"They'll be pretty."

"Maybe yes, maybe no. If they're lighter than Tuyen, they'll look like baby ghosts."

Luu Hai, perched in the high branches of the banyan, had promised the cadre he would keep watch while the village feasted. Although the Americans were scarce now, there was a possibility that a small unit would patrol the paddy lands, the partly destroyed bamboo and coconut groves, the tatters of hedgerows. Hai, instead of roaming his eyes over the horizons, raised his right arm and traced in the air the shape of Thien's body. Aroused, retracing her shape more slowly, he decided her hips were wider than those of any girl in the village. On the left side of Hai's mouth, a tooth was missing, an incisor. He worked his tongue into the groove, the soft flesh that ached and tingled. *The widest hips in the village*, he thought, *the prettiest in the village*. Most girls Thien's age still had slender hips, boy's hips. The center of Thien's body was the shape of a perfect leaf. *Not a banyan leaf*, he told himself, *a lemon leaf. A girl the shape of a lemon leaf but one hundred times as wide.*

His arms winged from his sides as she glanced up at him. Thien whispered in Nhi's ear and Nhi nodded. Nhi called up the tree to her brother: "Look somewhere else, will you? You promised the cadre you would watch the fields."

So Hai scanned the horizons and spotted his night friend, Nam's buffalo, asleep beneath a tree.

Later, forgetful of Hai, Thien plucked a leaf from a small plant. Folding it lengthwise, rubbing its resin on her fingers, she breathed its scent. Thien liked to smell leaves. This one had a fresh smell, a slight pungency that complemented the feast-day mango and pineapple, salted fish and ginger. She noticed her own hair and Nhi's hair smelled of fruit. This morning they'd washed their hair, and now it had the rich smells of coconut milk, jackfruit, lemon. She relaxed until Luu Hai called down the tree, "You should eat something, some fish or something."

She looked up at him. "Watch the fields," she said, "the *fields*." She separated the flesh of the leaf from the central rib.

Thien wondered what he smelled from the high branches. Salted fish and ginger? Pineapple and mango? A girl's hair? In the noonday heat, it was hard to know where one smell began and where it merged with another. Thien hoped the smell of her hair did not arouse Luu Hai. Then she thought, *Maybe it's good if he smells me a little.* She felt scared and happy that a boy might smell her from high in a tree.

She began to eat. Head down, breathing softly, she thought her body smelled of flowers and fruit, fresh ginger and fish.

After the feast, village girls fetched tea and Cadre Duc again addressed his audience. He referred to the day ghosts as "the blind men in Cambodia. They do not even know how to walk on the land," he said. "They stumble over roots and vines, and fear every trace of shadow. They move from one place to another during the day because the night is their enemy." He paused and lit a cigarette. "You will not find one of them that remembers his dead, that honors his ancestors as we do. A human being who lives entirely for himself is a wandering ghost long before he dies."

Thien heard little until Cadre Duc mentioned the elephant. "As you know," he said, "the presence of this animal is an auspicious occasion. We have used elephants to help build the Truong Son Trail. They have been indispensable for certain construction projects, and have been useful servants in transporting the heaviest weapons and ammunition." He hooked a finger and gestured toward the beast that was gnawing the stalk of a banana plant. "On the Truong Son Trail we have used elephants and buffalo, bicycles and jeeps, and armies of men and women." He nodded. "We use whatever presents itself, whatever becomes available. The animal that has visited our village would be most beneficial on the Truong Son Trail."

Thien glanced at the elephant man who sat motionless, his eyes half closed. Last night he told Thien and her grandma that he and the elephant would return to Ben Cat the morning after the feast. Now Cadre Duc and other cadre might change his plans, escort him and the elephant into the jungles of Cambodia. Or they might station him and the beast fifty kilometers west on *Nui Ba Den*, Black Virgin Mountain, the part of South Viet Nam where the Truong Son Trail ended. Thien knew the elephant man had no power to influence the decision. Not even the grandfathers, Ong Quan and Ong Truong, questioned the strategies of those who planned the war.

Cadre Duc now spoke in general terms of the role of elephants "in the history of our struggle. For centuries they have been employed as carriers of cargo," he said. "They have transported weapons and supplies, transported wounded soldiers, and have carried virtually everything too heavy for human beings to carry. We Vietnamese have used elephants against Chinese invaders in the same way that we now use them against Americans." He lowered his head. "It's true that many have died, victims of the bombings. But we will continue to use the survivors to carry our supplies."

Duc flicked the ash from his cigarette. He referred to the elephant that had come to the village as *anh*, older brother. Thien wanted to say, "*Chi*, older sister," but she could not raise her voice to an elder, especially one in Duc's position. He called the animal "a valuable beast, a brother and comrade," but it was clear he did not know and would never know the elephant that had come to this village. Only in her mind could Thien confound him with questions: What does the elephant smell like? What do you notice? Is the sound on the earth loud or soft when she walks? How quickly can she eat a banana plant, every leaf and fruit? Is the skin at the back of her ears delicate, nearly human? Can she swim the Sai Gon River? Or is she so heavy and huge that she will drown in the deep water? Thien glanced from the elephant to Duc's wife, Cadre Minh, who was still considered beautiful at age forty. Nearly every village girl wished to be fair-skinned, delicate, an imitation of Minh, an adult version of her daughter Tuyen. But Thien felt no envy as a thought disturbed her: Cadre Duc, an arrogant husband, would never fully appreciate the scent of leaves or fresh fruit, the scent of ginger or salted fish.

He invited Cadre Hien, a lower-ranking official, to address the village. Hien's family, like Duc's, had come from the north five years earlier. Dedicated, well-trained, the two organized the villagers to resist the Americans. They were privy to party secrets, changes in tactics, intelligence information, which they doled out to peasants on an as-needed basis. "Tonight," said Hien, "we must be especially prepared to protect ourselves. Intelligence reports indicate that we are likely to be bombed shortly after midnight. As usual, the Americans have targeted the areas where they suspect there are tunnels, and the secondary targets are the rice fields and the village. The planes—probably two squadrons—will fly at high altitudes, beyond the range of our anti-aircraft. It is essential that you take shelter in the expanded tunnel beneath the village long before midnight. Bring your chickens and pigs—whatever animals you have room for. Cadre Duc and I would join you, but tonight we have a special meeting near the headquarters of the U.S. Army's 25th Infantry. Our village tunnel has been reconstructed, so we urge you to use it. You are less likely to be buried here than in the bunkers and spider holes you have dug beneath your homes."

Luu Hai wished Nam's buffalo were small enough to join

the families inside the tunnel. He thought of the youngest buffalo in the village, a female—two-months-old and fifty kilos—that could be lowered through a trapdoor under Cadre Hien's house. Eyes closed, Hai worked his tongue into the soft flesh where his tooth was missing. In the shade of high branches, he imagined Le Minh Thien crawling through a hole in the earth, scrabbling on her hands and knees into the main passage of the tunnel. The sensation of his tongue against the exposed flesh became too pleasant. He forgot why she needed the earth to shield her, why she might die soon. He saw himself moving slowly as if in water through a darkness made beautiful by the presence of a girl.

10
The Insects, The Monkey,
The Animal With Wings

During the air strike, Conchola hid in the hollow of a fallen
tree. A cavity slightly wider and longer than his body, a moist
trunk that served as a bunker. The reverberation of bombs
fissured the rotting wood. Slats of light entered small cracks
and illuminated the movements of worms, ants, termites,
beetles. He whispered the names of saints: "*Virgen de
Guadalupe*, Saint Francis, Saint Jude...Saint of the Difficult,
Helper In Cases Despaired Of." More bombs buffeted the
earth, splintered trees. Conchola blinked and gaped as new
streams of light entered the hollow. Three beetles flattened
their bodies against the newly exposed wood. Conchola saw
bulbous eyes, thin green lines on black shells, sets of six legs
with furred edges. They began tearing shreds of wood with
snout-shaped mouths. For an instant he was unsure if the
whirring in his ears came from the mouths of beetles or the
wind of fires, or from fighter jets, bright streaks of sound
cleaving the air, dipping and rising. His hands pressed against
his ears, and then his fingers—spread wide—fenced his ribs
and heart. The jets kept yawing in over the trees, then nosing
up, looping, making another pass, and another, with their
seemingly endless spate of bombs.

Something skittered over the bridge of his nose. He
turned his head and saw a cross-section of the hollow: insects
in cell-like cavities, most of them motionless, dazed or dead,
a few of them tensing their bodies, probing the air with legs,
antennae. The nearest insect had V-shaped feet, a spot of
yellow on a brown shell. Its green eyes seemed as large as
human eyes, its antennae bright as swords, its pincers sharp

and dangerous. A soft whooshing sound rose from its throat. It raised its pincers, tensed, broke into a six-legged sprint, and disappeared down a crevice. Moments later Conchola covered his head as the earth rumbled. "Lupe," he prayed, "Guadalupe." He rolled onto his side as a great swath of light opened the tree.

A long-legged spider skated over shavings of wood. It made its way to a sac-like protrusion—maybe an egg nest—and poked the substance with its mouth. Conchola realized he was famished. He watched the spider feed itself until another bomb fell close to their position. The sky rained wood chips, dust, pebbles. A nearby tree, its main branches and trunk broken, gave a death song he knew by heart: the shriek of split wood, the snap of flames on leaves and seeds, the wind and roar of falling. The ground beneath the tree smoked, quivered. Roots snapped and snaked, thick worms that furrowed the earth's surface. Conchola touched his body, felt the weight of it. Face and chest, belly and groin. Shapes that seemed solid. He crawled from the ruined hollow and took cover between two live trees. Something sour in the air, hints of urine and blood, the moist fur of an animal's belly. Gut-ruffled, moaning, he breathed the scent of the one who had lain here. He pressed his face to grass, leaves, soil. "*Maestro*," he muttered, "*señor*," and convinced himself the tiger was alive.

The attack ended moments later. A bird chirped; something skittered in the grass. Conchola lay his hands palms up on the earth. "Lupe," he whispered, "*gracias*," but he could not stop shaking. His feet began to throb. Curled on his side, he removed his socks, probed the cuts on his heels. Maybe he'd been wounded again, grazed by shrapnel. Or maybe he'd been bruised by thorns and stones, the things he walked on after crossing the stream to warn the animals— "*Váyanse*, make tracks, spread wings. *Váyanse*." The thought hit him: I swam the stream, I can swim. He realized he was wet to the bone. He wormed his way out of his pants, his shirt, and lay on the ground naked. In his mind he jotted a quick postcard to the girls back home: *In darkness I swam the stream, crossed over. I'm alone now, a one-man patrol in a ruined jungle.* Bien rapto, contento. El tigre *is alone.*

He wanted to add something, but what? He thought of TV, a program he once watched with his mother and his Aunt Clara. After lightning splintered a forest, lit fires, reduced everything to ash, new trees and plants grew back richer and stronger and wilder. In his postcard Conchola wrote: *Devil's lightning, the worst kind. Animal scorch, tree scorch. Paw prints and ashes.* He paused. *Nothing like TV, nothing like anything you know of.* He shrugged, scratched his groin. *You'll never smell this smoke, will you? You'll never smell much of anything.* He grinned. *Well, the one true thing is I'm alone now, alone and lost and happy.* He got up and draped his wet clothes over a low-hanging branch. *Okay, my feet are cut, I'm naked and bleeding. Lost and naked and bleeding. Maybe you think I hate you, but I don't. I don't hate anyone.* His hands opened. *Here's why, my only secret. I was never alive until I knew paws and trees and flames.*

La gracia de gracia, *Antonio Lucio*

The sky brightened. He felt the pressure of light on his skin. He watched a brown spider spin silk, ferry itself from one branch to another. As it touched down on a pear-shaped leaf, its front feelers probed a vein—tree blood. The medic wondered how it survived, how the tree had survived, or himself. On a fallen branch a red flower had begun to open. Long petals the shapes of fingers curled over a yellow center. Conchola imagined giving this flower to a girl back home— Sara Peters. He imagined placing it in the palm of her hand, the sun-yellow and red in a flower the size of a saucer. Its yellow center appeared wet and swollen. Tentative, he touched the petals, cupped them, and then withdrew. He could never tell Sara Peters or anyone what was true for him. This flower made of red lips, yellow sun. This pressure of light on his skin. This spider with her long legs, her body round and smooth and perfect. If somehow he survived the war, returned home, how would he live? Who would he love? He imagined trapping a brown spider in a jar. He imagined showing it to Sara, pointing out the curvature of the legs, but what would she see? *Nothing*, he thought, *nada y nada. Can't share a miracle with a Bimbo.* He leaned his right shoulder into the spider tree, the broad trunk. The roughness and sexuality of the bark pleased him. Flesh, the substance of a thing, was contradictory. The bulk, the weighted mass— riddled with light. The wind and fire sounds had quieted. Turning slightly, mouth open, he rubbed his right cheek on the trunk of the tree.

His clothes were still damp when he put them on and began walking. He wondered if his warnings ("*Váyanse*, make tracks, spread wings") had saved any animals. He skirted the edges of fresh craters. Smells of burnt wood, smoke, tree blood. The soles of his feet absorbed warmth. Chunks of timber and root glowed and emitted heat like embers of charcoal. He spotted a blue feather, an amputated claw. He studied a tail, reptilian, a mantle of scales. Probed the tips of the scales, sliced open a finger, sucked blood, dropped the tail in his right front pocket. "Geronimo," he whispered, "*oye. I'm impossible to kill.*"

By now the platoon would have forded the stream. Led by Lieutenant Bateson, they most likely had a double-mission: first, find Conchola, capture him; second, find blood trails, blown bunkers, dead gooks, and assess the effectiveness of the bombing. *Bunch of losers*, thought Conchola. *Bone dumb but for Billie Jasper*. He shrugged. *All that saves Jasper is he once saw the tiger, the throat wound and chest wound, and once rouged his face with tiger blood.* He considered this. *Saved Billie's ass, gave him something to live for. He's still learning, though, still getting his bearings. He needed me to point out the booby-trapped one-*

five-five round that would have showered him through the trees.

Conchola found a monkey beneath the crown of a fallen tree. Two branches jutted like scissors over the corpse. The animal lay on its back, eyes closed, thighs splayed open. Conchola saw it was female. He knelt down and straightened her legs. She had lost her lungs, her chest. They were wounds now, white chunks of bone, vertebrae, flecked with something stringy and pink—maybe tendons. White fur crested her dark face, the backs of her hands, her feet. He patted her shoulders, then lay his hands on her belly. Her fur coat was warm, well-oiled. Thick and brown and healthy. He reached to wedge open her eyes. They still held light, tree light, and he had a feeling her body—so newly dead—did not yet know what had happened. "It's okay," he whispered. "You're on Easy Street, baby. Swear to Jesus." He closed her left eye, then her right, and patted her thin shoulders. *Don't worry*, he thought, *no se preocupa. You're still more wild and beautiful than all the Bimbos I ever loved.*

He couldn't force himself to wander any farther. Exhausted, he lay near the animal, closed his eyes, and collapsed into sleep.

In the late afternoon, the rain began. A steady monsoon downpour that saturated the remains of the jungle. Conchola wandered until he spotted an animal that needed help. Approximately a foot long, it had a mouse-like face, webbed feet, a furry membrane—something like wings—that stretched from its front paws to its back. It looked like some sort of rat-bat, an airborne rodent, a flying squirrel that once traveled the trees, roamed with monkeys. Now it lay on its belly, panting, its wings spread flat on the stump of a banyan. The medic noted wounds: the membrane, the furred wings, ruined by holes the size of pennies. He wished he'd brought bandages, basic supplies. The animal raised its head, made a snuffling sound, and Conchola saw a streak of blood, a throat wound. "Yeah, you got some scratches," he whispered, "nothing serious. You just need to keep warm, keep the rain off your body." He leaned forward so that his head and shoulders sheltered the animal. *There*, he thought, *I'm your roof, I'm your tree. Better than nothing.* The mucus and blood in the animal's throat hissed, bubbled. "Yeah, clear it out," said Conchola, "keep breathing. Rule *número uno*: You got to make room to breathe."

He talked to her gently. He went on about good times and bad times, how this was one of the bad times. "The best thing about bad times," he said, "is you know they'll end. They stay with you a short while and suddenly fly off like a flock of birds, *pajarillos*." The throat wound wheezed flecks of blood. Dying from wounds and shock and exposure, the animal shook uncontrollably. The medic tried to create warmth with his hands. Lacing his fingers over the animal's spine, he said, "There, there," but the trembling became more violent. He reached and tore a leaf from a fallen branch. He chewed it into soup, spat it in his left hand, and offered it to the animal. The nostrils twitched, flared, but the mouth wouldn't open. "Come on, Rat Bat," he whispered. "Rule *número dos*: Don't die on me, *no se muera. Nunca se muera.*" Conchola waited a long time before he lost hope, lowered his face, and slurped green soup from his palm.

There was a club-sized branch near his feet. He wondered if killing the animal, relieving it of its suffering, would be a gift of mercy. He remembered the wounded crab he had tossed in the stream. He had spared the creature from being blown to bits by C-4 explosives, but maybe the result was greater torment. The broken branch on the ground was the perfect size: as thick as the wide end of a baseball bat, as long as his forearm. Rat Bat made a soft, shrieking sound in its throat. Conchola said, "Yeah, it hurts, I know it hurts. Dream time, baby. You're on your way to a better world, a new world. A world where you open your wings and fly as high as you like any morning." The animal's eyes blinked, flickered. "I swear to you, baby, even the noonday sun won't seem so tall anymore. You'll orbit around new suns, new stars—no problem with wounds or worries." He lifted the club from the ground. "Here we go, baby, lickety-split and Hail Mary. Lift you light years away from all this sorry shit."

He sighted the back of the neck and swung hard. In its last moment the animal tensed, opened its mouth, scraped its claws and paws on the stump of the banyan. Conchola heard a rushing sound overhead. He dropped the club and the questions came unbidden: *Is there a heaven? Is there a refuge? Is there a place for this animal?* He touched the wings, the bony ridge of the spine, the small tail. For a moment his hands were healer hands, resurrection hands. Salvation. But in the end he could do nothing but lean his shoulders over the corpse and shelter it from rain.

At dusk the sky cleared. The eyes of the dead animal remained vigilant, wide open. Small mirrors, they reflected tree limbs and leaves, stars and shadows. Two stars shone straight above. They brightened, flickered, as the sky grew darker. Conchola prayed for the animal's soul. He heard scraping sounds and chirps in bushes and trees—birds, monkeys, squirrels—the scattered survivors. He burrowed his hands in earth. Cool wet rain and earth. Maybe a few worms inside, a few snakes, a few beetles. *Okay*, he thought, *let it be true. A real heaven, an honest-to-God heaven.* He looked at the dead animal, the dark form, and half whispered, half sung, "*Si, un cielo*, a heaven." His strong fingers burrowed deeper into earth. He arched his neck to look at stars.

11
Into the Earth

The mother pig would not fit through the narrow opening that led to the main branch of the tunnel. She screamed as village boys swaddled her in three sewn-together hammocks and lowered her into the shelter through a trapdoor beneath Cadre Hien's house. Thirteen piglets awaited her, squealing and grunting, groping for her milk-swollen teats the moment she touched earth. Hai and his friend Qui wrapped the two-month-old buffalo in a hammock and lowered her to the shelter. The smaller animals—piglets, chickens, ducks—had been shooed or carried into the tunnel through small passages. Wicker baskets, inverted, served as cages for ducks and chickens, but a few were left to wander. The villagers settled themselves and their animals in places where the tunnel widened. Formerly, the shelter had been poorly built, a death trap where twenty-seven people had died, but now A-framed timbers buttressed the walls and ceiling. Three candles burned; Ba Ly lit incense. The sweet smoke mixed with smells of excrement and sweat.

Thien sat with Nhi and several girls across from Luu Hai and his mother and the baby buffalo. The girl pictured the elephant—partly protected, partly exposed—munching bamboo leaves and hay. Three hours earlier, the elephant's master had coaxed the animal into a bomb crater where he shackled her. Thien had brought stalks of sugarcane and bamboo, and she and the old man had rolled huge mounds of hay into the crater. The animal would have ample food, but her upper body—her shoulders and the dome of her spine—rose nearly a full meter over the earth. Now Thien wondered if the elephant knew how to protect herself. Would she stand

and flap her ears when she heard the whistle of bombs? Or did she know enough to press herself to the earth, lean against the wall of the crater, raise her trunk over her head for protection? Thien tried to calm herself by picturing the animal enjoying her food. She imagined the trunk snaking beneath a mound of hay, seizing the hay, lifting as with a hook. The curled trunk, swinging high, then falling, plunged a bundle of hay the size of a child's torso down the cave of the open maw.

The villagers had brought pillows, sleeping mats, sacks of rice, baskets of fruit, baskets of eggs. Some of the mothers and small children were already asleep. Tuyen, Cadre Duc's daughter, began to jabber about Trung Trac and her sister. All the villagers knew the stories of the Trung sisters, the warrior women who rode elephants into battle, who used animal disguises to confound Chinese invaders almost two-thousand years ago. Tuyen's parents had trained her to remind the villagers, especially the youth, of their country's heroes. Her voice, however, was mild, a counterpoint to the grandiosity of legend. "Who revolutionized the methods of eagle claw fighting? Who knew the death dance of the preying mantis, the whirling of the drunken monkey?"

The girl beside her said, "Trung Trac, Trung Trac and her sister."

"This is correct. The sisters revolutionized eagle claw fighting. They defeated the Chinese invaders."

Luu Hai, resting his left hand on the forehead of the young buffalo, said, "Sometimes Trung Trac became a bird; her hands and feet grew talons."

"Perhaps."

"She explored every forest," said Hai. "She knew the birds, the spiders, the monkeys, so hers was a large army."

"Correct."

"And she knew the smells," said Thien. "She could smell danger, she could smell safety."

Tuyen appeared confused.

"She knew the difference," whispered Thien, "between what was true and what was mere words."

Fair-skinned Tuyen blushed.

"The Trach sisters were wise," said Luu Hai. "In daylight when a tiger came near, they gathered with small animals in forest shadows."

"Are you making this up?" said Tuyen.

"No, I heard it from Ong Quan. They huddled together and waited for the sun to vanish."

"He told me this before," said Nhi.

"It's more true now," said Hai, "so listen. Trung Trac and two monkeys crept out in the dark to scratch the tiger's hind legs. Later, at midnight, the praying mantis stung the softness of the belly." He nodded. "Near dawn, Trung Trac and an eagle slit the tiger's throat with talons. At sunrise, the water buffalo and the elephants sniffed the tiger's corpse and moved off with the Trung sisters to bathe in streams."

Tuyen tried to resume control of the discussion. "The Trung sisters often lived in shadows. Like in Cu Chi, they built tunnels and spider holes, many places for waiting."

Luu Hai, stroking the buffalo's forehead, said, "Ambush sites."

"Yes, ambush sites. Places for waiting. Regrouping."

"Eagle claw fighting," said Hai, "osprey fighting." Claw-like, he slashed the air with his hands. "Their best weapons came from the light above trees."

His mother told him to stop making so much noise. Ma Xuan held a watch near a white candle—12:48. Cadre Hien predicted the bombing would begin shortly after midnight, but maybe the Americans had changed their minds, or had flown their most powerful planes to Cambodia. The cadre sometimes received inaccurate reports. Their predictions were mostly correct, but they could not know everything. Maybe the village and the fields would be bombed tomorrow at noon. Maybe the Sai Gon River and the shoreline would be bombed. Maybe the bamboo and coconut groves would be bombed. Maybe everything near Cu Chi would be bombed, and maybe this would happen without any warning. Once, the Americans bombed the rice fields and the river and came to the village three days later with truckloads of food. They handed out meat stuffed in cans, packets of sugar and salt, boxes of Coca-Cola. Ma Xuan remembered their burned skin, their red faces that lacked the strength to be touched by sun. She had prayed to the Buddha that they return to their own land, that they leave her family and her village forever. Three weeks later, their planes came with more bombs. They bombed the trees near the river, they bombed the river and the fish, they bombed the fields, and they killed her family's buffalo. That was one of the days when the cadre had not given the villagers any warning. Maybe the Americans themselves did not know exactly when they would bomb, when they would bring food, when they would go away.

Most of those who were awake fanned themselves and chattered. Luu Hai, petting the buffalo and glancing at Thien, worked his tongue into the tender flesh where his tooth was missing. He leaned forward as Thien whispered to his sister, "I hope the elephant's okay. I hope she's eating."

"That's all she does," said Nhi.

"No, she remembers things, she smells things. The river mud, the bamboo—things like that." Her voice lowered. "Sometimes I think she likes to smell me. When I come near she moves her mouth and trunk, breathes me in." She giggled. "I wonder how I smell to an elephant. A piece of fruit or a salted fish."

This excited Nguyen Luu Hai. Salted fish? Fruit? Was this what a girl smelled like? She didn't mean for him to hear, could never imagine ears this careful. He waited in vain for Thien to say something of interest about himself.

He shooed a noisy rooster away from him. Ducklings squabbled; thirteen nursing piglets made sucking sounds. Hai listened for the thump of bombs, but the earth above remained silent. He placed his right hand on the side of the two-month-old buffalo. Breathing gently, making soft, slurping sounds, she slept now. *Dreaming*, thought Hai, *remembering her mother*. The round warmth of the animal set him at ease.

Minutes later the buffalo rose to her feet. The small light in the tunnel swayed, grew dim with dust. The animal made confused, snuffling sounds. She began to run, but there was no room. She pushed against the body beside her that pushed back until she flopped down, folded her legs and sat. Sounds of wings and wind, coveys of birds. She heard stalks and trunks torn from the earth, and it seemed the things above her, the things that shadowed her—the grass, the soil, roots, trees, stones—were changing shape, flying and falling. She heard dirt cascade down a crevice, fill a new hole. Nearby, in small baskets, trapped animals babbled. A rooster, turning in tight circles, whistled and crowed, then leaned toward the roar of thunder. The buffalo drank the dust in the air. Something huge lifted the trees, the fields. The body beside her—the one that had forced her to sit—was holding her, warming her, but it did not have the same smells and shapes as her mother. The body kept making odd sounds she could not understand. At times the sounds were harsh, grainy, something like wind, or like bits of storm dust whirled above paddies. The body held her neck and her spine and she felt the warm smooth weight of it. Its sounds and scent were peculiar, they were not her mother's, but nor were they something to resist.

At once the fields and trees and birds stopped trembling. The thunder lifted, rolled off through the sky, and the land resettled itself, replanted its roots, stopped shifting one way, then another. The buffalo felt the body beside her give way. Bawling, she stumbled to her feet and flicked her tail. She looked in all directions as the body beside her kept making its sounds, touching. The body was good, she decided, the body would not harm her. She felt a pleasant scratchiness on her ears and throat where the body touched gently. Next the body touched her spine, her upper parts, and the feeling was mostly good.

Dawn.

After the world underground quieted a long time, she was put in a sack, a small darkness that fit her body. At first she was afraid, but then the earth opened and there was light, a whole sky of it. She looked out from the dark sack and saw warm light over her body. The light entered her, swelled her throat and chest, quickened her breathing. Soon the feeling of being lifted toward light partly thrilled her, partly scared her. She called out as they lifted her in a sack to the bright surface of the earth.

She was allowed to stumble off on stiff legs. She moved as fast as she could through light that blew through the sky and into her body. The air smelled different than it had ever smelled. Here and there the ground was warm, oozing smoke, and there were holes she had to walk around to move toward her mother. She heard her mother moiling in her pen, kicking up dirt, calling out in a low rumble. She found the gate of the pen swung open, her mother near a dark hump of straw where she had last seen her. Tied to a pole, her mother could not run to her. But she kept calling, rumbling, and the familiar sounds emptied the small animal's body of fear.

She shuddered slightly as her mother licked her face, washed her. She walked between her mother's legs, tongued salt from the underbelly, the skin near the breasts. The top of her head rubbed against a breast. She fastened her mouth on a teat, suckled and gnawed, and closed her eyes as she pulled the milk inside.

The elephant turned and looked at a small wound on her left shoulder. She had never seen blood on her body, but the smell was common. She had smelled the blood of other elephants, other animals—pigs, buffalo, cattle. The land itself sometimes smelled of blood.

She curled back her trunk to siphon the smell of singed hair, blood. At first the pain had been mild, a mere distraction, but soon something small and hard began burning the flesh inside her. It was as though a giant fire ant had stung her, cut and twisted with teeth. Or as though a bird with a beak of fire had eaten from her flesh.

12
Tree Burial, Scouts, Tiger

Cradling the dead animal, pressing her wings to her body, he lowered her into the grave he had dug by hand. He tossed in a clump of moist earth. "*Vete,*" he said, "*ya vas al cielo.* Already watching me from heaven." Moments later he retrieved her, brushed the soil from her eyes, stretched her wings, imagined her flying. "*Pues,* you lived in a tree," he said, "so that's where you're going. A tree." Again he cradled her, carried her, and questioned his right to kill her. Maybe it was a great sin to take away the stars too soon. Maybe it was a great sin to take away the trees.

Conchola lay the animal in the crotch of a stout tree. Confused, he spread her wings as in flight, then pressed her claws into the flesh of the bark. "There," he said, "you can climb or fly, whatever you like." He wondered if her family would find her before she was buffeted aside by the first strong wind.

He walked in the night and startled the survivors. He heard long wings batter the air, rise. And there were occasional whoops and cries, throat shrieks, the strident alarms of monkeys. *Nos vamos*, he thought. *Travel the trees, spread wings. Train your ears to hear planes ten-thousand miles in the distance.* He walked slowly, wandered for what seemed a long time. He realized he had gone nowhere when he nearly stumbled into the grave he had dug for the animal with wings.

He walked a short distance from the hole, lay under a banyan tree, and waited for sleep. Shivering, curled on his side, he wished he had brought his poncho liner, something to warm his body. *Any animal*, he thought, *cualquier criatura de la selva, would know where to find shelter.* There were probably caves nearby, or spider holes, or thickets warm as blankets. Conchola considered the tiger. Mundo would never wander the earth, imagine he was traversing a great distance, only to stumble over a hole, a fresh-dug grave. The tiger knew every inch of this jungle, every sight and sound, every smell. Conchola wondered if Mundo would lay near the dead animal as though to keep her company. In an attempt to orient himself, the medic breathed the smells and named them: *wet soil, leaves, rotting flesh.* How could he distinguish this place from the rest of the world?

When the rains returned, he sat up and leaned sideways against the tree. The overhead branches offered little protection. Soon water rivered the folds and creases of the bark. Rain soaked his hair, dripped down his forehead, purled his throat and chest and belly. He tried to cheer himself up. In the morning the platoon might find him, offer him food and water. Three or four heat tabs to warm cans of chicken, warm his cupped hands, nourish his body. More likely, though, the lieutenant would shoot him for desertion. Conchola would need to claim that he slipped and fell in the stream, that he was carried away by strong currents. Maybe the lie would be easier to believe than the truth. Only Billie Jasper, his one friend, knew he had crossed over in an attempt to flush the tiger from the area to be bombed.

He found a way to drink. Hunched over, he cupped his hands against the trunk and the rain gathered. Water rolled down the fissured bark, pooled in his palms. He waited for the first mouthful, then lowered his head and drank. *Tree tea,* he thought, *animal tea. A slight sting on the tongue, a mild bitterness.* He wished the girls back home could see him drinking the rain, *agua pura.* He made a bowl with brown hands, let the rain gather. Distracted, half lost in dreams, he saw in his two hands a gesture of prayer.

The rain let up an hour before dawn. He curled against the banyan, dozed fitfully, and woke every few minutes. Once, he watched three figures glide across the land. At first he believed they were animals, small and quick. Their hooves touched earth, sprang, and gave no sound but a muted clopping. They passed between the empty grave and the stout tree where the dead animal rested. The figures changed from beast to human when he saw thin black lines, barrels of rifles slung from shoulders. As they turned, paused, he heard the air in their nostrils. Maybe they smelled him, this human one. Or maybe they smelled the animal with wings, the death smell, the empty grave, the overturned soil. Lucid now, his wide-awake stillness mirrored their animal stillness. He held his breath, waited. In one motion, precise mimicry, the scouts sprang, glided, and he followed with his eyes until they blended and vanished in the darkness of trees.

He saw the tiger at first light. The long body, fire stripes, orange and black, thirty meters from where he rested. For a time the beast watched him. The sun had not yet climbed the sky. Something Conchola could not name brightened the undersides of leaves, branches, the vein-like crevices of bark, the orange soil, the tips of his fingers. The tiger flattened his ears and moaned. Soft thunder, ripples of wind. Fire orange and black. *Trueno*. The body was a storm, beauty and rage. And the light of the eyes, animal light, made Conchola tremble. How much truth did he deserve? The medic, belly down, held the earth as he would an animal, held the flesh of the soil that might ripple and rise, cast him skyward digging fistfuls of light, *luminoso*. He breathed in when the tiger breathed in. The firm belly swayed, bulged, bow-shaped to earth, as light haloed the long body. Air rasped in and out of the wounded throat. Conchola grunted when the beast raised his head, sniffed. Maybe by now the human one smelled of leaves and rain, trees and soil. An animal with wings, a stream, a monkey.

For a few moments he lost all fear. He watched the trees on either side of the animal, the leaves that brightened not from the east, the light at the edge of the world, but the light of the body. He sniffed his forearm, the nearly healed wounds, and small hairs—spiked with light—bristled. He could have touched himself and been satisfied, touched the earth, satisfied, but now he carried in each cell pure desire and pure fear, fear that the first light would vanish. He stood and came forward as though to meet a friend. The beast flicked his ears and tail and gave the medic the momentary thrill of being felt down the length and depth of the four-hundred-pound body. *Queda*, thought Conchola, *rest your wounds now*. Swaying, he lifted his arms and called "*Mundo, Rey del Mundo*," but the tiger had already vanished into great dark trees.

13
Pictures

After a night in the earth, no mound of grass or straw to lie on, no lights familiar (moon, star, cloud), the animals were shooed or carried from the tunnel. Strutting roosters fanned their wings, cackled. Hens flitted about, noisy and skittish. And the mother pig, who almost always had her nose snuffled to earth, glanced twice at the sun, delighted by the familiarity, the delicious heat that made her long for water and mud and coolness. Soon she would wallow in a puddle, but now she flopped on her side to let her piglets suckle. She shifted so the smallest one, the one who had not learned to clamber over the others to fasten its mouth on a teat, found her milk and was fed. The air smelled mostly of ash, but they were alive, they were hungry. And the sun bent through curls of smoke without losing any strength.

She lay her head on the ground and let her body go limp. She listened to small purling sounds, her milk leaving her, her belly rumbling, her teats swelling and hardening, nipples popping from mouths, then again being pulled, suckled. Her piglets strained as though her milk would run out. They slurped, gnawed her teats, and now and then she grunted with pain. Her piglets soon filled themselves, but they wouldn't let go. Squirming, nuzzling, they pressed their thirteen snouts and mouths into the softness of her length.

A squabbling procession of ducks roamed the village until three boys herded them to a pen. Other boys ran to their buffalo, checked the animals for wounds, and Thien beat the elephant man to the elephant. From the edge of the crater she saw the grazed shoulder, three flies dipping in and out of blood. "A small wound," she muttered, her tone a question. She scurried down the slope and into the hole.

Luu Hai petted Nam's buffalo until she stopped raking her back hooves over the dirt. "Come on," he said, "you're lucky, you're alive. The bombing's over." He led her from her pen, paraded past Thien's house, and hoisted himself onto her spine. As the sun greened the fields, slanted under a tall cloud, he rode the buffalo toward the crater where the elephant stood shackled. Soon Hai saw the giant's arched back and raised trunk. He maneuvered the buffalo to within twenty meters of the crater, shifted his weight, and knelt on the mountain-shaped spine.

Now he stood. He had often balanced himself on Great Joy while the animal kept walking, but the spine of Nam's buffalo provided a smaller surface. Hai swayed, worked hard to steady himself, as the buffalo lumbered toward the crater. He heard whispers, Miss Thien's voice, and then he saw her in the hole crouched beside the elephant. He remembered the day when Thien towered over everyone, when she passed through the fields and looked down on the buffalo boys from the spine of her beloved. Now the elephant, shackled, half-buried, seemed less impressive, while Hai, standing as tall and as still as he could, had risen nearly three meters above the ground.

He sang his Sun Song softly, but not in whispers. He made sure Miss Thien could hear.

In my next life I will be the sun, I will light the fields.
I will eat java birds, rice birds, before they steal our harvest.
I will be the green of the rice, the yellow of sunlight.
I will have the strength of a bull buffalo, the body of a mountain.
I will carry a rice field and a pretty village girl on my spine.

Balanced shakily on the female buffalo, he called, "Miss Thien, Miss Thien!" but she greeted him with silence. Luu Hai peered over the edge of the hole and saw the wound on the elephant's left shoulder. "*Ngung*" he said, "*ngung*," and Nam's buffalo halted. Hai crouched on the animal's spine, then slid down and straddled her rump. *Where?* he thought. *Where will we find a bandage the size of an American's chest?*

He said to Miss Thien, "I'm sorry, I didn't know she was hurt. I wouldn't have been singing."

She remained silent.

"She'll get better," said Hai, "believe me. I've seen animals with wounds a hundred times worse than this."

The elephant's master, trailed by three village boys, approached the lip of the crater. "Not so bad," said the old man. "Enough to keep her off the Truong Son Trail a few weeks. Or maybe Cadre Duc will have new plans for her."

"She needs rest," said Thien.

"And disinfectant," said the man. "Clean rags and some kerosene."

Luu Hai slid off the buffalo, hit the ground running, and called over his shoulder, "I'll get them, Ong! One minute!" Spurting ahead, bare feet spanking the earth, he left in his wake a whirl of dust.

The roof had been blown off Cadre Duc's house, a wall had collapsed, but repairs were underway. New poles had been cut, and the roof—after some patching—would be lifted in place and temporarily secured with rope made from a tree (*cay may*). Luu Hai asked Cadre Duc's wife for kerosene and rags. The cadre hoarded kerosene, for it could be used to disinfect wounds when nothing better was available. She said, "Who's hurt?" and Hai told her. Cadre Duc's wife hesitated for a moment. She opened a small cabinet and gave Hai a jar of kerosene and a bundle of rags.

The elephant's master secured the rope ladder around the elephant's girth. His supplies in a sack strapped over his shoulder, he climbed onto her and doused the edges of her wound with kerosene. The beast, trunk raised, seemed ready to trumpet or wail, but her master stroked her ears, then her neck, and she kept quiet. "Almost finished," he said, "stand still now. Soon you'll have something to eat."

Once her wound was treated, he climbed down, unshackled her, and coaxed her up from the crater. He and Thien and Luu Hai guided her to a banana plant on the south side of the village. In a matter of minutes, the elephant stripped the small plant of fruit. For her main course they led her to the bamboo grove between Thien's house and Nam's house, but there were new craters here and the best bamboo had been devoured by bombs.

They followed her to the shade of coconut palms near the village well.

There is a medicine of smells. The elephant swayed back and forth, twitched her tail, as she remembered smells of water and salt, moist clay, smells of birthing. She remembered the child that once lived in her, that swam inside her and grew large, that one day fell down in leaves that smelled salty. A circle of female elephants had touched the infant with their trunks. They helped it stand and licked it and tasted it and took its smell into their bodies. The calf, along with the water and blood smells of the mother, carried the smell of a river cave where the elephant families often gathered. The cave held water in deep holes; its walls smelled of salt, fish, moist clay—smells still partially present at the birth of this daughter. The wounded elephant remembered the strong, rich smells of birthing. Now she carried inside her the opposite smells, smells of burned flesh, small fires, but maybe these would soon vanish. The wound had surprised her: the violence of the light, the knife-wind that cut her shoulder. But she had seen wind and light do this before, cut the flesh of animals. Repeatedly, she had seen wind and light kill enormous animals who once smelled as bountiful as she and her child.

Cadre Duc returned at midday when the peasants were taking their lunch in the shade. Accompanied by Ong Quan and Ong Truong, he walked through the village, surveyed his repaired home, and walked into the fields to take note of the damage. There were dozens of craters the peasants would need to work around, and three places where the bunds would have to be rebuilt before the paddies again retained water. "Nothing serious," he told the grandfathers. "But the next attack is likely to be severe."

He passed the word to have everyone gather for a ten-minute meeting in the shade of the banyan. The bombing had blown away several of the lower limbs, those Luu Hai had used for climbing. Today the boy had to shinny up the scarred trunk, latch onto lesser branches, and monkey his way to his lookout perch. He wondered if Cadre Duc had given Thien permission to miss the meeting. He spied her eighty meters away, squatting flat-footed near the wounded elephant, her elbows resting on her knees.

"The Americans are scheduled to return in two days," said Cadre Duc. "If they don't tangle themselves in the Cambodian jungle and lose their way, we can expect them to patrol through our village and fields late Monday morning." He lit a cigarette. "We have an abundance of materials from their unexploded shells, but we need more volunteers to transform these materials into a variety of booby traps." He looked from face to face. "Later this afternoon, several cadre will be here to assist us. All of us—old and young—need to study the revised map that includes the locations of new traps. We must know every step of our homeland so as not to unwittingly harm ourselves."

Mid-afternoon, setting a trip-wire with his cousin Nam, Hai heard a sound far above. There were two dots in the sky, small and black, and he guessed they were enemy helicopters used for observation. Hai took two steps aside and began pulling weeds. Nam leaned over, picked up a trowel, and neither boy looked up as the sound grew louder. With sidelong glances, Hai saw that the villagers had resumed their fieldwork. Cadre Duc and the other cadre squatted, made themselves small, hoping the observers would identify them as elders. The enemy had grown accustomed to a countryside absent of young men, a countryside of women, children, and elders. To Hai, the cadre looked small enough to be mistaken for grandfathers. Seen from the sky, their faces bent to earth, hidden by the brims of hats, they might appear harmless and benign.

In tandem the helicopters swept down over the village. They made several passes above the fields, then hovered over the village well and the wounded elephant. Thien positioned herself between the animal and the enemy. Head raised, eyes unshielded from sun, she stood her ground as the dragonflies dipped closer. She heard the elephant man say, "Don't move," but she stepped forward and held up her hands to show the pilots she had nothing. The dragonflies, each piloted by one American and with one American passenger, hovered a long time. One of the pilots nodded to Thien and waved. The American, most likely amused by the sight of the elephant, nosed down within twenty meters of the beast. Thien saw his smile, his mouth moving, talking. She saw him hand something to his red-faced passenger, and then she saw a camera. The passenger leaned forward, pointed the camera at the elephant, and seemed to take several pictures. The elephant lunged and wailed when the pilot dipped his machine closer. Her trunk swung back near her left ear. A millisecond later it unfurled, lashed, and Thien heard a high-pitched hum, a roar like a dozen scythes swung in unison. Three times the elephant flailed her trunk at the men and the machine that hovered beyond her reach. "Stop," said Thien, "before they shoot you." But she wished the trunk had been long enough to tear the machine from the sky.

Minutes after the dragonflies left, Cadre Duc ordered Hai and Nam to help him construct a trip-wire booby trap near the village well and the elephant. "The Americans are stupid," he said. "When they come on foot, they'll want to be photographed near the beast, feed it a few leaves—this sort of thing." He grinned. "Day ghosts," he said, "circus soldiers. We'll give them ten thousand names. Their naiveté is their weakness, you understand? They'll see the elephant and forget the ground on which they walk."

He handed Hai a spool of wire. The explosives, removed from a one-five-five shell, were crammed in a rusted can of Coca-Cola. Cadre Duc prepared the firing device, the detonator, and Hai and Nam attached the trip-wire. With Duc's guidance, Hai stretched the wire over the top of a bund and partly concealed it with grass. "Good enough," said Duc. "The circus soldiers are half blind. On Monday they'll stumble around, trip the wire, and after one or two of them bleed to death the others will do their best to destroy the well and burn the village." He pointed to his left. "So we'll greet them near the well with a thirty-second ambush, leave them with a half dozen more casualties to attend to. By the time they regroup to ignite our huts with Zippo lighters, we'll be back down the tunnels for the day."

Later, when he saw Hai's expression, he said, "The village will be rebuilt or relocated, as needed. And I wouldn't worry about an elephant who is unlikely to survive the war."

That night Luu Hai crawled through the tunnel to Nam's buffalo pen. He huddled beside the animal, slept briefly, and woke a few minutes before midnight. Through an opening in the wooden slats, he saw three stars. He remembered an old monk who told his mother that three was the best number, but now he believed the opposite. Today Hai had helped Cadre Duc plant three booby traps, and the third—the one near the well and the elephant—might bring disaster. The elephant might die, the well might be destroyed, and the remains of the village could be lost in less than an hour. Hai pictured flames, the roofs and walls throwing sparks and ash, and he heard death screams of chickens and ducks, pigs and buffalo. Maybe tomorrow night, the night before the Americans returned, he would help bring the small animals into the tunnel so at least these would not perish. But would the day ghosts hear the animals rooting, pecking, squabbling? Would they risk entering the tunnel, or use explosives to bury everything and everyone in it? Cadre Duc believed the village would soon be destroyed, so he was taking more chances. He wanted to see how many Americans could be maimed or killed before there was nothing left to defend.

Hai watched the sky, the stars. Maybe tomorrow night he would enter the main tunnel, but instead of crawling through to Nam's buffalo pen he would branch off into a narrow passage, the one that snaked farthest down in the earth, the side tunnel that made several loops before it rose to a small mouth some ten meters from the village well and the elephant. Hai pictured himself crawling out through that mouth and into the grass. If he were lucky, if there were no cadre around, he could reach the booby trap and unhook the wire without triggering the detonator, the explosives. On Monday morning, the day ghosts would arrive and take photographs of the elephant. They would drink water from the well, fill their canteens, bathe, and wander off toward another village. They might hit other booby traps as they passed through nearby hedgerows and fields, but hopefully they wouldn't turn themselves around, march into the village, and destroy every life in their path. Hai knew the village and fields would be bombed again, as they always were after the enemy suffered casualties. But some peasants and buffalo would survive, some always had. Tomorrow, if the cadre didn't assign him elsewhere, he would strengthen the pen of Nam's buffalo by piling thick bags of dirt along the walls.

Hai placed his left hand on her side. The animal, asleep,

moved his hand with her breathing. The boy thought of Le Minh Thien, her round face, her hips, her love for the elephant. He imagined nudging the girl and whispering: "Tomorrow I'll disarm the booby trap near the well; I'll crawl out in the night and unhook the wire." Hai snaked his tongue into the soft flesh where his tooth was missing. He pressed hard, invited pain, swished his tongue until his gums burned and tingled. He imagined Thien watching him, pulling back, wondering if he was telling the truth or creating a story. Hai's hand moved to the spine of the buffalo. "Every word is true," he said. "No story." He knew the girl didn't love him; she loved the elephant. But she might love both of them if she found out Nguyen Luu Hai was braver than anyone she had known.

His sleep was restless, intermittent. Once, when he woke, he rubbed his eyes and said to himself: "Do it first, tell her later. How can you brag about something before it is done?"

He rested against the female buffalo, felt the rhythm of her breathing, and dreamed.

14
Hunters

The markings on the earth were readable: the tiger had walked here, stood here, scraped claws on a fallen trunk, dripped blood, lain down in grass, walked among trees and vanished. Conchola touched drops of blood, fresh prints. Pugmarks. He sniffed wet fingers, smeared blood over his throat, lips, scars. He imagined the tiger lifting his great head, breathing the dank air, smelling his own blood on the flesh of a human. The medic searched for a blood trail, more prints, but found nothing. How did a four-hundred-pound animal, *un varón*, vanish in air? Or did invisible tiger tunnels riddle the red earth?

The wounded beast, from a cave near the stream, watched the sky darken over trees, and for the first time he trembled not from hunger or the pain of wounds, but from fear of a predator, fear of being hunted. He moved farther back in the cave when webs of light leaped above trees. He no longer trusted the sky, the power of storm clouds, their veins shot with light, the churning mass that could not be predicted. Maybe this midday sky was no different from ancient skies. Maybe it would hunt trees, fell a few at a time, break them with wind and light, smudge them with fire. Or maybe this was the new sky that would lash without warning, the sky that would hunt and blow fire through every animal and tree, every bush and leaf and eddy of water. The beast smelled old smells that streamed through the trees and into his cave. Dung and moisture, rainwater, the detritus of leaves. He smelled his wounds, but he did not yet smell ashes, charred flesh, or the death clouds—bitter and black—that emptied the lungs, forced the breath from the body. The new sky often lashed repeatedly at trees and animals it had already broken. A careless hunter, it devoured some things whole, but left most to lie in fragments on the ground, unburied and rotting. The new sky spared nothing, gathered nothing. The tiger curled his half-ruined body under a lip of stone on the far side of the cave.

For a long time rain fanned over the earth, the sky flickered, but no trees caught fire. The tiger, exhausted from watching what he could not control, allowed his eyes to close, his body to grow heavy. He slept briefly, his legs twitched in his dreams, and the movements woke him. His ears flattened against the sides of his skull. His lips curled, his claws unsheathed, as he leaned toward knots of darkness. He had no way to powerfully respond. He could not chase sky and cloud, leap, sever a spinal cord with fangs, but his hunter's body—electric, a play of muscle and nerve—assumed the pose of stalking, waiting. The rain was clear, revealed no smell or shade of darkness taken from blood. Maybe this one thing—rain—would never betray him. Now as lightning fissured the clouds rain fanned in long gray streaks, bright streams. Regardless of how many trees and animals were lifted by clouds or left to rot on the earth, the sky had been unable to change the pattern or smell of rain.

After the storm, a group of two-leggeds passed near the cave. The tiger heard them and smelled them before he saw them, clumsy animals moving noisily, scaring away whatever they hunted. He had seen them several times, had stalked them, but their smell and size still puzzled him. They were larger than the two-leggeds who once lived here, who vanished before the new ones arrived. The new ones, with longer bodies, stretched to the height of certain tree trunks—the place where the limbs first branched and flared. While hunting, they rose high over the earth, but while lying down, asleep or at rest, they seemed no larger than a herd of deer curled in the grass. He had never seen them eat their kill, even a small animal. They smelled of the things they wasted—rancid meat, a foulness different from the smell of any other live animal. Twice he was near them when they made great noises and sent sharp lines of fire-wind through forests. They hunted the trees, the circles of trees, and killed several animals. In this way they resembled the new sky, but they had thick-veined throats, appeared soft, and maybe he could have killed them. Confused by their noise, their size and their smell, he had watched them, considered hunting them, but had always left them alone.

After they passed a safe distance away, he moved down to the stream. He lapped the water, waded, and the ground and tree animals responded to his presence. Three myna birds cleared the trees and flew east. A cat-sized monkey, his eyes on the tiger, climbed backwards up a banyan, and a muntjac, a small deer some ways off, tilted her head and froze. After acknowledging the tiger, retreating with swift movements or hiding in stillness, theirs was the silence of the hunted. The tiger emerged from the stream, shook himself, and lay still in tall grass.

He breathed the smells of damp earth, fish and frogs, grass. His throat thrummed, and with each full breath pain wracked his chest, made him shudder. He coughed; a frog jumped. The tiger looked at a sky that seemed partly knowable, harmless. No longer his predator. Soft gray, with clouds thin as leaves, it carried no sound but the sound of wind.

So he hunted. With luck he would find something wounded, something near death. Or else something that froze, confused by a smell, a sound—the direction of danger. Tail curling, twitching, the tiger made a trail through the marsh grass nearly twice as tall as his body. He lay flat when he heard the nearby grass ripple, tear. There was silence, then more tearing, rippling. He breathed in the scent of muntjac deer.

Three body-lengths he crept forward and there they were: a mother and fawn tearing the stems of grass. The mother froze, her eyes wide, ears straight up. Electric. The tiger noiselessly shifted his weight to his back paws. He sprang, arced, tore her neck, her throat, and she fell beneath him in a heap.

His teeth had clamped down in precise locations. He severed her spinal cord, small bones, but the pain of his wounds exhausted him. He slumped on the mother deer and rested on the warmth of her body. The fawn, alternately holding her breath and gasping, moved in a half-circle, then flitted toward a tree line. She hesitated, turned around, and saw the large animal that covered her mother's body. The sky began ringing, the trees hummed. She blinked, took small breaths through her nostrils, and sprinted for the trees.

The tiger feasted on the rump, the abdomen, then worked toward the heart. When he had taken what he could, he carried her remains to the tree line. Before he could rake leaves and earth over her carcass, he smelled and heard a two-legged animal. Although it made less noise than the others, it still kicked and rattled the earth, and its smell was unmistakable. This was the lone two-legged the tiger had stalked several times. It gave off the dense, fetid smell of other two-leggeds, but also smelled of marsh grass and blood.

The beast hid himself in a nearby tangle of reeds. Exhausted, he would not stalk the two-legged, would not attack, but he might scare off any animal who attempted to eat the remains of his kill.

The medic saw the body of the deer. A minute later he saw pugmarks, tiger prints, and knelt down to trace the contours with his fingers. He barely had the energy to smile. He sat beside the deer, Mundo's prey, and wondered when the tiger would return to finish his meal. It was evident the deer was newly dead. The eyes were clear, serene, and whatever flash of fear passed through them in the final moments was gone, temporarily absolved. It was a strange phenomenon Conchola had observed in the dead. He had seen it in the eyes of the animal he killed, the animal with wings. And he had seen it on the face of a boy, Mark Currie, who had been killed by a sniper at the base of *Nui Ba Den*, Black Virgin Mountain. The face and eyes reflected what was intimate, trees and sky. Death absolved them of fear, and the dead seemed not merely to mirror objects but to merge with them, dissolve. Conchola could not fathom the expressions of generosity, or why they must pass. Drawn inward, soon the eyes would glaze over, a thin film dulling their surface. Presently, he turned away before the eyes of the dead deer lost their innocence and became dull, dark holes.

In his mind he wrote a postcard home:

Mama, I'm doing my best over here. I have the tiger's blood on my face, his recent kill at my feet, and I doubt he's wandered far from this tree line. I'll wait for him, Mama, as I've nothing better to do. I hear there are people in Asia who believe you come back to this world after you die. Por ejemplo, *you can come back in the body of a bug, a little gnat or a fly. Or you can come back as a different human being in a different body, or as a wild animal—a tiger. I'm not coming back as no gnat or fly, Mama, I swear. Maybe for me, a Catholic, it's wrong to believe that instead of going to heaven or hell when I die I'll return to earth in the body of a tiger. Maybe I don't care too much what a priest would say to this, or what Jesus would say. Somehow I believe Jesus and the Virgin of Guadalupe would approve, but who knows? If I die, Mama, I'm coming back as a wild animal, a tiger. If anyone in the* barrio *asks about Antonio Lucio, you can tell them this is true.*

He fell asleep near the remains of the deer.

The tiger, from his shelter of reeds and grass, heard and smelled more two-leggeds. These were the ones who had passed earlier, who had hunted near the stream, and now they'd circled back, retraced their steps, for whatever reason. He remembered the two-leggeds—the one asleep near his kill and the ones approaching—often moved in circles. It was easy to stalk them because their movements were repetitious. They never surprised anything as they walked again and again over the same trails of soil and leaves and stones.

He lay still and waited. First he had smelled them, a moment later he heard them, and now he saw them. They were bunched together near the stream, their heads down, and he could see they were tired. The one in front glanced up at the nearest tree line, then hung his head. He came forward a little, his eyes on the earth. He stopped, looked to both sides, then sidled toward the trees.

This two-legged coughed and shivered when he saw the deer and the two-legged curled beside it. Other two-leggeds rushed forward, their feet thumping the earth, their throats loud, their bodies heavy. The tiger feared they would eat the remains of his kill, but instead they circled it, surrounded the dead animal and the two-legged who was waking. This lone two-legged slowly lifted his body and made sounds in his throat. Then all the two-leggeds were making sounds, stretching tall their bodies, raising the air with noises. They jostled each other, their throats loud, their bodies loud, and soon the sounds were unbearable. The tiger slipped off through reeds and grass, crossed the stream, and did not rest until he could no longer hear or smell the two-leggeds gathered near his kill.

Billie Jasper said, "So you trapped this thing? Then you *ate* it?"

Conchola considered lying. "The tiger's," he whispered. "Wouldn't take my master's food even if I was starving."

Warren nodded. "Lieutenant, sir, let me shoot this mother fucker. Just one time, sir."

"Shut up."

"No sense bothering with a trial, sir. Kitty-cat was AWOL."

"He'll tell it to a judge."

"Wasn't AWOL," said Conchola. "Fell in the stream and the stream carried me, sir."

Warren raised his M-60, held it waist-high.

"Put that shit down," said Jasper. "Won't need it."

"Matter of opinion."

"Put it down," said Lieutenant Bateson. "He's already got two or three nooses wrapped around his neck."

The lieutenant radioed command to report on the platoon's success. "Missing's soldier's been located," he said, "at approximately 17:20 hours. PFC Conchola has no weapon, no boots; we found him asleep near a dead deer." After monitoring a brief response, the lieutenant said, "Affirmative, put it on the books. AWOL in a war zone."

"Wasn't AWOL," said Conchola.

The lieutenant raised a hand to silence him. "AWOL," he said to the dispatcher, "as explained in earlier transmissions. I'll most likely press for a court martial once we return to Cu Chi."

Before signing off, Bateson studied his maps and gave the coordinates or probable coordinates of the platoon, a rough estimate of their location. "All accounted for at present," he said, "twenty-three friendlies. One sorry-looking medic without weapon and boots."

Now Conchola lied. He swore to the lieutenant, swore to his Mama and Jesus and Mary that he fell in the stream, slipped on stones, and the currents carried him outward. "Can't swim, sir. Tried to call for help, but my mouth was waterlogged and I was in shock and I thought I was dying." He looked around. "Sir, you think anyone wants to die this way?" He gestured toward the stream, the nearby trees, the shadows, the remains of the deer. "I counted myself dead, sir, one more sorry statistic. If the stream didn't drown me, then the gooks'd shoot me or the tiger'd eat me, and either way I was bone-dumb dead."

"Bone-dumb," said Warren. "Got that right."

"Stuff it," said Bateson, and fixed his eyes on Conchola. "You telling me you fell in the stream? Dropped your drawers to shit and keeled over?"

"There it is, sir. The bare truth of it."

"Stupid," said Bateson. "Beyond stupid."

"I know, sir."

"An accident," said Billie Jasper. "Could've happened to anyone."

"Bullshit."

Conchola shrugged. "Okay, sir, couldn't have happened to anyone. But what judge in the world will call me a liar when I say I wouldn't swim off down some jungle stream in the dark of night?"

The lieutenant swallowed.

"Wouldn't do it, sir. I'm not suicidal."

"Just stupid."

"All right, sir, stupid. But not suicidal." He raised his arms, made a cross. "Can't swim, sir. I'm helpless in water."

"Helpless in lots of places."

"Fine, sir, agreed. But the last thing I'd do is leave behind my rifle and boots and try to swim off alone down a jungle stream."

The lieutenant looked at the ground for a time. "You do cause problems," he said. "On a regular basis."

"Took the words from my mouth," said Warren.

"Yeah, who saw the booby trap?" said Billie Jasper. "The one-five-five round?"

Conchola nodded.

"Anyone else would've walked right into it," said Billie. "Would've blown himself up and left nothing but spittle."

Conchola bobbed his head. "There it is, sir."

"Saved my sorry ass," said Billie. "Don't deny it."

"Kitty luck," said Warren.

"No, sharp eyes," said Billie. "Maybe he ain't sure-footed in the dark, but he's got cat eyes. Admit it."

"Let's dispense with the chatter."

"I could walk point," said Conchola. "I wouldn't mind, sir."

"Yeah, you mess up you blow us all away."

"Won't mess up, sir, I promise. I could do what I do best: see what's ahead of us, see what's around us. I could walk us all the way back to Nam."

Hunched over, the lieutenant looked at the carcass of the deer. Conchola guessed at the man's thoughts: A medic never walked point, never. But a medic who screwed up the way Conchola screwed up begged to be punished. It was true Conchola spotted a booby-trapped one-five-five round in a nest of reeds. He saw what no one else could see, and spared the life of Billie Jasper. It was also true a judge would believe him if he claimed he fell in the stream and was swept away, his throat too waterlogged to call for assistance. *Your honor, I was terrified, helpless. The night was dark, I slipped and fell, and the currents carried me outward.* Maybe the lieutenant was thinking clearly, weighing options. Or maybe he was just staring at the corpse of the deer and thinking of how easy it was to die here. Maybe he was thinking of himself, of how the remains of his body would look, or of how no one would really care if another lieutenant was wasted. When he finally spoke his shoulders bunched, his voice wavered. "Tomorrow they'll fly us to Cu Chi," he said, "so your time with your tiger's nearly over. Maybe you'll tell your story to a judge, or maybe you'll walk point—I'll decide later." He cleared his throat. "But if you piss me off, if you cause any more trouble, I assure you the consequences will be severe."

Billie Jasper had carried Conchola's boots and M-16. The weapon was disassembled now, so Jasper sat on the ground, arranged the parts in his lap, and put it together in less than a minute. He gave the weapon to his medic and his medic thanked him.

"Watch my back," whispered Conchola. "I'll watch everything in front."

15
Hero

Each night Ma Xuan prepared the family altar. She cleaned the red cloth that covered the shelf facing the front door. She arranged offerings of fruit, mangos or bananas, and when possible she brought a special gift in a white bowl—a cube of ginger, a hard-boiled egg, candied coconut sliced in shavings thin as paper. Already praying, she would dust the framed picture of her husband, the picture of her and her husband's parents, and she would light a white candle and three sticks of incense. Each night she honored her ancestors with food and prayer, incense and light. And each night she called her children, Hai and Nhi, who bowed to the altar with her, their palms on the bare floor, their foreheads near their palms, their posture an expression of reverence—the body of a family not much different than earth, fields and graves, *que huong*, ancestral homeland. The umbilical cords that once joined her to Hai and Nhi were buried in this earth.

Ma Xuan made sure her children prayed correctly. After three bows, Luu Hai would sit cross-legged on her right, Nhi on her left, and their spines would be straight, their faces slightly lifted. She knew of families whose prayers were insincere. The children sometimes squatted flat-footed, their arms slumped on their knees, and their quick bows were more like casual nods of greeting. Ma Xuan reprimanded her own children the moment they lacked attention. Each night, after listening as she recited introductory prayers, they too invoked the compassion of Quan Yin and the wisdom of Lord Buddha. As Nhi and Hai continued praying, she would snuff the candle so it could be reused through several weeks of praying. Her family of three would recite in darkness the memorized

119

prayers, the traditional prayers, the prayers to bless and protect the ancestors. Each night Ma Xuan concluded by speaking aloud the names of the dead so they would be remembered. The knelt-upon earth held seeds, bones, names, offerings. It was home to her large family, her ancestors who gave and received blessings from the Other Side.

Tonight she had brought one gift to the altar, the mangos picked from a tree near her home. She prayed names in the dark, her children listened, and she ended with prayers for her husband who died violently and could not be properly buried. A proper burial required that a body be whole. A body should rest in the earth where it worked and near the home where it lived, and should be unbroken so the soul could pass from the home of the body to the home of spirits. "We ask for special help for Nguyen Van Phong," she whispered, "my husband and my children's father. We ask that he be accepted into the next world, that he not be held back and left to wander." Her husband had lost his left leg and arm, but now Ma Xuan pictured his wholeness, his body firm and supple. She again spoke his name, and the names of his parents and grandparents. Three times she bowed to the altar, her children bowed, and then she left them. She parted the curtain that divided the room and lay down on a reed mat that served as her and her daughter's bed.

Luu Hai leaned closer to Nhi and whispered, "Tomorrow, if I am not here, will you tell Thien to remember me?"

"Remember what?"

"Just tell her to say my name and remember Luu Hai. Tell her I tried my best for her."

"What are you talking about?"

"I have to take a risk," said Hai. "Tonight I'll try to disarm the booby trap, the one near Thien's elephant."

"It's not hers."

"Well, you know what I mean. The elephant's in danger."

"We all are."

"But the elephant has no chance. If the Americans are

caught in that trap, the first thing they'll do is put one-hundred bullets in her chest."

Nhi touched her brother's wrist. "Instead the cadre will put one-hundred bullets in you. They will kill you."

"No, they'll think the trap failed. An American stumbled over it but it didn't blow."

"Don't be stupid."

"It happens," said Hai. "It's happened before."

"Not often."

"An easy job, almost too easy. Just lift the wire and let it lie loose on the bund."

Nhi pointed toward the altar, the dark shelf. "You want your picture here tomorrow? Should I pray you don't become a ghost?"

"You won't have to."

"We already pray too much. We have to say extra prayers because of how father died."

"I won't die."

"Then why ask that Thien remember you? You know you could die."

He looked away.

"Should I give her your picture for her altar? Is this your wish?"

"I won't—"

"What would Ma say? What would the grandfathers say? You can't help the elephant or help anyone by making yourself dead."

He feared she was right. Maybe the booby trap would explode as he lifted the wire in an attempt to disarm it. Or maybe one of the cadre would observe his efforts, and after a quick trial maybe Cadre Duc himself would shoot Nyuyen Luu Hai for treason. Ma Xuan would then place the one picture of her son on the family altar. She would lean it on her husband's picture frame because she had no frame for it, nor the money to buy one. He wished Ma had a more handsome picture, a smiling one she could offer Miss Thien. The only picture of Hai was too serious, a mirror of his father. The bunched brow, squinched eyes, firm jaw—the face of a peasant. The boy imagined a more satisfying picture: Luu Hai riding his buffalo, Great Joy, over the green fields near the banyan tree, the cove of the Sai Gon River shining in the background. Would Thien place this picture on her altar? Would she light a candle and incense and bring bowls of fresh fruit? He imagined a perfect picture, himself and his buffalo, but then he imagined something better. If he survived, if he did something brave and Thien loved him and married him, she would be a member of his family. With every breath a wife cared for her husband, body and soul, living or dead. And if Hai disarmed the booby trap and was not blown up or caught by the cadre, he would tell Thien how he crawled out in the night to save her elephant. He would speak modestly, a few words at most: "It was easy; I knew I could do it. But I had to keep my hand real steady when I lifted the wire."

After further consideration, he decided the feat would be more impressive if told by someone other than himself. Nhi was Thien's best friend, so Nhi would surely tell her. Nodding, relaxed now, he pressed his tongue into the narrow groove where his tooth was missing. Hai licked at raw flesh, let it ache and sting, as he imagined a picture of himself and Great Joy riding on a bund between ripening fields.

His sister rose without a word and went to Ma Xuan. In a moment she might shake mother's shoulder, reveal his plan, and the two might grab him and hold him in their arms and not let him go anywhere. The boy sidled to the corner of the hut used as a kitchen. "*Dung lo*," he said to himself, "tomorrow they'll thank me." He slipped behind the cookstove and down the hole that led to Great Joy's pen and out toward the main branch of the tunnel. Groping, feeling his way in the dark, he thought of how surprised Miss Thien would be once Nhi informed her how the elephant was saved.

He passed through the main branch of the tunnel where two nights earlier the peasants and their animals had gathered to escape the bombing. Root smells. Urine. Dregs of pig shit, duck shit. The odors dissipated when he clambered through a narrow side-passage and into a small chamber. He slithered up through a maze of crannies and spider cracks that rose toward the village well.

He paused near the mouth of the passage. Crickets sang in the grass and fields, and a bird flung open its wings, screamed and cackled over the Sai Gon River. Hai heard the upthrust of wings and pictured an osprey arcing away from whatever threatened it. Maybe it had plunged its talons into a fish too large, a fish that almost pulled it down into the currents. He didn't know if an osprey fished at night, nor did he know its call. *Fisher-bird*, he thought, *fly high, keep flying*. He scuttled forward until he saw a sphere of dim light over the hole.

A scraping sound, a sound like fingernails on the surface of leather. He rose from the tunnel, listened, and lifted his head high enough to see the dark outline of the elephant. The beast seemed aware of him. She raised her trunk, curled it, and though he ducked down in tall grass she must have noted his scent. He heard whispers and craned his neck to see the elephant's master reaching to brush both hands over the animal's left ear. He was certain the old man neither saw him nor heard him. Maybe the master had received permission from Cadre Duc to stay with his beloved animal on the last night of her life. Maybe he too considered disabling the booby trap, unhooking the wire, but he most likely had no knowledge of these things.

Hai saw no one else. The starlight was dim, the moon mostly hidden by clouds, but he could see the silhouettes of bushes and trees, the stones of the well, the rice bund some ten meters away, the great bulk of the elephant's body. He felt a sudden heat and quickness in his legs. Between clouds there were stars, the Silver River, and his body felt like swarms of stars, small lights, a part of the sky drawn inside him, intimate and powerful. He wondered if he could reach the bund and unhook the wire without alerting the old man. It occurred to Hai that he had been unwise to blurt his intentions to his sister. By now she'd told Ma Xuan, and if tonight Hai succeeded, if tomorrow the booby trap failed, the cadre might hold a thorough investigation. They might question everyone, even small children who could speak but a few words, and they might demand answers. Hai felt guilty that he had not considered Nhi's safety. He'd seen her merely as a messenger, the one who would tell Miss Thien of his bravery. But now Nhi too was in danger, could be sentenced to death, for failing to alert the cadre of her brother's actions. Tonight or tomorrow, if Hai was alive, he would discuss this predicament with Ma Xuan and his sister. Only when the danger passed, when the cadre stopped searching for someone to blame, could Nhi tell Miss Thien and the elephant man how the elephant was saved.

He crawled toward the booby trap, the bund. It had rained earlier, the ground was moist, and he made soft, swishing sounds as he parted the grass with his face, his body. Frogs always sang louder after a rain, crickets too, and for a few moments Hai barely heard his own movements. In his peripheral vision, he saw the dome of the elephant's spine, her raised trunk curled at the end, pointed in his direction. He couldn't see the elephant's master, but pictured him standing near the animal. Sweat ran down Hai's forehead, blurred his vision. He paused, curled on his side, wiped his face with his hands. The moon had come out from behind the clouds.

He reached the bund and lay still for a time. Behind him he heard the elephant eating, tearing leaves and stalks, but the crickets and frogs had gone silent. After several moments they began singing again, a cover of sound that allowed him to whisper a prayer that came as natural as breathing: "May the Buddha protect my family, my village...every animal." He saw the trap, the dark wedge of a Coca-Cola can, a thimble of light reflected off one edge. He rose to his knees and held his hands near his face to see if he could trust them. His fingertips moved slightly, but his palms remained steady. He massaged his hands, rotated his wrists, let his fingertips lighten. Each hand must place no more pressure or weight on an object than a single blade of grass.

His face was within inches of a loop of wire attached to the can. Another wire, blade-thin, threaded the loop and stretched across the grass of the bund. Hai placed his left hand on the backside of the can. Breathing softly, he clasped the loop of wire with his right forefinger and thumb. He felt the opening in the loop, the place through which the trip-wire could be unhooked, released. Whispering his prayer to the Buddha, he lifted the strand of wire, the metal warm on his fingers. His prayer, as natural as breath, was saying itself. And Luu Hai was smiling and happy and he thought of Thien and his sister and his village and the elephant as he lay the wire attached to nothing on the grass of the bund.

He crawled back through the tunnel and into his home where his mother and sister greeted him near the cookstove. Ma Xuan hugged him, then slapped him, and interrupted when he apologized. "How could you do this? You didn't ask my permission. You didn't ask the permission of your elders, your village."

He stared at the floor.

"You think you're brave? You think someone admires you?" She slapped him again. "You smell like sewage. Take off your clothes and go to bed."

In a dark corner, stripped naked, shivering, he heard her mumbling: "No food tomorrow; you'll work and go hungry. You think you can do as you wish, take fate in your hands? If your father were here, he would beat you until you bled."

At dawn, the girl removed the wooden disc from the village well. The elephant warbled, unfurled and lifted her trunk, and paid no attention to the pain in her shoulder. Water smelled best at the beginning of the day. Well-water was best of all where it was quiet and deep, where it tapped a spring of pure water. The body of the nearby river did not smell as good. In light or darkness, the river smelled partly of death, partly of birth, but there was a smell beneath it that came from the quiet pools and the soil, the places that birthed the river. The animal tried to enjoy this smell before other smells intruded. She watched the girl lower a bucket into the well. Her master began rubbing her, putting medicine on her wound, and the acrid smell disturbed her. She leaned forward and swished a loud burst of air through her trunk. The best smell was the smell of birthing, the smell of water. The smell of a newborn calf was good because it held some of the water that birthed the river, the best water of the earth.

Thien helped the elephant man fetch three cart-loads of hay that Nam's buffalo hauled to the village well. They piled the hay between the well and the elephant, and they hand-fed her stalks of sugarcane and bunches of bananas. "We'll need a whole mountain of hay," said the elephant man, "to keep her out of sight of the Americans." They went back for another cart-load, but the situation was hopeless. The elephant still towered above the hay, her upper body clearly visible. If by some miracle they were able to conceal her, they knew their efforts could be erased hours later. Cadre Duc and Cadre Hien would probably inspect the site before the day ghosts arrived. Most likely, they would order the villagers to remove any obstacle that obstructed the elephant from view.

"When the ghosts arrive," said Thien, "I'll stand near the elephant and warn the enemy of danger."

"No, you won't."

"Just raise my hand, wave them off. One second."

"Forget it."

"I'm not afraid to die," said Thien, but her voice became tentative. She did not wish to risk her life for an effort that would probably fail. Nor did she wish to save Americans, give a warning that saved the enemy of her village, the enemy of her country. She began to say something else, but her words came out as mumbles. "Yes, I think you understand," said the elephant man. "The cadre would execute you and toss you in a hole."

An hour later Cadre Duc ordered the mounds of hay removed. He showed village boys a map of the area, a rough sketch of the well, the elephant (a circle with a tail), the rice bund, the tunnel opening that would serve as the site of ambush. Now in pencil he drew an X on either side of the tunnel. "Spider holes," said Duc. "One meter deep will be sufficient." Before explaining their purpose, he ordered Hai and Qui to begin digging. "Fast," he said. "Let's see how well you've learned to dig."

Later, when the boys were almost finished, Cadre Hien arrived. After Duc and Hien shared a cigarette, they walked side-by-side past the spider holes, the tunnel entrance, the village well and the elephant. "Our post will be the tunnel entrance," said Duc, "and two other cadre will be in these holes, somewhat more vulnerable. Anticipate a thirty-second ambush, maybe less. If the day ghosts hit the trap and cluster around their casualty or casualties, we'll have a brief opportunity to inflict greater wounds."

A flush spread over Hai's face as Cadre Duc looked toward the rice bund. Duc inched forward, squatted, and briefly studied his map. He shaded his eyes with his right hand. Rising, he wiped sweat from his brow, then stepped forward to inspect the trap. Hai, whose life might depend on an air of insouciance, sang a work song he had learned from Ong Quan, the oldest man in the village, the one who knew the most songs:

The rice in the fields, wet and green.
The sweat on my body, wet and brown.
The buffalo works, the sun works; who is singing?
The buffalo sun is singing to the fields.

He began to repeat the song as Cadre Duc bent down and lifted the loose wire from the grass. Thien, feeding the elephant sugarcane, and the elephant man, dipping a cup in a bucket, had no idea what the cadre had discovered. Hai stuttered and sang louder ("bu-buffalo sun"), ended his song mid-sentence, and no one responded when Cadre Duc said, "Who did this? Who would do this?" Duc knelt down and reconnected the wire, reset the trap. "Unfortunate," he said, "but we'll investigate later. Whoever tried to alter our plan has made a very grave mistake."

An hour later, villagers gathered under the banyan tree to hear Cadre Duc dispense his instructions. Since empty fields would arouse suspicion, several peasants would remain in the fields to mislead the Americans. Cadre Duc chose Hai's family and Nam's family for fieldwork. "Bring your buffalo," he said to Nam. "as though it were any other day. Let her wallow or roam, but lead her back toward your home approximately one minute before the Americans reach the well and the elephant. The others assigned to the fields must continue working, or pretending to work, near the entrances of tunnels. When the booby trap explodes, when the ambush is sprung, be prepared to find your escape routes into the main tunnel beneath the village."

As the peasants dispersed, Thien followed her grandma along a buffalo path that led to their home. Luu Hai climbed halfway up the banyan tree, squatted on a wide limb, and waved to the girl who did not see her admirer. The boy spotted the elephant man crossing a bombed field, trudging toward the village well and the elephant. "*Xin loi*," said Hai, "*xin loi*. Another animal's almost dead."

16
Tame Elephant

They sat in the shade of a banyan tree that towered above the rice fields. Billie Jasper wrote a postcard to his girlfriend. PFC Warren dismantled his machine gun, cleaned the barrel and firing mechanism, and teased Conchola about tigers and kitties. "In Cu Chi you better worry about kitties," he said. "The tunnels are too small for big cats, so the gooks got all these kitties." He sighted down the barrel. "Fierce little fuckers, no mercy. I heard about a medic who wishes the kitties killed him. He made the mistake of squatting near one of their tunnels, opening his legs a bit. One of them gook cats took a swipe, ate for her breakfast this thing the size of a finger." He held up his right pinkie. "Same-same," he said, "the size of a dink's dick. Lost all two inches in one little swipe."

Conchola, smiling, said, "Sorry to hear about your Daddy," and then he ignored him. The rice fields, what remained of them, had blossomed. He'd been here before, this same patch of earth, but the paddies had never appeared this generous. Conchola could not recall an earth this green. He put on his bush hat and squinted at glades of rice, paddy water, a few peasants who braved the midday heat to do whatever task was needed. The green rectangles of the fields had been broken by bombs. The nearest crater was filled with spring water, circled with tall grass. A boy and a water buffalo approached the crater. Behind them, a woman and child, maybe fearing their hoes and shovels would be mistaken for rifles, patched a leaky rice bund by hand. Conchola watched the buffalo ease itself down into the lake of the crater. The boy called to the animal, talked to it, and after a minute or two of coaxing the mud-soaked beast clambered onto a bund and let the boy ride him. Conchola remembered the last time he was here he saw a boy and a buffalo. Before the Cambodian invasion, what seemed eons ago, he had watched a boy rub the snout of his animal, then hold his hands near the slobbering mouth so the beast would lick them. Now Conchola assumed this was the same boy, the same buffalo, until he remembered the first buffalo had horns that could eviscerate a man, a great dark head twice the width of his own shoulders. The animal before him was smaller, perhaps female, and he did not see any other buffalo in the fields near the village. He watched the boy hurry the beast toward the thatch huts on the far side of the fields. The air quieted, the paddies baked and shimmered, and the sun was at twelve o'clock.

Billie Jasper wrote FREE on the upper right corner of his postcard. "Get ready for a wedding," he said to Conchola. "Me and Lucinda Sayers."

"*Felicitaciones.*"

"My best man," said Billie. "Couldn't happen without you."

"I'll be there."

"She's so pretty maybe you won't believe her."

Conchola grinned.

"No, you won't," said Billie, "you won't believe her. Like if she walked up and shook your hand, you'd think you were seeing her in a dream."

Conchola opened a can of peaches, a can of pound cake, and nudged Billie's elbow. "Maybe my girl's prettier."

"You don't have one."

"And sweeter too. Sweet as peaches and syrup and bowls of fresh sugar."

"Sweet as baby food," said Billie. "You once worked in a baby food factory. Beech Nut."

"So?"

"So don't tell lies about no girlfriend. The one time you told me the truth you said you chased the wrong girls."

Conchola paused, then nodded. "White ones," he said. "But now I got myself what I need. A brown girl."

"In your head."

"*Perfecto*. She loves me true."

"Yeah, but mine's real, a real girl. Lucinda Sayers."

"I believe you."

Billie sat straight up. "Baby, her hair," he whispered, "you should see her hair." His eyes narrowed as though the shine and luster hurt them. "Long," he said, "this long," his hands rising, then separating, measuring. "The shiniest, most beautiful hair all the way down her spine."

Warren leaned over his disassembled weapon. "You mean like a monkey? Little monkey girl with a perm?"

"Fuck off."

"Yeah, well, just thought I'd ask. Don't try to tell me her hair is gold and straight all the way down her spine."

Jasper stood, then Warren, then Conchola.

"Troops," said the lieutenant. "Set your asses down. Drop it."

"Sir?" said Warren.

"Drop it, I mean now. I won't be tolerating any more bullshit from you or anyone else."

Lieutenant Bateson attended to a call on the radio. Before nightfall, he would have to lead his platoon through the nearby village and across fifteen kilometers of mostly open farmland. The paddies were dotted with hedgerows, clumps of bamboo and palms, but they appeared benign in comparison to the jungles of Cambodia. The lieutenant's main concern was water. The platoon would head south, away from the river, where water might not be easily accessible. He looked over his map, felt the strain in his eyes, the familiar pressure. "Okay," he said to his men, "fill your canteens, enough lounging. We'll be moving out in five minutes flat."

Conchola walked out from the banyan's shade, Jasper

behind him. They started toward the spring-filled crater, but Conchola halted when he saw the village well and an elephant over the fields to the south.

"Billie," he pointed. "You see it?"

"Oh, yeah, Cu Chi Zoo. What they charge for admission?"

"Wild elephant," said Conchola. "Bet you a month's pay it left its forest and wandered in here."

"Or fell from heaven."

"No, its forest probably got bombed. The animal had no choice but to leave its forest."

"Whatever."

"It's wild," said Conchola. "I'm sure of it."

"You would be."

"It wandered into this ville after its forest was pretty much ruined."

Warren and a few other guys spotted the animal. "Elephant," said Warren, "gook elephant," and rummaged through his rucksack for a camera. "Kitty killer," he said, "beautiful. Send a picture to Meow Man's mom."

The elephant and the well were approximately eighty meters away. Conchola dropped his rifle and pack, took out his canteens, slung an aid bag over each shoulder, and he and Billie stepped onto a bund and began walking toward the animal. The medic called to Lieutenant Bateson, "Be right back, sir. Get our water up ahead. I remember that well has fresh water." The platoon was in disarray. Warren and several others traipsed after Conchola and Jasper. Some of the men huddled near Lieutenant Bateson who stood on a bund near the spring-filled crater. "Conchola," said the lieutenant, "hold it up, that's an order. We'll enter that ville together and we'll enter as a team."

Conchola halted and used an empty canteen to shield his eyes from the glare. "Wild elephant," he said to Billie. "You can tell by the way it's tensed."

A few minutes later, the men formed as a platoon and

Conchola led them toward the well and the elephant. The medic was not watching his steps. The elephant turned, began moving away, and Conchola glimpsed someone—a man or a child in a white shirt—who slapped the animal's right flank. Conchola was disappointed that the beast might be tame. It was apparently being led away by its master, a wisp of a figure, and within seconds the two vanished behind a stand of palm trees. The medic thought he heard whispers, gook sounds, singsong voices. He quickened his steps and moved toward the palms, the well. The lieutenant called, "All right, slow the pace, slow it down a bit." And a split second later Conchola stumbled across a wire.

The explosion hurled him forward on his belly. The shooting began; he lay still, helpless without his weapon. He had his medical supplies, his morphine and bandages and gauze, but he had no way to defend himself. He turned his head to the side and saw blood on his left hand. He watched blood drip from his palm, color the grass. "Jesus," he said, "what the hell." Conchola reached with his good hand, grabbed one of his aid bags. "Billie?" he said, "you with me?" He heard someone behind him coughing, wheezing, struggling to breathe.

The shooting stopped. Billie bled from both eyes. He bled from his throat, his chest, his abdomen; his breathing was erratic. The booby trap had sent an arc of shrapnel behind the one who tripped it. Billie was blind. His right hand groped for his face. When he was hit he fell from the bund and into the paddy, and now he lay face-up in shallow water. Conchola pulled him onto the bund and turned him on his side. He sealed the chest wound with plastic, covered it with a bandage, and began to wrap the abdominal wounds with layers of gauze. "Lucinda," he said, "remember your girl, Billie. Remember her hair. Remember what you told me." Over and over he whispered, "Lucinda, Lucinda," as though her name were medicine. "Lovely Lucinda, lovely Lucinda.

Maybe you can marry your girl a few months sooner than you thought."

He bandaged the eyes with gauze. Billie's body twitched and stilled, twitched and stilled, and his breathing became more shallow. "Okay," said Conchola, "ready to fly, baby. Back to the world in a jumbo jet. You'll be ten thousand miles away by morning." Billie's body shook in a way that reminded the medic of the animal with wings, the one he killed out of mercy. He touched Billie's chest and said, "Stay with me, baby, stay with me. You'll be in Carolina in a matter of hours."

A kid named Bowers was hit, the lieutenant was hit, but Conchola stayed with Billie. His friend's shoulders shook, his arms and legs shook, and every few seconds his body arced slightly, his throat and chest lifted. Conchola said, "Okay, baby, one more thing. The tiger." He gripped Billie's left elbow. "Tell me who saw him first. *You* did. You saw him, Billie. His throat wound, his chest wound. And then you saw him vanish." Conchola waved his arms. "Our *maestro's* out there, he's alive. Guts and balls, Billie, guts and balls. He'll always be alive."

He bent down and began to remove the gauze from Billie's eyes. He wanted Billie to see his face, to see the light of the fields, the sky and the trees, the force of the sun, the sharpness of midday shadows. Maybe Billie needed to look carefully into the shade of palms trees to remember the morning he saw the tiger. Conchola removed the last strips of gauze. "*Mira*," he said, "look," but he knew Billie saw nothing. A substance the consistency of jelly coated the sockets and the bridge of the nose; the outer quadrant of the left eye was intact, but there was no pupil. "Okay," said Conchola, "I'll make you a picture. I'll help you to see it." He began to describe the tiger, the fury of eyes, the beautiful light, the ringing in the trees, the feeling that this was Geronimo, that no bullet or bomb, no fire or fragment of metal could kill an animal this powerful. "Come on," said Conchola, "come on. You ain't with me." He did his best to breathe for Billie when Billie stopped breathing. And twelve times he struck the chest with his fists in an effort to revive the heart.

Warren pulled him away and said, "Numb nuts, he's gone. You're humpin' a corpse. The lieutenant's hit, Bowers is hit. What are you doing?"

Conchola looked at him.

"Shake a leg, grab your bags and shit. People are bleeding."

Conchola tossed an aid bag over his shoulder.

"Dick in a sling," said Warren. "Sorriest medic and point man I ever seen."

The lieutenant was hemorrhaging from a wound to his right thigh. Conchola took deep breaths, steadied his hands, and clamped the femoral artery with a hemostat. Bowers was not badly hurt. Conchola bandaged his right hand, his right forearm, and said, "We'll trade places, all right? I'll go back to the world with these few scratches." For a minute he forgot about Billie, forgot his mistake of walking point without watching where he was going. He finished with Bowers, then went back to the lieutenant. "Say goodbye to us, sir, send us a postcard. Send us pictures of the girls."

The lieutenant's radio operator called for a medevac and Conchola triaged the casualties: one routine (Jay Bowers), one urgent (Lieutenant Bateson), and one terminal (Billie Jasper). The radio man said, "No, two routine. Look at your hand, doc. You're bleeding."

Conchola glanced at his left hand. "Forget about it," he said. "All it needs is a bandage." He sprinkled the wound with disinfectant, wrapped it with gauze, then went and sat beside Billie, a few meters from the village well.

Conchola felt a tightness at the base of his skull. He was mumbling, "*Lo siento*, I'm sorry," as he bent down and touched the hair that curled above Billie's forehead. The hair was alive. It responded to his touch, prickled his fingers. He ran his hands through it, then touched Billie's face, his cheeks, the places that were not broken. He smoothed a wrinkle on his friend's filthy shirt. Already the death smell was strong. Conchola breathed it in, made no attempt to avoid it. He leaned over the body and thought, *Tell you something, baby. Maybe I'd trade places, maybe I wouldn't.* He kept touching Billie's hair, his face, and sometimes he talked to him. It seemed a long time went by before the medevac arrived.

When Billie was gone, when the lieutenant and Bowers were gone, Conchola walked up to the well and filled his canteens. It was hard to believe a live elephant had stood beside coconut palms, a few meters from this well. At first it appeared restless, wild, but then it obeyed a man or child who coaxed it beyond the tree line. Conchola tried to retrace the events. The elephant had looked real, but maybe it wasn't. Maybe what he saw was not an elephant but a projection, an image—something flashed on a screen or a billboard to draw the platoon forward. He stepped into the shade of trees, knelt amid trees. *No, it must be real*, he decided. *There's no screen or billboard, nowhere to cast an image.* He walked out from beneath the trees and looked toward the fields. The fisherboy was gone, the peasants too, and there was no buffalo wallowing in a crater. The light, the green of the rice fields, the color of grace, meant nothing now. For a long time he stared at the light, leaned into it, invited pain. "Billie," he said, "Jesus. That elephant wasn't even wild."

After the canteens were filled, Warren and a few others arranged blocks of pentrite and blew up the well. Sergeant Stevens, the new platoon leader, gave his first command via radio: he called in napalm and white phosphorous on the ville.

17
Graves

She followed her master through the village and onto a wide path. He steered her into a grove of bamboo as the planes approached, and he tried to divert her (nearly succeeded) with moist leaves and stalks of sugarcane. Three kilometers away the village burned. The elephant remembered the animals she had last seen: the small baskets crammed with chickens, ducks, piglets that made a cacophony of sounds as their masters carried them to tunnels. She remembered a small human who crawled from a hole and tried to shelter a water buffalo in a grove of bamboo. A larger human rose from the dark, caught up with the small one, slapped his face, shook him, rattled his shoulders. The two led the buffalo to its pen before they disappeared down a different hole in the earth. Now the elephant heard shrill squeals, the voice of this buffalo. Spear-shaped flames struck mud and leaves, rose in splinters. They were taller than any the elephant had seen, taller than any tree or stalk of bamboo, and their bulging heads curled open like the petals of poison flowers. Birds spun through the sky with such speed the air caught fire, the earth shuddered. Had they folded their wings, lighted in a field, the elephant would have summoned her strength, charged full-speed, and trampled these small things into the earth.

Soon the sky quieted, birds vanished in clouds, and her master led her toward the ruins.

The roof of Nam's buffalo pen had been blown into the branches of a tree. The animal, a wall of flames behind her, charged the gate and collapsed, her legs twisted beneath her.

She smelled the singed hair and layers of skin that had already peeled from her body. Panting, she raised her hindquarters, bellowed, then crumpled on her side, dazed and gasping. The buffalo disbelieved her incapacity. Half blind, one eye smudged in the earth, she strained to see the sky with the other. Shaking and roiling clouds drove by. She hoped for rain to cool her and quench the fires at the back of her pen, but the clouds funneled, piled up thicker and blacker than rain clouds. Tendrils of heat flared through her throat, her skull. Her hooves shifted, twitched, but she had no strength to lift herself, plunge through the gate, charge whatever it was that set fires, that heated the earth until it peeled the flesh from her body. She called once, tossed her head, then lost control of her movements. The air strummed her chest, breathed her. Her flanks shivered, pulsed; her mouth hung open. She tried to rise but she couldn't; she tried to lie still but she couldn't. It seemed a long time passed before the fires quieted, flurried into ash, small flecks. Then the flies came, swarms of them orbiting her right eye, her snout, dipping down to taste the tips and sides of her tongue. She tried to exhale, shoo them with her breath, but she had no strength. They busied their legs and mouths on her eye, her snout, her tongue, and dove down to sample the thick folds of her throat.

Peasants emerged from tunnels and counted the live animals. Collectively, they still had three adult buffalo, one small buffalo, six roosters, nineteen hens, seventeen ducks, thirteen piglets, and the squealing mother pig now being lifted from the tunnel by six boys, three on each side of her. Women and children scavenged charred sheds and homes for tools and supplies. They unearthed three plows, four slightly damaged carts, thirteen hoes, twelve trowels, nine shovels. Luu Hai and his cousin Nam dug Nam's buffalo grave with spades. They worked fast, their rage apparent, as others gathered what could be gathered: photographs of ancestors, sacks of chicken rice, white rice, hammers and anvils, incense, candles, hammocks, reed mats, baskets, tatters of clothing. Luu Hai's mother could not find the photograph of her husband. Their thatch roof had collapsed, caught fire, and black palm leaves covered the dirt floor, bright with embers. With thongs to shield their feet, she and her daughter poked the ground with sticks, turned up fragments of things—a broom handle, the lip of a broken bowl, a packet of sewing needles, a spool of black thread, a small pot with no handle. The house and its contents had been ignited, repositioned, and little could be salvaged. Under a sheet of metal, the former lid of the stove, Ma Xuan found a blackened frame but no photograph of her husband. She picked up the frame and dropped it, the metal too hot to touch. She groaned, nearly cried out, but restrained herself in the presence of her daughter. "We'll come back for this later," she whispered. "Remember where I found it." She thought of her husband, killed violently, dismembered, and now his photograph reduced to vapor. She did not have another photograph, only this charred frame with nothing inside it. She poked the ground with her stick. She dug down until she tore up clods of dirt that made gnawing sounds, muted screams.

Thien sprinted toward the elephant and her master. She dodged to the side of the path, clipped a few leaves of bamboo, and offered them to the animal. "I looked everywhere," she said to the elephant man. "I ran through the village and saw no sign of you." In a mood of exhilaration, she failed to notice four cadre observing them from the shade of sugar palms. "You saved her," said Thien. "She would have been nothing but ash if you'd kept her shackled near the well."

The elephant man waved to the cadre, his distant audience. "I would have led her farther," he whispered, "if there were somewhere to conceal an elephant for several days, several weeks. The cadre are unlikely to congratulate me for saving her. If they decide I'm a criminal, you and the other villagers must care for this animal on your own."

Thien turned and saw Cadre Duc and three other cadre approximately thirty meters away. "Did they hear me?"

"It probably doesn't matter. I'll tell them what happened, or tell them what they wish to hear." He shackled the animal's hind legs, showed Thien how to do this. "The elephant's loyal, but they'll kill her if she tries to protect me."

"How could—"

"Listen to me. You're in charge. You understand?"

"Yes, Ong."

"Keep her by your side and feed her some leaves."

Thien obeyed. As the elephant's master approached the cadre, she picked fresh bamboo leaves, bunched them together, and the elephant grabbed them with her trunk. The girl feigned disinterest, turned her back to the men. But she listened to every nuance of the brief exchange she would later refer to as a trial.

"You led the elephant away with whose permission?" said Duc. "Who granted permission?"

"Sir—"

"Our ambush was in place. We were in our holes, and could not have stopped you without exposing our positions."

"I tried—"

"You'll be silent until I finish," said Duc. "Our forces inflicted three casualties when we should have inflicted ten or twelve, half the platoon. No one instructed you to move the animal; the instructions, in fact, were to the contrary. The Americans would have bunched up more had the elephant remained in the assigned position." He cleared his throat. "I suppose," said Duc, "you were attempting to save the animal's life."

Thien turned so she could see the men. After a pause, after it was clear that Duc had finished, the elephant's master explained his motives. "Sir, I was trying to endanger as many American lives as possible. I knew they would follow the elephant, move closer to the ambush site, and trip the booby trap because of their distractions. All of this happened, sir: they moved fast, tripped the wire, suffered losses, and were too confused to accurately retaliate." He glanced at the elephant. "Had I considered earlier the strategy of leading her away, I would have explained my proposal and requested your permission. As it was, I acted alone; I had no time for requests. By leading the animal away, I was one-hundred percent certain I would put the enemy at greater risk."

Two of the cadre chortled. "Well put," said one of them. "A good story."

"Lies," said Duc. "The excuses of a traitor."

"Sir," said the elephant man, "I would never betray my country."

"You already have," said Duc. "Last night, or before I arrived this morning, who unhooked the booby trap near the well? Was this done to endanger the lives of Americans?"

"Of this I know nothing, sir."

"At this point, a denial is counterproductive. Your actions prior to the ambush are equivalent to a confession."

"I didn't—"

"Enough," said Duc. "We allow testimony, but we never allow begging. Before our eyes you led the elephant away, and you unhooked the wire while no one was watching." He motioned to the two men standing on his right, then the one on his left. "Do you agree? Do you believe this is true?"

They nodded. One of them grinned.

"Then take him with you," said Duc. "You know the penalty for what he has done."

Penalty? thought Thien. *A bullet through the brain? Instant death?* She considered unshackling the elephant's hind legs, inciting a charge, as three cadre led the elephant's master into the rice fields. The animal seemed disoriented, confused, as though awaiting a new command, a sequence of instructions. Her right foreleg swung back and forth, back and forth, but she did not trumpet or wail or try to break the chains that bound her. Two cadre lifted the elephant's master onto a rice bund, then led him toward the swamps north of the river. He did not turn back for a last glimpse of the girl and the elephant. Almost dead, *chet roi*, he followed the tallest cadre, the one with a pistol secured to his belt.

Thien began to unshackle the elephant's hind legs.

"Keep him in chains," called Cadre Duc. "The animal is to remain near the village."

Thien looked at him.

"Later he'll be needed," said Duc. "You'll be provided with instructions."

She bowed.

"You'll keep him within one kilometer of the village. Is this understood?"

"It is, sir."

"If I see any sign of him elsewhere, you'll endanger both the animal and yourself."

He wrote something on a slip of paper. A future plan? Something that involved Thien and the elephant? She glanced toward the swamps north of the fields, the shaggy outline of hedgerows the elephant man now entered at gun-point. She turned, closed her eyes, alert for the sound of a gun, the moment of execution. She heard java birds, rice birds, the hum of flies, cicadas, the breathing of the elephant. She went to a bamboo stalk and plucked a handful of leaves. "Here," she said, "eat." The elephant rumbled, sniffed the offerings, then turned her head the other way.

She furled her trunk and wheezed. Minutes earlier she lost sight of her master, but it was more disorienting to lose his scent. Swishing her trunk from side-to-side, then forward and back, she found no trace of the smells that issued from his body. She missed the smells she knew best: the moisture and oil of his skin, the slight sourness of his sweat, his breath, the smell of hay that saturated his clothes, the hands that touched her and spread the smells of her body. Warbling the air through her trunk, the elephant inhaled the scent of ash, bamboo leaves, salt, sweat, smoke, fish, lemon. Smells of danger, smoke and ash, were predominant, so she worried for her master. She would have protected him, shielded him, had he not chained her back legs. Three humans reeking of smoke and sweat led him to an area she could not enter. She had expected them to turn back, lead her master to her side, but they glided over the land until her master was gone and no scent in the air was identical to his.

Swaying, she fanned her ears, stomped her right foreleg, and yawped and bawled for her master's return.

"You must control the elephant," said Cadre Duc. "Is this something you're capable of?"

"I am, sir."

"Has anyone trained you? Are you certain you can control him?"

Her, thought Thien. *I'm certain she's a cow.*

Duc glared at her. "Yes or no, answer up. Can you control this animal or not?"

"Yes," she said, "but I'm not her master. The elephant obeys her master the moment he gives a command."

She saw possibilities. Maybe the elephant man's life would be spared because he was indispensable. Maybe Cadre Duc had some other plan for the animal, a new way to use her in an ambush, or to draw unwary Americans toward another booby trap. "Sir," said Thien, "she trusts her master; only her master can control her completely." She knew Duc would kill the elephant, divide her meat among his fellow cadre, if he did not see in her a higher purpose. "She's well-behaved," said Thien, "and very smart. She trusts me a little, but her master can give her any command you wish."

Cadre Duc stared at her for a long time. "You'll have to demonstrate reasonable control over the animal. Is this understood?"

"It is, sir."

"Unfortunately, you miss the elephant's master. You wish to save both the elephant and its master."

She looked past him to the fields.

"His error will not be pardoned," said Duc. "He will not return to this village or any other."

She flexed her knees to control her trembling.

"This leaves you in charge of the elephant," he said. "Keep him near the village and away from the fields and most likely you'll survive."

Duc allowed her to unshackle the beast and lead her closer to the village. Thien remembered how the elephant man gave simple commands (Come, halt, stay) in a quick-fire voice, a staccato of repetition. Now she said, "Come-come-come," and the elephant obeyed. The animal kept curling her trunk over her shoulders, testing the air behind her. But she followed the girl toward the south side of the village, the land that was mostly ash.

A single gunshot echoed from the swamps.

All day Thien remained with the elephant while most of the villagers repaired paddy dikes. She practiced three commands (Come, halt, stay), and tried to reward the animal with a stalk of sugarcane each time she obeyed. The animal ate two stalks, then refused the girl's offerings. Once, rather than heeding Thien's command, she guttled the air through her trunk and made a sound—"Karoosh, karoosh!"— like a burst of storm-wind blown through a valley. The leaves of a palm trembled. The elephant sniffed her, breathed the girl's scent through her trunk and mouth, but seemed disappointed. Eyes closed, she swayed back and forth as Thien talked to her, patted her left foreleg. "I'm sorry," said Thien, "your master's gone. I miss him, too, but he's gone. He's not coming back." She hesitated. "We'll have time for our sadness when the war is over, all right? For now you need to obey me, you need to listen. Do what I tell you and maybe we'll survive."

An hour before dusk three helicopters hovered above the village. Luu Hai, who had been working in a field near the river, crawled over a bund, slid down a slope, and hid himself in the shallows. He called to Ma Xuan and Nhi, "Here, over here," but they lay still in the nearest paddy, in a few inches of water. Hai emerged from the river and slithered up the bank to help them. "Safer," he gasped, "safer in the shallows." But they were both too frightened to move.

Ma Xuan whispered prayers. Hai scanned the paddies and saw Nam and Nam's mother kneeling behind a rice bund. He saw others lying motionless in the fields, bellies to earth, heads tilted above the shallow water that flooded the rice grass. For several minutes the dragonflies hovered. Hai assumed they were gauging their prey, determining the best lines of attack, which group to kill first. Qui was in the crown of the banyan tree, the lookout tree, but maybe the dragonflies had come in so low and fast he had no time to shout a warning. After yesterday's ambush, it might be one day too late for peasants to go about their work, hoeing and pulling weeds, rebuilding bunds, transplanting rice, saying with their daily chores *Don't kill me, I'm a farmer*. One too many booby traps, one too many American casualties. Luu Hai crawled toward his mother and sister, but no one else in the fields moved.

One of the dragonflies poised over the north side of the village, one on the south, and now the third skimmed out above the fields. Hai heard a scream. He turned to his left and saw Thien and the elephant in the shade of a palm tree. Trunk and tail extended, the animal skirted around the tree, flapping her ears, screaming—the peal of her voice louder than the *whish-whish* of machinery. Thien stayed near the tree, her arms raised in a command (Halt, halt!) as the beast spun around and around, trumpeting and bellowing. Hai shut his eyes and imagined the worst: the flash of light, the deafening thud, the dead body of Thien, the shreds of her clothes, the strewn bones and flesh of the largest animal he had ever encountered. But he heard no explosions, no rockets, no bullets. No eruptions of fire. What he heard above all else was the elephant trumpeting, screaming, roaring, the thump of her giant feet waking the earth.

Ma Xuan blurted, "Lord Buddha, Dear Lord," and Hai opened his eyes as paper fell from heaven. Blue and gold, yellow and green, sheaves of paper fanned and fluttered. They brightened the fields, the edges of the village, the branches of the banyan. Hai saw new colors in the leaves near the lookout perch. The dragonflies swept over the banyan tree, over the village and fields, and one of the pilots lifted his arm and waved.

Now a loudspeaker began broadcasting from the helicopter that hovered above the banyan. The peasants heard a woman's voice, three words of English, "Hello, excuse me," and then a man's voice, a message repeated twice in Vietnamese:

You must leave this area for your own protection. Beginning tomorrow afternoon, everything will be burned, leveled, and whoever remains will be in great danger. The Viet Cong have used this village as a staging area for at least five years. Tomorrow morning you must gather your belongings and relocate thirty kilometers south, at a newly constructed hamlet. There you will be protected, well-nourished, and will have no need to leave the compound. If you cooperate, you and your family will be provided all essential items: sufficient water, three meals daily, emergency medical care on an as-needed basis. No person in your family will be interrogated for long periods, nor will anyone be subjected to torture. Most importantly, you will not have to remain in the new hamlet indefinitely. Once the Viet Cong leave the area you now occupy, you may choose to stay in the hamlet or return to rebuild your land. Your American escorts to your temporary home will arrive tomorrow at approximately 8 a.m.

The elephant stopped circling. Thien wished she would once more trumpet or wail, but she merely flapped her ears as though to fan the human sounds back to where they came from. The girl picked up a yellow leaflet and read the same message broadcast from the helicopter. The elephant sniffed the paper, sniffed Thien, and then touched her wound with the tip of her trunk.

Peasants gathered leaflets from the fields and even those who could not read studied the marks that described their future. Ong Quan and Ong Truong compared several leaflets, each a different color, and tried to determine if the marks on one were distinguishable from the marks on the others. The hope was for a better choice: a rice field rather than a hamlet, a field they could farm, a field closer to ancestral graves, a small area separate from the war, or at least partially protected. Every mark on every leaflet was scrutinized. Those who could read became authorities who informed those who could not that all leaflets, regardless of color, contained the same message. Luu Hai, the last reader to lose hope, studied each sheet of paper the villagers handed him. "No," he said finally, "all the same, word-for-word. Each page has the same message." An old woman muttered, "I'll die here, I'm not going." Others echoed her words, or similar words. Ma Xuan said, "How can we abandon our ancestors? Who will tend our ancestors' graves?"

Soon Cadre Hien and other cadre came into the fields, passed through the village, and informed the peasants there would be a meeting tonight at the former site of the village well.

At dusk, village girls fetched buckets of water from bomb craters. They hauled the water to the meeting place, boiled it in a caldron, and served the cadre chrysanthemum tea in small cups.

Thien was free to care for the elephant. She followed the

animal to the river and watched her wallow and drink. When the girl waded in, touched the elephant's trunk, the beast reared back and squealed. "No," said Thien, "quiet. Don't draw attention." The elephant slurped water into her trunk, held her trunk high, and showered the girl's shoulders and chest. Thien, stunned by joy, jumped up and down in the shallows. "Again," she said, "please! Good heavens!" The elephant, trunk still high, glanced at her sleepily, backed away, and lumbered to the shore.

Thien needed to treat the wound. "Down," she said, "down. On your belly." After feeding the elephant three stalks of sugarcane, she was allowed to clamber up on the wet back and dab the edges of the wound with a clean shirt soaked in kerosene.

Sugarcane in hand, she led the beast toward the site where the villagers had gathered. Cadre Hien and several comrades stood on a mound of rubble, the former well. Thien was relieved that Cadre Duc was nowhere in sight.

Hai sidled up and whispered, "Where's the elephant man? I haven't seen him."

She pointed over the fields to the marshes.

"In the swamps?" said Hai. "By himself?"

Thien touched a finger to her lips. "A quick trial," she said. "Cadre Duc questioned him."

"Why?"

"Duc says he unhooked the booby trap last night. This morning he led the elephant away from the ambush site without the cadre's permission."

Hai had trouble breathing.

"Duc had him killed," said Thien. "Less than twenty minutes after we came up from the tunnel."

(Hai remembered the shot. He and cousin Nam had straightened up for a moment, paused from digging the buffalo grave, glanced at each other, then returned to digging.)

"I was helpless," said Thien. "If I'd unshackled the elephant, let her charge, the cadre would have killed us all."

Hai tapped his fists together. "I'll find the old man," he said. "Least I can do is find him and bury him."

"I already asked three people to look. They told me it was dangerous."

Hai shook his head.

"I need to stay with the elephant," said Thien. "I can't sneak out there myself and search the swamps for his body."

"I wouldn't want you to."

"I asked Qui and his brother to look. I even asked your sister to look. They said if the cadre saw them, they too would be dead."

Hai cupped his hands near his mouth. "The one they executed never touched the booby trap. Never even touched it."

Thien leaned closer.

"After the meeting," said Hai, "I'll find him and bury him. I have an idea of where he might be."

Cadre Hien's assistants lit kerosene lamps and the meeting commenced. Hien, on a mound of stones, a dais of rubble that used to be a well, assured the villagers their lamps would not attract enemy planes or helicopters. "They will leave us alone for one night," he said, "and attempt to gather us in the morning. By tomorrow at noon, if you insist on staying, you will be executed, or if shown mercy, you will be confined to prison and tortured. In the morning you can choose to cooperate with Americans, ride in their trucks to a new home of concrete and barbed wire, or you can choose a different option. Cadre Duc was called to Tay Ninh, but I spoke with him and several other cadre before they departed. Approximately thirty kilometers west of here, there's a well-developed tunnel system in the Renegade Woods. The Americans, despite patrolling the area repeatedly, have yet to discover the tunnels. Beyond the shelter of the woods, you will find fields of rice that resemble the fields near this village. You can work in these fields on most days, and will not be in danger unless the Americans launch an offensive. What is certain is that they are about to destroy your ancestral home. Even before today's incident, they had planned to evacuate the village, drop their most powerful bombs, and destroy every tunnel they are aware of. After tomorrow's bombing they will send in mop-up teams, defoliate any remaining plants and trees, and they will leave the earth as barren as possible. This morning's operation was risky because we knew the village would soon be abandoned. Of course when the Americans and their machines are defeated, you are obliged to return to your ancestral home, grow your rice and raise your families. I assure you the move to the Renegade Woods will be temporary and successful. Although you will suffer certain hardships, you will not—unless you choose—live in concrete cages constructed by the very people who invaded our land."

The grandfathers applauded. Ong Truong said, "Death to the Americans! Death to the invaders!" and the villagers joined the death-chant. Cadre Hien flapped his arms as though he were sowing grain. "Yes," he said, "death to the invaders. But discipline yourselves and postpone the celebration." He raised his arms over his head and the crowd quieted. "Remember you have unfinished work," he said, "numerous preparations. You can celebrate your victory tomorrow night when you have ample time."

His colleague, Cadre Chi, clarified logistics. "Tonight," she said, "the main roads and trails in this area have become American ambush sites. Aware that you have no wish to follow their orders, the enemy expects an exodus to the east, toward Sai Gon. Instead, you will move west on a trail not listed on their maps. You will stop when you reach a place of tall trees, a place with hectares of unused paddy land. En route, you may encounter small groups of enemy soldiers, but you are unlikely to meet heavy resistance if you remain on our trail."

She distributed maps to the village elders, Ong Quan and Ong Truong. Quan, given three maps, kept one for himself, gave one to Luu Hai, and another to Ba Ly, the oldest woman in the village. Although Hai did not wish to be shouldered with responsibility, he received the map with a show of pleasure. Ong Truong, also given three maps, shared his extras with Nam and Qui. Cadre Chi said, "The map is simple, anyone can follow it. The important thing to remember is that you must keep yourselves and your animals moving throughout the night to reach the Renegade Woods by morning. You have four pack animals—three buffalo and one elephant. Gather your belongings and secure them to the beasts."

Ong Truong said, "Will any cadre be coming with us? Will we be guided?"

"Follow the cattle path toward Black Virgin Mountain," said Chi. "Most of the leaders of this area have already been re-stationed in bases to the north."

Cadre Hien approached Thien and the elephant. He appraised the animal, walked around her, and said, "The wound is mostly healed, yes?"

Thien stared at the ground. "I believe so, sir."

"Then hitch the elephant to one of the carts," said Hien. "If tonight it proves its worth, it will soon have the privilege of being a working elephant on the Truong Son Trail."

Before leaving, the villagers lit candles and carried them to the fields. They tended ancestral graves, burned incense, and arranged offerings of fruit and flowers. Little could be scavenged, but they found a few mangos and oranges, a few bananas, and jasmine was in bloom in the remains of a garden. Ma Xuan lay a fresh spray of jasmine and three oranges on her husband's grave.

Ears erect, eyes wide, two rabbits hunched near a tomb. Their ears shifted toward the sound of insect wings, the lurch of a spider, a thin voice, a flame shortened by wind. Something small hopped through a nearby hedge. Heads tilted, the rabbits twitched their ears, calibrated each sound. For a split second they froze, haunches flexed, eyes bright. In unison they bounded onto a bund and tore the grass with their teeth.

Luu Hai carried a shovel into the swamps north of the village. Frogs leaped from his path, leeches clung to his calves, mosquitoes swarmed him. He feared the cadre might spot him from small rises, from nests of stalks and brambles, but he feared more the thought of water snakes coiled near his feet, their pinpoint eyes and quick fangs, their movements too silent to alert him of their presence. He waded through a knee-deep marsh toward a cove of trees. He expected the master's remains were nearby, in a hollow beneath a *sau* tree, where three months earlier Qui's father was found. Something plied Hai's left calf, maybe a sprig of grass, a minnow, a snake. He lifted his leg from the water and swatted himself. Nothing fell away, but his calf itched, prickled. He sloshed toward the cove of trees and rose up on solid ground.

Hai removed the matches he'd fastened to his waistband. He struck a match, cupped it with his hands, and moved forward. Every few steps he paused, knelt on one knee, studied the land. Amid grass and weeds, he found scraps of clothing and debris: a knife-ripped pant-leg, a torn blouse, spent shells of pistols and rifles, the sharpened blade of an axe—no handle. A hole in the earth, dug by hand or gouged by a shell, had filled with water. He held his match over the pool and startled a golden-spined minnow.

His mother called him. Three times she called her son, but Hai remained silent. What would he tell Thien? That he could not find the body? That the old man might still be alive? That the cadre might have confined him in one of their prisons? The more difficult part would be to admit his responsibility for the elephant man's fate. He had crawled out in the night to disarm a booby trap because he loved Thien, because he wanted to save the elephant and the village, but mostly because he loved the girl and wanted her admiration. Now he felt ashamed that his desire resulted in suffering. Still, he reasoned, the old man had led the elephant away from the well and the ambush site in full view of the cadre. This alone would mean prison or death, for dozens had been jailed or executed for lesser crimes. The peasants, who did not know the locations of the prisons, had been told by Cadre Duc that they were in far away provinces which he refused to identify. But maybe the prisons didn't exist. Maybe those accused of crimes were buried in unknown graves. Qui had found his dead father in these swamps, in this cove of trees, but how many others were missing? Hai lit one last match and held it against the darkness. He glanced at the scattered rubbish, the spent shells, the torn blouse, the sharpened blade. These were messages, intimations, but none of them offered evidence of the elephant man's fate.

He tossed the match, sloshed back through the swamps, and into the rice fields. Ma Xuan was calling again, and now the boy responded. "A shovel," he said. "I left a shovel out here."

He scampered over a rice bund toward the candlelight of graves.

18
Digging A Hole

After the casualties were evacuated, after the well was destroyed and the village napalmed, the platoon headed east through open paddies. Conchola no longer walked point. He trudged after the platoon, his legs leaden, the last man in a long line that traversed rice field after rice field. Every few minutes he bent down as though he'd dropped something, as though it were hidden in the grass. He remembered lifting Billie into a body bag, patting his left wrist, bending forward before closing the zipper. He remembered a silver necklace, a crucifix, the way the cross lay at an angle against the upturned flesh of Billie's chest wound. He kept telling himself he should've secured the necklace in the sack tied to Billie's wrist, the sack that held Billie's wallet and watch, three envelopes, two pens, the postcard for his girlfriend. He should've taken the time to write neatly on each envelope— *Lucinda Sayers, Billie always loved you.* Instead, he nodded to Billie, patted his wrist, zipped him in, and helped carry him to the chopper. Lieutenant Bateson, barely conscious, and Sergeant Bowers, head bowed, had already been loaded. Warren said to the bleary-eyed lieutenant, "Don't worry about Meow Man, sir, he won't be screwing up anymore." Then the chopper lifted, Billie rose, the wounded rose, and Conchola watched the dark shape grow smaller and smaller until Warren tapped his wrist.

"Buford," said Warren. "You feel a little like Jimmy Buford?"

Conchola turned his back to him.

"Yeah, painful," said Warren. "Terrible. Sorry to bring it up."

But he did bring it up two hours later. The platoon, exhausted from the heat and the strain of sludging through paddies and hedgerows, rested in the shade of trees, a grove of eucalyptus. Conchola took off his helmet, sat on it, and Warren settled in beside him. "Jimmy Buford," said Warren. "Sweet kid, uh?"

Conchola shrugged.

"Had to be," said Warren. "If he was mean, if he didn't feel any guilt, he'd be alive still."

"Save it."

"Yeah, I would," said Warren, "if it wasn't so important. In the Nam every mistake costs another life. Isn't this true?"

Conchola spat.

"There it is," said Warren. "You mope around and scowl and spit because what can you say anymore?"

"Fuck you."

"Yeah, well, two words," said Warren, "not much," and hung his head, a mockery of sorrow. "Jimmy Buford, this really sweet boy, kills his friend, wastes him. A firefight, a little scrap, and Sweetie Boy panics. All at once he curls in a ball and shits all over himself. Then he fires his weapon this way and that and shoots Dickie Soens in the head."

Conchola smirked.

"Yeah, you didn't smile much when it happened," said Warren. "Remember Lieutenant Bateson assigned Buford to walk last, watch our tail?"

"Ancient history."

"Six weeks ago," said Warren. "The LT had Buford walk last because who in hell could trust him?"

Conchola looked at the ground.

"One mistake," said Warren, "and he's the Lone Ranger. Got nobody to talk to. But like I say Jimmy's real sweet, minds his manners. Two weeks after he wastes Soens, he stands up in a little skirmish and takes a bullet through the head."

Conchola said, "You're too dumb to die," rose to his feet, and walked away.

"Hey," Warren called after him, "hey, man." He raised his arms. "What's the big hurry, man? What's the problem?" He shrugged. "At least Sweetie Boy was polite."

In his mind, Conchola wrote a postcard home. *Maldición. Mala suerte. Perdido.* One day I'm in thick jungle, I'm trailing the tiger or he's trailing me, and the next I'm in farm country —rice paddies, hedgerows, no place for a wild animal. I lost my way, got confused, and the one boy I care about is on his way home in a body bag. I zipped Billie in, shut out the light, helped carry him to a chopper. He was the only one besides me who knew anything about tigers. For all the rest, Mama, the Cat's just something wild and dangerous that moves alone through the jungle shade.

Conchola considered writing to Lucinda Sayers and Billie's family. He remembered Jimmy Buford, out of respect, wrote a letter of condolence to the family of Dickie Soens. Before sending his letter, Jimmy passed it around to some of the guys, Conchola included, maybe because he wanted to show he had enough courage to take the blame, to admit what was true, what would never change—he had killed a man for nothing. Nobody teased Buford, not even Warren, but they stayed clear of him. One of the golden rules of survival was to avoid those who made serious blunders. Now Conchola wished he'd broken this rule, given Jimmy some encouragement, a few words of comfort. The kid couldn't take the separation, the awareness that he was off-limits, *persona non grata*. He never learned how to bide his time, lick his wounds, how to be alone. In a brief firefight near *Nui Ba Den*, Buford, six-feet tall, appeared timid, delicate, as he tottered to his feet, took baby steps, said, "Okay, okay," and invited a bullet through the head.

In the late afternoon, the platoon set their ambush beneath coconut palms at the edge of a paddy. Conchola got out his entrenching tool, began digging, but the sound of metal slicing the earth disturbed him. He and Billie had always dug together, shared the same foxhole, or dug separate holes not so far apart that they couldn't whisper a conversation. At night there was nobody else Conchola ever talked to, nobody who heard him and whispered back to him. Billie wore a crucifix, a silver necklace, but he seldom talked religion. Conchola wondered what a priest or minister would say, what hope he would give, before the gravediggers readied their shovels and broke the silence of the coffin with clods of earth.

An hour later Sergeant Stevens said, "You need a hole that big? You gonna bury yourself?"

Conchola filled his shovel.

"Enough," said Stevens. "You don't need a hole so deep you can't raise your rifle and shoot something crawling toward you."

Warren came over and squatted on his haunches. "Sad sight," he said to the sergeant. "Must be missin' his buddy."

Conchola snorted.

"Zapped and zipped," said Warren. "*Xin loi*, Billie boy. Airborne Ranger."

"Enough," said Stevens. "Let's get hold of ourselves."

"But he's diggin' for two people," said Warren. "A grave for two people."

"Conchola," said Stevens, "consider this an order. Drop your entrenching tool, stop feeling sorry for yourself, and drag your ass out of that stupid hole."

He hacked at the earth one last time before he obeyed.

Through the night the medic lay on the ground, face-up, and revised his letter of condolence. He wrote nothing on paper, but sometimes his lips moved, tested the shapes of words, and he wondered how they would sound to Lucinda Sayers and Billie's family. He tried to picture Billie's people gathered in some small town in the Carolinas. Scrims of cloud edged a gibbous moon, and he searched the billows and plumes till he saw faces. He believed Billie's Mama would have a pretty face, round and sweet as pie, but his Daddy would be a rake of a man, skinny as his son, his face nearly as long and flat as a sliced pickle. Maybe the clouds over the moon that now fanned and streamed, kited taller and taller in high wind, would remind Billie Lucinda Sayers, her hair long and black and flowing. Conchola imagined when Billie's people heard what happened they would convene on his front porch or in his Mama's kitchen. Cross-town friends might hear them rousing themselves, singing and praying, a voice or two that raked like a claw, or that swung out over trees and fields, hoo-hooed like an owl. Maybe all night Billie's people would lean on each other, hold each other up, gather in a circle. Conchola wanted to hear them singing praises, listening and talking, honoring Billie with stories, everyone taking his turn, or her turn, and doing Billie right.

He sat up as though to nudge his way in and share his story. "Sure, we were close," he would say, "me and Billie. At night we'd share a foxhole, or we'd dig in a few feet apart so we could watch over each other, whisper and jive, keep from getting spooked by odd noises and shadows." He wondered if he should tell about the time he and Billie rouged their faces with tiger blood. "Yeah, lucky charm," he would smile. "We each wore the blood of the beast, dabbed our faces for protection." There were some things they might never understand. He prayed that Billie had seen the light of trees, the leaves lit from beneath, losing their shadows. Maybe at night Billie saw that the soil itself, the dark walls of their foxhole, held grains of light, webs of light, roughly the same patterns of brightness and shade as the blood that filled veins, arteries, the flesh of animals. *When something's true*, thought Conchola, *it's larger than words. The more true it is, the harder it is to tell it.* He prayed this light bathed Billie, entered wounds. Tree light, animal light, Jesus—lover of mercy. He doubted his words made sense. Maybe he should just say that he loved Billie, that he was sorry, that Billie's death was accidental. "Yeah, charms wear off," he would shrug. "We left the Cambodian jungles and were in open land the day we lost Billie." He would pause, bow his head, then look Billie's Mama in the eye, steady his gaze, place the blame on his shoulders. "My fault," he would say, "my fault, for believing we were safe here." He pictured the elephant that drew them toward the trap, the ambush, but the mention of it would provoke too many complications. "Okay," he'd whisper, "here's all that matters: Your son died in a land of rice fields and thatch huts, and he remembered you in his last moments." He would search the faces of the crowd until he found the prettiest girl, Lucinda Sayers. "Yeah, you're the one, honey. I heard so much about you I swear to God I already know you." He would bow to her, sing praises. Maybe say something about the loveliness of her hair, of how Billie once lifted his hands as though he could touch each strand, each fiber and curl, from the other side of the world.

Thin clouds crossed the face of the moon. Conchola wished he were lighter, bird-like. A body that could rise and be drawn by wind, carried west toward the jungles of Cambodia. He heard Warren snoring, heard another guy edge away from the group, heard a stream of piss rain down on the grass. In the company of men Conchola was unhappy, always would be. In Cambodia, lost and alone, he had had the best time anyone could have in a place still at war.

At dawn the platoon gathered and moved toward the village that had been napalmed the previous day. At 8 a.m. a convoy of trucks would arrive, presumably the villagers would climb aboard, and be transported to a newly constructed hamlet. In case Viet Cong resisters escaped eastward, toward Sai Gon, the platoon would set up a blocking force approximately three kilometers from the village. Now they had to move quickly, find a suitable ambush site, position themselves before the enemy evaded their defenses. Sergeant Stevens ordered PFC De Angelo to lead the way.

Conchola, who walked last, who had lain awake through the night, surveyed the edges of the fields for the elephant and its master. How could the Viet Cong conceal an animal this large? Where would they shelter it? How would it live? He suspected the beast was an apparition, *un fantasma*, the ghost of a slaughtered elephant. Maybe its forest was destroyed, maybe the animal was killed by bombs, but could reappear to deceive the enemy, to conjure an image that seemed as solid as a living being. Maybe it walked the land in a body lighter than clouds, lighter than air—light as ghosts. But what about the man or child who commanded the beast, who led it away through a palm grove? He too could've been a ghost, someone needlessly killed, obsessed with revenge. Conchola paused and looked over the fields to a hedgerow, a frayed tree line, layered shadows. The elephant, if it conjured its shape and moved over the Cu Chi countryside, would rise far above this bombed stubble and cropped brush, these straggles of stunted trees.

The platoon trudged through a swamp, filed over a rice bund, and entered a hedgerow. Vines and saw grass snagged at ankles, leeches suckled calves. Conchola, head down, observed the placement of each foot, and moved slowly enough to see leaves of grass throw thin shadows. It seemed unfair that he couldn't retract his mistake, walk once more over the rice bund with Billie Jasper behind him. He remembered the tension of the wire on his left ankle, the clicking sound, the force of the explosion. They were going for water, gaping at an animal ghost and going to a well for water. *Virgen de Guadalupe*, he thought, *Saint Francis, Saint Jude—why didn't you warn me?* He wanted a second chance to observe each step, monitor his breath, use the sharpness of his vision, the alertness of his body. The tiger, still alive,

probably never allowed himself to become too relaxed, or to
be drawn too quickly toward the sight or sound of something
unfamiliar. The beast drew each breath through his entire
length. No breath was careless or light, no movement lost to
distraction. Now Conchola walked quietly, his steps sure, his
eyes on the webs of grass and vines that could hide a wire, a
mine, a bamboo pit—each stake filed to a point, dipped in
poison. They called the pit a tiger trap because of its
dimensions, long and wide, large enough for the body of a
tiger. Its surface—rectangular, grave-sized—was camouflaged, a one-inch layer of woven grass and leaves that
concealed the pit, the stakes, the openness made for falling.
A single misstep hurled a man forward, plunged stakes
through his vitals. *There's one way I won't die*, thought
Conchola. *A tiger trap. Impalement. It just isn't meant to be.*

Walking and praying, he asked Guadalupe to help Billie
and Lucinda and Billie's family. Maybe some of Billie's
people would already be gathered in his Mama's kitchen or
on the front porch when the man in uniform came into the
yard and said, "We regret to inform..." Conchola slowed his
pace, shook his head, wiped sweat from his brow. He pictured
Billie and himself back on that rice bund, moving toward the
well and the vanished elephant, proceeding with caution. He
noticed the flex of his arches, the slight curl of his toes as he
touched the earth with one foot, then another. Now he stepped
within an inch of a black bug that climbed down a blade of
grass. He noticed a snail the size of his thumb nail, the head
of a leech, the vibration of the ground, the softness that
yielded to the weight of his body. He breathed fully, moved
in slow motion, and when he looked up he saw the platoon
had traversed the hedgerow and entered another paddy. He
watched them a few minutes, then hid near a low shrub. "Go
on," he muttered, "*vayan*." He plucked a blade of grass and
placed it between his lips.

Soon no one in the platoon would remember him. Or if
they did, it would be when they returned to the world and

told their buddies about the boy who got lost twice, the second time forever. He could picture Warren cocking his head, slouching over a bar, saying, "You won't believe it, this kid we called Meow Man. This kid who believes he got clawed by a tiger. In Cambodia, middle of the night, he goes off to take a dump, squats down, keels over and falls in a stream. *Xin loi*," Warren would say, "swept away. So we scour the jungle in search of this kid who has some sort of hard-on for a tiger." Shrug. "After two days, we find this little kitty-cat of a boy asleep near a dead deer. Jesus H, I mean that's the sort of company he keeps. Doesn't care what he sleeps with, live or dead. No matter. The second time he gets lost, and the last far as I know, he disappears in the open paddies." Another shrug. "Lights out, man. Dick in a sling. Worst case ever. This last time we didn't try too hard to come to his rescue. For all I know the cat's still out there, dick in a sling, wandering around alone."

Conchola watched the platoon straggle into another hedgerow and disappear. He knelt quietly, lay down, and curled in the weeds and grass. At eye level he saw a white flower, bell-shaped, that held an insect as though in a hand of spread fingers. The insect was small, but had disproportionately large eyes, a black shell, thick feelers. Conchola guessed it was a beetle, an infant beetle. It circled slowly around the stamen of the flower, crossed over to one of the petals, peered over the edge. "*Compañero*," said Conchola, "lose your tribe?" Maybe the beetle saw him, looked back at him. He watched it for a time before he fell asleep.

19
Animal Trail

The elephant and the adult buffalo hauled carts laden with chickens, ducks, pigs, small children, elderly women. They carried baskets and bowls, pots and pans, Buddha statues, sacks of chicken rice, white rice, bags of seed, jars of water. In the elephant's cart, Thien and Hai had arranged pyramids of coconut and jackfruit, bundles of sugarcane, and Thien had buried green bananas in a sack of un-husked rice so the hardened fruit would soon ripen and be ready for eating. Now as they walked near the elephant, kept pace with her, Hai offered a nervous declaration. "Miss Thien," he said, "if something happens, I promise to help you. If there's an ambush, or if planes come, or helicopters, I will keep you and your grandma safe."

He could not wait for her reply. Heart thumping, hands sweating, he skipped ahead to the lead animal, Qui's buffalo. The beast carried harrows and hoes, surplus harnesses, anvils, shovels, scythes, and the *ma* rice that filled baskets, the month-old shoots ready to transplant if the peasants found a moist paddy upon reaching their destination. Hai remembered the end of his Sun Song, the words too bold to be sung aloud: *I will have the strength of a bull buffalo, the body of a mountain. I will carry a rice field and a pretty village girl on my spine.*

Ma Xuan had assigned Nhi the task of fetching water from the canal. Presently, Hai watched his sister carry two buckets on her shoulder pole, hurry up the bank, and set them at the edge of the path in front of Qui's buffalo. As the cart passed by she held up one bucket, then another, and Tuyen— stationed inside the cart—took the buckets and began watering the rice plants. She bent over each shoot, tended it carefully, as the buffalo and the cart moved forward. The beast carried earth, water, rice, mounds of supplies—the remnants of a village. What the peasants could not fit inside carts they'd strapped to the sides and spines of buffalo. Kitchen knives, kettles, cups, packets of dried fish, bags of salt, bamboo fishing poles, blankets, pillows, saws wrapped in canvas, mesh bags filled with tongs and pliers and hammers. Luu Hai, singing his song in silence, wished he could haul the peasants and their belongings onto his spine and move steadily along the path.

The two-month-old buffalo carried sacks of rice husks to be used for kindling. When she tired, Hai wedged the sacks in the elephant's cart between the mother pig and a passel of chickens. The adult buffalo in front of the elephant carried on her spine sacks of betel nut and areca leaves, *tam* rice, mangos and corn, lemons, baskets and yokes, sheets of fabric. The elephant, because of her shoulder wound, had only a wide net (a harness) draped over her back. In the front of her cart, Ba Ly perched on a bundle of sugarcane. She chewed betel nut, spat the juices. She ordered Thien to guide the elephant so the wheels of the cart would avoid potholes and ruts.

The animals moiled along a cattle path that paralleled a canal. The elephant, sometimes wider than the trail she walked on, brushed against bushes and trees, but she did not stop to forage. Several times the girl waved handfuls of leaves near her trunk, but she would not take them. To the elephant, the girl smelled better tonight, pleasantly sour, salty and cool, as though she'd rubbed herself with jackfruit leaves, daubed herself with lemon. The wind that blew from her mouth had a similar smell to that of the elephant's master. There was no smell of grass, though, or hay, and the oil and moisture of her skin smelled sweeter. She often touched the elephant's flanks, so her hands had the mud and water smells of the elephant's body. The girl tried to lead but her voice—at too high a pitch—was difficult to interpret. The sounds pushed from her throat echoed the pining of cicadas, the whine of wheels. Straining forward, the elephant hauled the cart in hope that she would soon locate the scent of her master. She allowed the girl to walk close by, appear to guide her. But the three adult buffalo led the way, hooves thumping the earth, raising the night dust already moist with dew.

A water-filled bomb crater obstructed the path. Work teams brought out shovels and hoes, cleared a new path, and the animals and carts lumbered around the crater. Ma Xuan walked near her son and told him to pay attention. "Stop watching the sky," she said. "The moon and stars are not the ones who may kill us." Ma Xuan had little hope the peasants could defend themselves. Carts banged and rattled, animals panted and gasped, and the thrum of buffalo hooves could probably be heard more than a kilometer in the distance. Stands of trees and hedgerows, mostly destroyed by bombs, offered scant cover. The elephant made little noise, but her size—her raised head and the dome of her spine—rose over the small trees and could be easily spotted. Maybe the only hope was that Cadre Chi had received correct information. If the Americans believed the Viet Cong and their sympathizers would flee toward Sai Gon, they would concentrate their forces between Cu Chi and the southern capital. At dawn the invaders would fill the sky with observation planes and target everything that moved, animal or human. Tonight the peasants had to force themselves and their animals to keep moving so they might reach their new home before the Americans could see the land.

Still walking, Ma Xuan used the light of the sky to study the map Ong Quan had given her son. A band of stars, the Silver River, arced from the northern sky to the south, and the moon, beginning to wane, forded the river near its center. The villagers would have to continue west along the cattle path until they reached a forest approximately twenty-two kilometers from Black Virgin Mountain. According to Cadre

Chi, they would distinguish it from other forests because it had thus far escaped heavy bombing and defoliation, because a few groves of banyan and tamarind remained, and stands of coconut palms and bamboo bordered twelve hectares of paddies. The map showed little detail, just a few splotches to signify stands of trees, tunnels, untended paddies. If the peasants succeeded in replanting the *ma* rice they had brought with them, two months would pass before they reaped a small harvest. Maybe her son and other villagers could supplement remaining food supplies by catching snakes and eel, fish and frogs, rats and lizards. *But will this be enough?* she thought. *Will we survive?* Ma Xuan worried less about the buffalo who thrived on grass, and the elephant who seemed to devour everything but the heartwood of a tree.

And there was a concern equal to survival: the ancestors, the dead who must be cared for. She walked beside the elephant cart and informed Ba Ly of her intentions. "We must continue to tend the graves," she said. "One night soon my sisters and I will return on this same path, or through open paddies. A few of us will move more quietly than this herd of animals and people."

"Yes, you'll move quietly," said Ba Ly. "But if the cadre are correct what will remain of our village?"

"They may spare the graves. If not, if they destroy the graves, who but us will rebury our ancestors?"

Ba waved her hands and shook her wrists, a gesture of negation. "The enemy will be waiting," she whispered. "They'll kill you as you try to return, or they'll kill you at the gravesites."

"We are that easy to kill?"

"No, but you might need to pray and make offerings without tending graves. You cannot benefit the ancestors by taking such risks."

Ma Xuan hesitated. "The risks are small. A few of us can tend the graves and hide in our village. Once a month, maybe twice, we can return to our village."

Ba rubbed her right palm over her face. "What village? What will remain?"

"We don't know yet."

"So much is already gone. Our homes, our well. What else is there to go back to?"

"The fields," said Ma Xuan, "the graves. We must have the decency and respect to rebury any ancestor who is tossed from the earth by bombs."

She forced herself to keep walking. The peasants could load in a cart bits of earth, bits of paddy mud and *ma* rice, but they could not carry their ancestral home, the center of things, the *que huong* that could not be moved from one location to another. The ancestral home was the place of birthing, of death, the land that held centuries of bones, bloodlines, that knew each ancestor from first to last breath, that formed the cord to join the dead with the living. If the graves were abandoned, how could the ancestors offer guidance? How could the dead be honored, made important? How could the survivors flourish? The ancestors, buried where they were born, where they had worked and lived, perhaps shared one deep fear—to be uncared for. Only if they were uprooted by bombs, or if no one remembered them in prayer, or made the proper offerings of fruit and rice, altar money, incense and flowers, would they roam a Land of Shadows in search of a place that still knew them. Ma Xuan prayed that her husband forgive her negligence, that all her ancestors forgive her. "I will do my best," she promised, "to see that each one is remembered and honored and fed."

Walking, head bowed, she pictured her husband's grave as she last saw it—lit with candles. If she returned at night and the Americans found her and killed her, maybe they would unknowingly allow her remains to lie near those of her husband. But she knew they often removed bodies, trucked them to their camps where enemy commanders photographed them, counted them, and perhaps ordered them to be burned in pits or buried in unmarked graves where no family member could claim them. These nameless dead, wandering ghosts, were destined to harm themselves and the living. Her husband, partly dismembered, was at least buried where he had lived. The land knew the weight of his steps, the strength of his hands, the play of his fingers over grains of *lua* rice as he determined whether a field was ripe for harvest. No buffalo or teams of buffalo could carry this knowledge in carts. No human being grew large enough to harbor her home in her body. To know the land and be known, one must live and die in the same place, and one must rest on the land when the last breath bowed to it. If enemy bombs overturned her husband's grave, Ma Xuan would rebury him, or whatever remained of him. If she died in her effort, she would at least die with noble intentions. Months might pass, or years, before the peasants returned to their homeland. Ma Xuan could not wait for the day when the Americans surrendered. She would honor her ancestors, tend their graves, risk her life to do so. She walked faster now, her gait supple and sure. *The next time someone dies*, she told herself, *we will dig a deep grave so the body will not be uprooted by even the most powerful of bombs.*

The two-month-old buffalo lagged behind her mother. Moaning and grunting, she stood on the path, then folded her legs and sat. Luu Hai tried to shoo her forward. "*Di*," he said, "*di-di*," but the calf was sleepy. He and Nam lifted her in their arms and carried her to the cart of her mother. She stumbled over sacks of rice, then lay down between four baskets that made wicker cages for ducks and chickens. The mother buffalo snorted, swallowed, licked the air with her tongue. Luu Hai swatted her rump and said, "Keep pulling, keep pulling." So the peasants, led by the animals, lost little time as they rounded a bend and continued their journey west.

The young buffalo had never ridden in a cart. Her new height startled her, and when the cart passed under small trees she saw the moon and stars sway between branches. She had

never seen the sky move, turn its body like an animal. The
cart creaked, bounced in and out of ruts, and nothing stayed
still for more than an instant. She heard her mother's
breathing, felt the heat of her, and was amazed how fast they
moved on a path twice the width of her mother's body. The
moon lit the surfaces, the grass and stones, the mud slabs
that slid toward her and vanished. She glanced at the moon
as it moved through another tree. Its light passed between
the darkness of leaves and limbs, then made bright, crooked
pools on the path, the same shapes as the gaps between
branches. Until now, the night she had known was a time for
rest. She had not watched the sky as it swayed, or the earth as
it rolled toward her under the hooves of animals. After a long
time she closed her eyes, too tired for her vigil. But in sleep
she felt inside her the motion and light of the sky, the steady
shifting of stones, grass, air. All things moved, changed
shape, and did not pause to rest. Even the trees, their limbs
and trunks, were unsettled as the light between branches
bounced and jilted over the surface of the earth.

The cadre had left the peasants four rifles and a dozen hand-
made grenades. Hai, following Thien and the elephant,
pointed his AK-47 at the darkness of distant tree lines.
Several women and girls who did not ride in carts carried
grenades in net bags slung from their shoulders. Others
carried scythes or machetes, as though in an ambush they
would survive long enough to defend themselves in hand-to-
hand combat. Hai, given a rifle, a map (which he'd
surrendered to his mother), had trouble paying attention to
the war. He chided himself for not mourning the fate of the
elephant's master. He believed the man was dead, but death—
despite all he had witnessed—remained elusive. Hai pointed
his rifle at a star. He loved a girl who might one night love
him. He loved the moon, the Silver River, the shapes of trees,
the smells of night, the smells and sounds of animals. He
passed between Thien and the elephant, smiled to the girl,

and could not resist taking pleasure in the fullness of her body. Pointing his rifle at a brighter star, he worked his tongue into the soft flesh where his incisor tooth was missing. He wondered if Thien knew her own beauty. She seemed to take herself for granted, to give her body little care or attention. Hai thought of the soil beneath *ma* rice, the darkness against the green of newly transplanted shoots. The stems, in daylight, glinted bright as knife blades, but pale roots sank down and fastened themselves to darkness. Hai imagined stooping in a paddy, sinking his hands in the earth. He imagined digging down to the grit of the soil, the night colors no less interesting than the glow of a tended field. Thien, in the bowl of her hips, mirrored the darkness beneath *ma* rice. And in daylight when she speared seedlings into paddy mud—a sight he had often seen—the brightness of rice grass lit her face, gave her face this same brightness. Why did she seem as casual as an animal who had never studied herself in a mirror of water? *No, she does not know her beauty*, he thought, *she takes herself for granted. If one day she asks me, "Why do I need you?" I will point to the light of ma rice and the darkness beneath, and I will bow low until my face comes level with her hips.*

Ma Xuan tussled his shoulders and said, "What's this about? Pointing your rifle at the sky, bowing from the waist. You're supposed to be a leader."

"I am, Ma."

"Then stop dreaming," she said, "pay attention. You're nearly fifteen years old and behave as though you're six."

Hai lowered his head in a display of subservience. *No, I'm already old, Ma, I'm in love. But you would not believe this if you heard it.*

He disciplined himself and moved toward the front of the column. He remembered Cadre Hien warning the peasants about the possibility of mines, unexploded ordnance. The moon—partly a blessing—lit the cattle path, and maybe it would allow Hai to see the rim of a bomb or a shell before the peasants and animals triggered an explosion. If the elephant stepped on a bomb of some three hundred kilos, she and Thien and the rest of this moving village would rise in the air, a tangle of limbs, a confusion of bodies. He whispered to Qui and his sister who walked beside the lead cart: "Watch for bombs and shells; let the moonlight help you." If the Americans flanked the path, lay hidden in hedgerows, the peasants had little chance of survival. But at least they could use the moon to search for glints of light, fragments of metal, the edges of shells or bombs that protruded from the earth.

The buffalo made restless, snuffling sounds. The elephant rumbled, snorted, as Hai and Ma Xuan dispersed among the animals and peasants. They called, "Halt, halt," but everyone—beast and human—had already halted. The elephant swayed, raised her left foreleg, now her right, but did not advance. Qui's buffalo, nostrils flared, flicked his tail, tamped his back hooves on the earth, then raised his head and grunted. In the silence that followed Hai listened for enemy movement. The cicadas began singing, the tree and water frogs sang, and he did not feel in his body the dangerous stillness that often preceded an explosion. For a moment he felt invulnerable. As he darted past Thien, he volunteered to investigate, move forward alone, but Ma Xuan, from beside the lead cart, said, "You'll follow me." Hai did not wish to hear this command. He preferred to be the lone scout who would forge ahead, gauge the dangers, then report his discoveries to Le Minh Thien and the peasants. He knew, however, that whatever ruse he gave his mother would not dissuade her. He glanced at Thien, shrugged, and said, "*Khong sao, khong sao.* We'll see what's in the way."

The two scouts smelled the body before they saw it. A girl Nhi's age, Thien's age, partly clothed, on the path near a large crater. She lay face-up, her legs turned outward at the knee, her heels touching. The moon lit the thatch roofs of three nearby huts. Ma Xuan called, "Hello, hello, hello." When there was no response, she whispered to Hai: "We must give her a burial; her family is gone."

They retreated to inform the peasants and organize a workforce. Hai and his mother would dig the girl's grave; Nam and Qui and other buffalo boys would hack out a new path so the animals and carts could bypass the crater. The elephant, moaning, flapped her ears and scanned with her trunk. Among the animals, the carts, Hai could not smell the dead body. *A girl*, he kept thinking, *a girl. No older than Nhi, no older than my sister. No older*, he said to himself, *than Le Minh Thien*.

Hai and his mother began digging the grave in a field near one of the huts. "A terrible fate," said Ma Xuan. "No family member to bury her." Once the hole was deep enough, she would not allow her son to carry the body from the cattle path to the grave. The girl's shirt was torn, one of her breasts exposed. The size and shape of an anthill, a small mound rising from her chest.

Ma Xuan called for her daughter to come forward and help carry the body to its resting place. Hai felt a thumping pain in his gut. He stood by with his shovel, but once his mother and sister lowered the girl into the ground he could not bury her. "Please," he said, and handed his shovel to his sister. Nhi and Ma Xuan began raining soil on the body as he turned away and wretched. *Another death*, he thought, *one more. I should be used to it*. But this one—a girl no older than Thien—her foul smell sickened him. Bent over, he vomited until there was nothing left to vomit. Then he stumbled to the cattle trail, grabbed a machete and helped chop saplings and brush along the verge of the path so the animals could skirt the crater, haul their loads, and lead the way toward the Renegade Woods and the black mountain, *Nui Ba Den*.

Before they left, Ma Xuan entered the hut nearest the grave and left a note on a small table that had been the family altar. *We found a girl, a dead child, and buried her in the nearby field. Look for the small mound in the paddy. We will tend her grave whenever we pass this way again.*

Shortly before dawn, they took shelter in a small grove of tamarind trees. The peasants discussed whether this was the Renegade Woods, the place of tall trees, but Cadre Chi had spoken of a forest, hectares of unused paddy land, whereas this was merely an island of foliage, a small oasis. "But for now this is where we must hide," said Ong Quan. "If we keep going, we may be in open land when the sun rises." Ong Quan and Ong Truong deliberated. Come morning, in open land, the peasants could take shelter in whatever holes they could dig, but observation helicopters would spot the elephant, the buffalo, the carts heaped with belongings. The grandfathers agreed to circle the carts around the trunk of the tallest tamarind and wait for the next night to complete their journey. "No choice," said Ma Xuan. "If we are seen in the open, there will be no one to dig our graves."

Peasants unhitched the animals from the carts and hurried them to the canal to drink and bathe before sunrise. While the elephant rolled and wallowed in the shallows, the buffalo trudged farther out, their heads and horns pitch black over the surface of the water. Luu Hai led the two-month-old buffalo into the shallows. He petted her ears, her spine, slathered her flanks with mud. He whispered, "You're too young yet, I can't ride you." So he found Qui's buffalo, the only bull, up to his neck in water. Hai hoisted himself onto the wide back. An eye on Thien, he crouched, then stood tall, his balance perfect on the spine of the buffalo. Hai whistled until the girl turned to him. He winged his arms, caught a breath, rocked forward and back, and dove for the deep.

Thien treated the elephant's wound when the beast emerged from the canal. She said, "Lie down," and the elephant surprised her by obeying, folding her hind legs, then her front, and allowing Thien to scramble up onto her spine.

The animal seemed to understand the girl offered medicine. Thien, thinking ahead, decided she would get out a jar of kerosene if the Americans patrolled near the tamarind trees in daylight. If the elephant smelled medicine, maybe she would lie down again, and in this way shelter herself behind the cart piled highest with belongings. Now Thien daubed the exposed flesh with kerosene. The wound had to sting and burn, but the elephant issued no sound of complaint. "Next comes breakfast," Thien whispered, "bushels of tamarind leaves. And maybe a few bananas as dessert."

Luu Hai, his hands filthy with the canal muck he'd brought up from the bottom, prayed in silence: "Mother of Mercy, Quan Yin, spare the life of Le Minh Thien. Spare the lives of all of us." He plastered the muck over the flanks of the two-month-old buffalo. He patted her rump and said, "Go on now, go on. Your mother will teach you to bathe in mud."

Hai prayed for the girl Ma Xuan and his sister had buried in a rice field. He wanted to feel a profound sadness for the elephant man, but he mourned more for the girl and for the death of Nam's buffalo. The buffalo was his companion, his night friend, and he longed to be near her again, to touch her and smell her, to sleep where she slept and feel the warmth of her body. She was in the ground, in a soon-to-be-bombed field, and the elephant man was probably in the swamps, in the muck beneath water. "May the old man be spared further torment," Hai prayed. "May he escape the water demons and swamp demons, the fetid smells, snakes, leeches." Hai vowed to burn altar money for the elephant man and the girl, to one day make offerings of *Nang Thom* rice and fresh fruit, joss sticks and candles. He cupped water into his palms and berated himself for not praying first for his father. "May *cha's* grave be undisturbed," he whispered. "May *cha* be peaceful and happy." He tried to remember his father's face, but all he saw was a dull gray sphere, a face like a stone. Hai opened his hands, gave back the water to the canal. He shivered when he thought of the girl Thien's age and Nhi's age buried in an abandoned field.

Thien watched him swash through the water and onto the shore. Earlier, before they left their village and fields, he whispered to her that he had not found the body of the elephant's master. Hai had tried to comfort her with possibilities (the old man being questioned at a Viet Cong base camp, being held as a prisoner), but she could tell he doubted his own words. Now as he came forward along the bank, she remembered his assurance that the elephant's master had not tampered with the booby trap. "The one they executed never touched it," he had claimed, "never even touched it." For once Hai's words were believable. Perhaps he alone had disarmed the booby trap, unfastened the wire. But he couldn't have known the elephant's master would be blamed.

He walked past her on the bank, turned around, and said, "You're good with the elephant, Miss Thien. She mostly obeys you."

"She mostly does as she pleases," said Thien. "She misses her master."

He lowered his eyes.

"But I won't blame you that he's gone. I'll never blame you."

Hai was confused. "You mean the body? You won't blame me for not finding it?"

Thien hesitated, then shook her head. "No, something else," she whispered. "I believe I know who unhooked the wire."

She did not await a confession. He had wanted to spare the elephant, the well, the village, so he disarmed the booby trap—she remembered Cadre Duc's words—"when no one was watching." Thien did not understand why she admired his courage. One was taught to never act as an individual, to act in confluence with one's family, one's elders, one's village. Thien stepped in front of him, but he would not look at her. "The old man had no chance," she said. "Duc and the other cadre had already decided who to blame."

Hai's breath was doing odd things in his throat. "The body...I should have found the body." He squatted and picked up a pebble. "Not enough time," he muttered. "All I needed was some time."

She leaned forward and briefly touched his hand. Shivering, sweating, he gave her the pebble, this smooth shard dark as a cricket. The girl felt the shape of it, then lifted it near her eyes. In moonlight it was black but for glints of light on one edge, dull spots like a band of stars small and far away.

At dawn the peasants positioned themselves and their animals behind carts camouflaged with vines, branches, foliage. Thien fed the elephant yellow flowers and tamarind leaves. The buffalo cropped the tall grass. Nhi and Tuyen scattered *tam* rice for the ducks and chickens. Nam fed the mother pig, and then the pig allowed her piglets to suckle. Ma Xuan winced at the loud snorting and slurping, the crowing of roosters. The peasants had been somewhat successful in camouflaging themselves and their animals, but how could they stop these noises? Ma Xuan told herself she should have spoken with the grandfathers last night. She should have encouraged Ong Quan and Ong Truong to hurry the peasants and animals toward *Nui Ba Den*, the Renegade Woods, the trees that gave shelter. Had they not stopped for the girl, dug a deep grave to shelter her from bombs, they might have reached their destination. But it was impossible not to bury her, impossible not to pray. *Buddha of Heaven, how could we not do these things? We may be all she will ever have.*

They carved holes between the roots of the tamarind. Ong Quan and Ong Truong strategized on how to organize their defenses, who to trust with the rifles, the grenades, and again Luu Hai was assigned a rifle. Ong Quan set two scythes, three machetes, and one grenade beside each hole.

Hai climbed the tamarind tree and perched in its crown. He had volunteered to be the first sentry, the one who would scan the horizon for planes, helicopters, day ghosts, whatever might kill them. In the late morning cousin Nam would relieve him, and later Qui would climb the tree and relieve Nam so that each boy would have a chance to sleep. But Luu Hai, now wide-awake and well concealed in the leafy branches, thought, *She touched me. Le Minh Thien touched me.* He remembered giving her the pebble that she lifted to her eyes, that she held in her right hand, that maybe she would keep forever. This was his first gift that she accepted—a pebble. The salted carp and osprey he had brought for her and her grandma were different because Ba Ly accepted these gifts, because Thien herself never acknowledged them. The pebble was beautiful, polished smooth, gem-like. Hai hoped that she would hold it at night to her belly or chest, and that the stone would grow warm as she rubbed it on her skin.

Once the defenses were prepared, once the animals were tended, the peasants squatted under the tree and munched jackfruit seeds, rice balls, slivers of dried fish, small chunks of coconut and banana. They had to ration their supplies. They could not drink canal water, build fires, boil water, because the smoke would reveal their position. Each adult took one long swallow from a water jar, each child took three. Luu Hai, with his rifle, his maleness, considered himself an adult. He came down from the tree for his share of water, swished it in his mouth, savored the coolness. He held it in his mouth a long time as though water might grow as seeds grow, as though it might lengthen, fatten, burst its skin and become stream water, river water, or at least something ample enough to fill a ladle and begin to quench his thirst.

20
Blending

Conchola knelt under a small tree and spotted a chameleon. The contour of her domed skull, her profile, one eye aimed in his direction while the other (which he could not see) probably watched the sky, streams of smoke, distant fires. The place where Billie died—green paddies, thatch roofs, palm trees near a well—was in ruins now. The targeted area was approximately two kilometers to the west. For several minutes he watched the horizon, planes and fires, and when he looked down there was no chameleon. He wondered if she had crawled away or changed color, blended more carefully with her surroundings. He bent down and she appeared again, mostly brown, olive green, with the ridge of her spine the same color and shape as the prong of a slender twig.

Her throat swelled, tightened, puffed with air. *Listo*, he thought, *inteligente. Don't do anything but breathe.*

Three hours later, concealed in a hedgerow, he saw his platoon wading through a paddy. PFC De Angelo walked point, Sergeant Stevens followed, and Warren was in his usual place, the heart of the platoon, dead-center. A bullet through the brain might improve Warren. Conchola lay on his belly, aimed his rifle, but couldn't pull the trigger. He remembered Warren's words for Billie Jasper: *Zapped, zipped. Xin loi, Billie boy, Airborne Ranger.* The medic pointed his rifle at a clump of earth near Warren's feet.

The platoon halted when Sergeant Stevens barked out a command. Soldiers hunched over their packs in the middle of the paddy, each one a beautiful target. Stevens looked around, then cupped a hand to his mouth. "Give it up, Conchola. You're halfway dead, three-quarters dead. You either get your ass out here or..." He paused, apparently unable to find the right words. Warren called, "Here kitty, here kitty-kitty." Stevens, maybe finding the right words, said, "Yeah, fuck you, Conchola. You can kiss your ass goodbye."

The sergeant got on the radio. A helicopter flew overhead, zigged and zagged, but Conchola wasn't worried. He lay in tall grass beneath a tree, his body motionless, no more visible than a chameleon shadowed by a twig. As the soldiers resumed their march, bent down under heavy loads, he felt a moment of pity. The medic had jettisoned some supplies. He still carried his rifle, one aid bag, an entrenching tool, a poncho liner, a canteen, a can of chicken, a can of ham and limas. To make potable water he had iodine, a month's supply, so if he stayed near waterways he wouldn't need to haul extra canteens. Billie had died going for water, going toward a well and the ghost of a tame animal. From now on Conchola would stay alert. No animal or human, spirit or flesh, tame or savage, would deceive him. He watched the platoon cross the paddy and file one-by-one into a cove of trees. *Miserable grunts*, he thought. *You'd shoot your own selves if you could see how sorry you looked.*

The helicopter flew east, the last soldier disappeared, and Conchola was alone. He removed the gauze from his left hand. He probed his wound, the small gash between his forefinger and thumb, slightly swollen and infected. For a long time he studied the scars on the outer side of his left forearm. The markings were similar, or perhaps identical, to those a tiger would leave on the bark of a familiar tree.

He wrapped his hand with clean gauze. Alert for trip wires, mouths of tunnels, he crossed from one hedgerow to another. He made a careful detour around a patch of freshly dug earth. Beneath it there could be a mine, a tiger trap, a bed of sharpened bamboo, a place where the earth opened. For a few moments he had faith he could read this land, translate its messages, absorb essential information. *Billie, you can follow me*, he thought, *estoy despierto. Eyes like lasers.* He paused and remembered the elephant, *un fantasma*, a ghost animal that appeared fierce and alive and magnificent. Conchola wished his face were still rouged with blood. Ghosts had fears, vulnerabilities. The wise ones avoided those who smelled of the blood of a beast, especially a tiger. Conchola could not convince himself he was fully protected. The tiger blood had flaked off, drifted. *Somewhere in the ground*, he thought, *there's a spoon of blood dust, something finer than gold, witchier than witches, reina de las brujas, that would keep my ass safe.*

But he had Southeast Asia to himself. There were no rules now, no taboos, and no one could give him orders. In the Cu Chi area nothing was easier than scorching a ville, lighting up the paddies and watching them burn, but in Cambodia the planes and their bombs would never destroy mile after mile of jungle. There were still places the U.S. Army had no maps for. Or places for which maps were worthless once one entered the tiered canopies, the darkness so dense you felt you could shape it with your hands, create an animal that sprang from leaves and creepers and rot, that leaped from tree limb to tree limb, or that clawed the earth, pissed on trees, left its mark, roared and seethed and wandered. *Wild West*, thought Conchola. *Follow the sun's path till you're in the shade. At night find the North Star, bow to it, turn left ninety degrees, and you're headed west again. Vaya, west is left of north. Remember. If the night brings rain, monsoon rain, forget the friendly star, move as a hunter without a compass. Y escúchame, despierta. Use cat eyes to see the shade.*

He crisscrossed hedgerows, tangles of brush that divided one section of paddy from another. A few miles west of where Billie died, he came to another ville that had recently been bombed. Still some smoke here, small flames. Silence. The medic drew back, belly-crawled over a paddy warm with sun, ember and ash, and proceeded due west.

Dusk. A lizard watched him from behind a stone. In a nearby paddy, mostly bombed, two rabbits feasted on tall grass that bordered an unkempt tombstone. At the verge of a hedgerow, Conchola found spring water in a crater. He squatted, unbandaged his hand, bathed his wound. Two fish jumped, then another, and dozens of water bugs skated the surface. He wished for a net or a pole, a hook, a way to catch dinner. He took off his clothes to let the air cool him. Mosquitoes hunted in swarms, sampled his blood; his wind-milling arms couldn't shoo half of them away.

He eased into the hole with the fish and water-bugs. Stars in the pale sky. Dim light, somnolent. Growing brighter, shining, as the sky darkened. A single star, or perhaps a planet, cast a light strong enough to silver the ripples and swells of the water. Conchola, floating on his back, his arms fanned out from his sides, thought of distant light, light years of journey, starlight, planet-light, the reflected light that penetrated this crater, that maybe reached farther into the clearings of a jungle. Refreshed, he spun around, dove, vanished in water. He came up gasping, arms and legs wheeling, and saw above him a configuration of stars that resembled a tiger's face.

He paddled to the shore, dressed, painted his face and hands with repellent. He wondered if mosquitoes preyed on large cats, or if the fur and skin of felines were too thick for mosquitoes to nose their way in, suck tiger blood with needles. Flies and gnats might buzz the eyes, but the glare alone, the fury of light, should swiftly repel them. He remembered the mantled tail he found in Cambodia. He put his hand in his right front pocket and it was still there, a reptilian thing, the sharp scales that had cut his finger. He didn't know why he'd saved it, but now he pulled it out, held it like a pen in the soft light to see which end was most suitable for drawing and writing. After wrapping his right hand, making a glove of gauze to cushion the scales, he scratched into the ground a wide face, long fangs, whiskers, a raze of lines for claws. WARREN, he gouged, SILLY FUCK, WHERE'D I GO? WHERE AM I? He drew arrows (North, South, East, West), and four paws, each headed in a different direction. *Disorient the platoon*, he thought. *Piss them off. Confuse them*. Grinning, he carved into the earth huge block letters: GUERREROS, LOSERS. EL TIGRE IS IMPOSSIBLE TO KILL.

He sat down to a dinner of canned chicken with ham and limas. After this last supper courtesy of the Army, he would learn to forage, find trees that bore fruit, fish trapped in ponds, or hunt with his rifle. The disadvantage of hunting was the rush of a bullet, the way it broadcast one's position. If he fired but a single round, he would announce to the Viet Cong and the Americans, *Cabrones, here I am, I invite you to surround me*. He began to wonder if the weapon was worth its weight. Maybe he should leave it, toss it in the lake of the crater, or shove it barrel first into a moist paddy. The enemy, the Viet Cong or the Americans, would find it if he left it on the ground, and might use his weapon against him. The platoon would be back this way, if not to find the deserter, to continue their missions, search and destroy, their daily activity—now redundant—of pouring fire into ashes. An M-16 wouldn't help against a platoon or a squad, or even three well-trained commandoes. And if on his way to Cambodia, the Viet Cong surprised him, captured him, they might be more lenient if he was unarmed.

The simple food tasted delicious. He enjoyed the salt, the tanginess on his tongue, the quiet swallows. He thought of the girls back home, those he once loved. Their fair skin, deep blue eyes, golden hair. A sugary sweetness that would never know the grace of claws, the light of tree shade. He remembered what people were supposed to care about: money and TV, a nice house, a nice car, a little of this, a little of that, a mess of comforts. Maybe a man was luckier to be harassed by insects, chased by bullets, trailed by a tiger. Conchola saw the stars of the sky. In the morning he would see the sun or rain, he would cross through hedgerows, slip through paddies, and keep moving until wilderness shadowed him, stalked him, took him in or killed him. He told himself the girls were history, the platoon was history. There was only the memory of his Mama, the memory of Billie, and the importance of his journey. He acknowledged a certain loneliness. He wished he could tell Billie or his Mama why he abandoned his duties, why he couldn't go home anymore no matter what happened. He pictured his Mama's face, the kindness in her eyes. How could he tell her he no longer cared about anything his country cared about? How could he prove he was more alive than any man she would ever know?

He shrugged. *Mama, what would I do in the barrio? Buy a used Chevy? Check the listings for a tiger program on public TV? Open a Bud?* Maybe if Mama sat with him beneath these stars, close by, nearly touching, she would understand his reverence. She was pious, faithful, and he, her only child, sometimes prayed to the saints she believed in. *La Virgen de Guadalupe*, The Dark Madonna, *Madre Oscura*. Beloved Saint Jude, Helper In Cases Despaired Of. And the animal saint, silent and strong, Saint Francis of Assisi. He would be unwise, though, to tell her of his longing for the tiger, or to mention his current destination— Cambodia. Billie would understand, might even follow him if he promised to stay alert, but not his Mama. Mamas worry, they're trained this way; can't help it. He pictured his Mama's bowed head, her hands lifted to her heart, her dry fingers on the beads of her rosary. He glanced at his tattoos, the beads strung together, faint smudges in starlight. He shrugged. *Yeah, Mama, I'm sorry, sorry these couldn't please you. One thing, though, one last thing before I pick up and leave: You don't have to worry the only child you brought into this world never took his chance to live.*

He finished his meal, dug a hole, buried the cans. He tossed his writing instrument, a tail, into the crater, and a fish jumped. He followed this with his rifle, his ammunition, and the water rippled. On the rim of the crater, he found a long feather and the head of a snake. Snake eyes small, open. Dull and sleepy in starlight. He noticed a bowl-shaped depression in the earth, maybe the impact of a grenade, something recent. He tossed the snakehead and the feather into the water. The feather floated, rode the wake of a fish's tail. The snakehead turned and went under, sank down in the dark where it might be nibbled on at night.

He retreated to a hedgerow, curled in his poncho liner, and slept off and on for nearly an hour. He dreamed of Mundo, *la fiera*, the glare of the eyes, the wounds that he wished he could heal with his own hands. He dreamed the animal watched from a distance as Billie Jasper followed him toward a well. Conchola, calm and alert, halted when he saw a trip-wire half-covered with grass. *Stand back, Billie, stand back. You see it?* Conchola inched forward, pointed, and said, "Whatever you see won't kill you." He thrashed in his sleep, vaguely heard himself pawing, murmuring: "You can follow me, Billie, you can follow me. Through any sunlit field or shade."

He woke and the moon was up. He folded his poncho liner, stuffed it in his rucksack, and coated his face and hands with another layer of repellent. The moon, in the eastern sky over the paddies, cast angles of light into the hedgerow. The medic wondered how far he would walk before he reached the jungles of Cambodia. One hundred miles? Two hundred? Would he know he was in Cambodia? He set out with the moon behind him, the night quiet but for insects. For a few seconds, as he stepped from hedgerow to paddy, his shadow was tiger-sized, long and sleek, and he moved in near silence through moonlit grass.

21
Tamarind Tree

Before sunrise, when the first winds blew through, everything could be smelled. Buffalo hair, buffalo breath, hides caked with mud. *Ma* rice, green shoots. Coconut. Jackfruit. Unwashed girl. Tamarind. Mist. Sugarcane. Dung. Lemon. The elephant smelled the grit and brine of fields, the fresh root growth, the condensed sourness of grass seeds, rice seeds, the water and heat that milked them till they swelled, yielded, their sheaths broken. She smelled seed husks, the green flesh they once contained, the tamarind tree, bitter roots and moist leaves, the frogs and fishes of the canal, the weed beds and dank water. The girl gathered and fed her the tenderest parts of the tamarind. Pleasant bark smells, crushed leaves. The girl's face smelling of lemon, and her body the brackishness of a paddy, a pool of undisturbed water. This small one who had not bathed with soap in many days had finally begun to smell bountiful. She smelled agreeably tart, similar to the elephant's master. But her breath and the skin of her forearms were still sweet and clean.

In the high branches of the tamarind, Nguyen Luu Hai saw *Nui Ba Den* as the mist lifted. Black Virgin Mountain, a pyramid that rose from the paddies to the sky, a mound of stones with trees that grew from crevices—the crowns nearly black in the distance, the stones the mottled color of rain clouds. He pointed and called down the tree to Ong Quan and Ong Truong: "Black Virgin Mountain, Black Virgin Mountain; thirty kilometers." The grandfathers, after consulting their maps, determined they were within eight

185

kilometers of the Renegade Woods if Luu Hai's estimate was correct.

Most of the peasants continued to sleep. Boys curled on one side of the tree, girls and women on the other, and no one slept alone without the comfort of neighboring bodies. The buffalo lay together in an enormous nest. Qui's buffalo positioned his body as a shield, a blocking force between the elephant and the female buffalo. Many times the bull buffalo rumbled and woke, sniffed the air, and gaped at the gargantuan size of the animal he opposed. The elephant whipped its trunk around, smelled things, but did not seem especially interested in buffalo. Qui's buffalo would watch for a time as a girl pushed bundles of leaves into the maw of the giant. Later, satisfied that he and the females would be unharmed, the bull buffalo would close his eyes and return to his restless sleep.

Storm clouds would have been more welcome than a clear sky. The first planes appeared with the first sun, and Hai watched the rice fields to the northeast bilge with flames. He called down the tree, "*May bay, may bay!*" but the peasants already knew. Awakened by the sound of bombs rather than Hai's voice, they lay near the carts, and the children remained curled on the ground, some of them rolling over, remembering bad dreams, pressing closer to the bodies beside them. Qui's buffalo strained the rope that anchored him to his cart. The elephant, swaying, lashing her trunk side-to-side, made a sound like a scythe swung through dry grass. The planes flew farther west, targeted paddies and forests, fringes of green that had survived previous bombings. Hai, watching the horizon buckle with light, felt the trunk of the tamarind oscillate, adjust to movements in the earth approximately ten kilometers in the distance. His sister Nhi and his mother and Thien and Tuyen lay between the elephant and the cart that served as a shield. Tuyen began chattering about Trung Trach, the great warrior woman, as though a brave story would lessen her fear and the fear of those around her. "Trung Trach quietly applauded," she said, "when the enemy squandered his ammunition. In each moment of battle, she knew when to reveal herself and when to stay hidden in the earth."

Hai had heard this many times. In difficult situations, Tuyen was instructed to repeat the stories she had learned from Cadre Duc, her father, and Cadre Minh, her mother. If strict silence was not essential, if the enemy could not be alerted by the voice of a girl, Tuyen proceeded with stories. "You all remember," she continued, "the story of Trung Trach and the preying mantis. Today this tree that protects us is a tall spider, and we are its sturdy legs."

No, a tree's a bird, thought Luu Hai. *You climb up to give him your eyes. Fisher-bird eyes. Osprey.*

"A praying mantis," Tuyen whispered, "will not attack unless it's sure of victory. It may race about, distract the enemy with its circle dance, but it seldom strikes while the enemy is awake."

She rambled on about the wisdom and foresight of Trung Trach's battle strategies until Hai's mother interrupted her. "Trung Trach and her sister first prayed to their ancestors," said Ma Xuan. "They prayed near a sacred mountain, Hung Mountain, and they did not fight or resist anyone until their ancestors blessed them with their strength."

Minh, Tuyen's mother, said, "Yes, and we are the same. We pray near *Nui Ba Den*, a sacred mountain, and we ask our ancestors to bless us."

Ma Xuan nodded. "This is our way."

"Our ancestors give us counsel," said Minh. "They know our suffering."

"If we honor them."

"We cannot do otherwise," said Minh. "We pray to our ancestors, we honor them, and we do our best to live."

Bright rims of fire streaked the horizon. Ma Xuan wondered if the paddies east of the mountain, the forests northeast, the land they hoped to settle, was presently disappearing. Maybe the peasants would survive the day, reach their destination at night, but would fail to recognize it because their maps would be meaningless, their proposed home a graveyard. How much would remain when the first stars appeared? Would there be enough wood to build homes, enough trees to conceal the animals and huts of a new village? Maybe the peasants and their animals would have to continue west and find sanctuary in the jungles of Cambodia. Maybe Cadre Duc would find them and put them to work on the Truong Son Trail, repairing the damage of bombs as the elephant and the buffalo hauled supplies to the end of the trail—*Nui Ba Den*. The war would make the decisions, push people from one place to another. Here beneath a tamarind tree the survivors of a village, a community that once thrived, were as powerless as a storm-blown leaf.

Tuyen was again trying to comfort those around her with stories of Trung Trach, the warrior woman who could transform herself into a spider, a sword, a raging elephant. "*Biet roi*," Luu Hai called down the tree. "She could also turn into a fisher-bird, an osprey." Ma Xuan and the grandfathers and everyone else looked up at him. "A raptor," he said too loudly, "a fisher-bird. This is what gives a tree its eyes."

The bombing was far off now, the explosions muffled. "Watch the fields," said Ong Quan. "Watch the mountain. We don't need you jabbering about this or that from high in a tree."

The sky had already quieted when Nam scaled the tamarind to relieve the first lookout boy two hours later. Hai, as Nam slid by him toward the higher branches, said, "Watch for helicopters, watch in every direction."

Nam chuckled. "Raptor eyes? The eyes of a tree?" He

flapped his arms. "Go on, Luu Hai. Even an osprey needs some rest."

But Hai could not sleep when he came down from the tamarind. Thien was feeding the elephant sugarcane. Between the elephant cart and the tree, Hai's mother now lay with her daughter, her arms arranged protectively over Nhi's chest and abdomen. Hai sat on the ground near his mother. A baby cried until its mouth was fastened to a breast. Two small boys sword-fought with sticks. They made slashing sounds, spitting sounds, and Ma Xuan said, "Enough! Before the day ghosts hear you!" The boys waved their sticks, made stabbing motions, but were quieter. "Sit down," said Ma Xuan. "Both of you. The ghosts could be hidden in a hedgerow on the other side of the field."

Hai wished he could speak with Thien. He looked at her, she looked back, but then she turned to her elephant and he turned to Qui's buffalo. The bull was lying on the ground, his head slightly raised as he dozed. The other buffalo lay near him, and the two-month-old buffalo slept between Qui's buffalo and its mother. Hai enjoyed the thick, grassy smell, the tang of buffalo breath. He snuffled the air as an animal would, but he could not pick up the scent of Thien's body. To smell the one he loved maybe he must marry her and press his nose to her hair, her skin. Surely the buffalo knew her scent, the elephant, too. But all Hai could smell was animal breath, pungent grass. He wondered if he was more skilled at smelling things than the enemy, the day ghosts. It seemed impossible that the pilots of planes and helicopters had ever smelled fires, flesh, burned soil, ruined fields. From the sky maybe nothing could be smelled but sunlight or rain, cloud smells, sun smells—heaven. At times, the planes flew over the roof of the sky, their wings so high they could not be seen from the earth, and their rain of bombs and flames seemed to fall from nothing. By now the ancestral village was probably gone, but for what reason? Maybe an American killed easily and often because he smelled almost nothing. Maybe if he lived near water and fields, animals and plants, he would be more careful about what he bombed and destroyed.

Thien surprised him by speaking. "If we reach the place of tall trees, we must build a shelter for the elephant."

Hai hesitated. "You mean a pen?" he asked. "Like a buffalo pen but larger?"

"No, a shelter," she said. "We'll use a bomb crater, there's always a crater. And with thatch and bamboo we'll build a roof over the crater, cover it with earth, so the elephant will be protected."

Hai thought this over. "We could do it."

"You'll help me?" she said. "If we find enough trees and bamboo?"

"Of course."

"It'll be a lot of work," said Thien. "The roof must be solid."

"It will be."

She looked at him.

"Easy," said Hai. "For the frame we'll use the strongest bamboo—long poles. We'll layer the poles with palm fronds, then earth. Haul the earth with yokes and baskets."

"But first we must find the trees, the bamboo. Then we must ask Ong Quan and Ong Truong for permission."

"They'll agree," said Hai, "*khong sao*. The grandfathers will want *two* shelters, one for the elephant and another for the buffalo. Or maybe they'll want all the animals together in one enormous hole."

He smiled. *And there must be room for us*, he thought. *Three adult buffalo, one child buffalo, one elephant, one girl, one boy*. He remembered the strength of Great Joy, the steadiness of the bull buffalo. Hai was not the least bit tired now. He pictured the important work he would do, his body straining under the weight of yokes and baskets, the weight of the land that he would carry up a bamboo ladder and onto the roof of an enormous shelter. Slowly, with lighter, more human loads, the other peasants would follow, and the protective mound of the roof would assume the shape of a small mountain. One side of the shelter would remain open, a cave for the elephant and buffalo to enter and leave. Once the roof was piled with as much earth as the bamboo would sustain, Hai would layer dried palm leaves over the surface so day-ghost pilots would look down on a grayish splotch, a dun, lifeless color that mirrored places they already bombed.

He smiled at the sky. *Invisible*, he thought. *They'll believe we disappeared.*

He wished for the courage to ask Thien if she carried his gift, the pebble dark as a cricket. Maybe she carried it in the front pocket of her pajamas, or in the pocket of her shirt. Maybe she kept it where it was easy to reach, to press with her fingers. The pebble was like the body of a boy, hard and smooth, a quiver of bone. But it would warm her hand and bring comfort if she held it for a while.

22
Stalking

Antonio Lucio heard animals. The clucks of chickens, the honk of a duck or a goose, a snuffling pig, a rooster. He crawled through a hedgerow, scanned nearby fields, small islands of green amid craters that dotted the earth as precisely as punch holes in a game board. He heard the snort and swish of buffalo breaths, restless hooves, but he did not see animals. The broken fields concealed little. Sixty meters over a bombed paddy there were bushes, trees, a place the Americans forgot to bomb. Would a menagerie of animals—buffalo, chickens, ducks, pigs—withstand each other's company for the coolness of shade? Wherever there were animals there were peasants, Viet Cong. There might be a well-trained platoon lying in wait, or two or three buffalo boys surrounded by their animals. Most likely a tunnel, or a network of tunnels, burrowed beneath the trees and fields. He heard the gabble of ducks, chickens, the snort of a buffalo. He slithered through the hedgerow until he was downwind of the animals and the trees.

Maybe ghosts had convened in tree shade. *Un día de campo*, a picnic in the country. Food and shade, *fantasmas*. Animals and peasants. He heard a human voice, maybe a child, whisper, "*Xin hay im lang, xin hay im lang.*" He guessed at the meaning (Quiet, quiet), and imagined a runt of a kid, a buffalo boy, trying to control his animals. *Ghosts*, he thought, *fantasmas. Spooks on a picnic*. He heard a sharp, crunching sound, loud swallows. Maybe nothing out there but a few ghosts entertaining hunger, pretending to eat, munching the air and crackling it as though this breathed softness came from gristle and blood and bone.

The medic waited. Maybe something ordinary would emerge from the trees, sink its legs or hooves in the earth, leave an imprint with the weight of its body. But if these were ghosts they wouldn't leave visible prints, or anything more substantial than a single thread of coolness. Maybe the most effective way to disarm a ghost was to be aware of its proximity. The day Billie died, had Conchola been alert, he might have followed the ghost of an elephant into the shade of a VC village. The sun was fierce, merciless, but he might have discovered a single thread of coolness. Maybe a ghost could be startled, shaken. Maybe the elephant—nearby now, unaware of him—was pretending to eat and breathe beneath the coolness of trees.

The day passed uneventfully. He monitored animal sounds that inspired guesses: buffalo ghost, chicken ghost, bird ghost, imitation elephant. Twice he caught sight of something in slow flight through high branches. Possibly a monkey ghost, a shadow that blipped through his field of vision and disappeared in tree shade. In the late afternoon, he heard explosions to the northeast. GIs were probably blowing things up, small caches, tunnel openings, or any darkness that appeared suspicious. Conchola knew the strategy: kill the shade so the shade would seem harmless. But some GIs believed in spirits, *fantasmas*, beings who could not be buried. The shade resurrected itself, the dead came back; nothing was safe. You walked toward a well, an elephant appeared, the earth erupted. The work of ghosts, a covenant of spirits. They could kill you as surely as a live gook with a 30-caliber machine gun tearing your flesh to small bright bits.

He could not stay awake. He had walked all night, sometimes crawled, and his body softened into sleep, his muscles limp and light, his eyes closing without volition. In dreams he had periods of vigilance, his body alert to variations of tree shade, animal sounds, warm snuffling and scratching, snorts and chews and swallows. Briefly, at intervals, he heard human voices, a girl's whisper, a boy's, and there were dark faces amid leaves and branches. The girl fed stalks of sugarcane to an enormous elephant. She tried to coax the animal to kneel, make itself smaller, but the beast ignored her. The girl was pretty, her face soft and brown and quiet. The boy lay near a buffalo, fell asleep, and made moaning sounds as though he longed for a lover. Waking slowly, Conchola saw the faces of children, the bodies of animals, fade and vanish. Soft snorts and snuffles issued from the darkness of the tallest tree.

Dusk. Deep shade, dark limbs. The crowns of trees pale yellow. Awake, he saw the first animals appear on the land. A bull buffalo, two smaller buffalo, a calf, a pig, a family of chickens. He heard ducks, but he couldn't see them distinctly. Saw ropes, black lines of harnesses, child-sized humans rousing the buffalo, tossing lines over their backs, their chests, leading them forward. For a few moments the elephant—too magnificent—barely registered. A quick shadow darted around it, attached some sort of harness to its girth, and the beast began pulling. It pulled a cart that creaked, a burdensome cart piled with packages, belongings. From a distance it appeared that the elephant and three buffalo had pulled up an entire hedgerow by its roots, that they carried in carts tangles of brush, vines, saplings. Within a few minutes, the trunk of the tall tree lay bare, a thick vertical line—no foliage to conceal it. A procession, a convoy of spirits, rambled westward. Full-sized animals, miniature humans, mounds of leaves, branches, roots—everything moving. Human ghosts had harnessed part of the earth to ghost animals. They'd darted around the beasts, then spurred them forward with slaps to the rump, singsong voices, whispery commands. The animals moved, the earth moved, and now Conchola absorbed the resonance. Tremors passed seventy meters over a bombed field and up through the ground, up through his body. The buffalo grunted, snorted, their breathing labored as though what they hauled bore true weight, the weight of earth and branch, root and vine, the weight of packages strapped to their spines, the weight of rounded hills that rose from carts, the weight of their own bodies. In silhouette, burdened with cargo, they had the humped shape of pack mules. He heard hooves, buffalo drums, a pleasant cadence. The elephant walked silently, or with no sound he could hear, but its breath—the wheeze of air in its trunk—was like a powerful pump sucking the earth, pulling up water. He counted three adult buffalo, one small buffalo, one elephant, and approximately thirty figures, four of them with rifles. *Ghosts with rifles?* he shrugged. *Maybe dangerous, maybe not.* For a brief time he believed everything before him was supernatural, a display of spirits. After the last animal and its cargo disappeared behind a hedgerow, he rose to his feet, rubbed a finger over his scars and tattoos of rosary beads, and said, "*Tigre*, time to move."

He walked to the tall tree the ghost animals and their guides had encircled. Here he found the imprint of wheels, hoof prints, buffalo prints, and the deep round marks of elephant feet that confused his belief in ghosts.

He stepped up onto the path along the canal. Maybe ghost animals could briefly bear weight, leave their marks in order to confuse whoever and whatever attempted to follow. He found animal prints and wheel prints that made no sense. For five yards there would be nothing, no mark on the earth. Then suddenly he would see a hole half a foot deep, an elephant print, small bare feet (human), and a succession of buffalo prints within the rail-shaped tracks of wheels. It seemed the procession partly flew, partly touched earth. He still heard animals, their strained breathing, but he could not see them on the path in front of him. A steady breeze blew from the east. He would have to stay downwind of the menagerie, move in a half-circle across hedgerows and fields, maintain a safe distance. *A safe distance from ghosts, Billie? How far? Maybe beyond the range of a bullet, a mortar, a wire hidden in high grass.*

He followed his boot prints back to the hedgerow, ducked inside its shadows, and began walking. He asked himself impossible questions: Could ghosts see in darkness? Do they need a small light? Could a tiger follow their trail? Could a tiger stalk them? The air smelled of rain, moist leaves. Clouds darkened most of the sky, but he could see well enough to avoid tripping over vines, creepers. Bent over, he crossed from hedgerow to field, no bushes for concealment. Within a few minutes, he spotted the ghosts on his left flank. The caravan of animals and cargo reappeared, inky blotches. Hillocks. The groans and snorts of beasts again seemed genuine, a skillful imitation. He crept closer, knelt behind a bund, and saw two ghosts—humans—sweeping things away, swinging brooms. The sight at first baffled him, then took on logic. The sweepers did their best to erase wheel marks, buffalo prints, elephant prints, human prints. They and the caravan beyond them were not ghosts for all bore true weight, the weight of flesh, and they wished to erase from the earth their signs of passage. Not enough time to smooth deep prints that gouged the earth where it was moist and pliable. But they swept away as many marks as possible so those that remained would confuse whoever followed them on the trail.

He was fortunate to have seen them before they saw him. Those who bore weight would clear the path, trigger any traps, mines, attract GI ambushes, and maybe stop and compare strategies with the Viet Cong who lay waiting. He would follow them at a safe distance as long as they headed west, toward the wilderness of Cambodia. He doubted they would go that far; they most likely had different intentions. A longing for wild animals was rare, seemingly unshared. Those before him were refugees, homeless wanderers, who would probably settle in the first deep shade not yet destroyed by bombs.

The medic crept to the path they walked on. He lost sight of them, but still heard the struggle of animals, the sounds of labor. The elephant siphoned rivers of wind through its trunk.

Buffalo hooves thumped the earth, and now and then Conchola heard groans, ragged snuffles. He estimated the menagerie was eighty meters ahead of him, a safe distance. *Seguro, Billie, seguro. No one knows who or where I am.*

23
Geronimo

The moon in the eastern sky. Nhi and Tuyen, walking backwards, sweeping the path with brooms. Erasing wheel marks, the imprint of hooves, human feet. Bobbing their heads like birds, alert for movement in the fields, the hedgerows, movement on the path before them. At the same time they saw a crouched form that resembled an animal. "A calf," whispered Nhi, "a stray." "No, a dog," said Tuyen, "a village mutt. Not a sniffer." They froze and observed movement on the cattle path some sixty meters away. The Americans sometimes used animals, well-trained dogs to sniff out Viet Cong tunnels, routes of passage. The dogs knew the scent of Vietnamese hair, skin, sweat, blood, clothes, but the peasants often confused them by washing with the same soap used by American GIs. The Cu Chi cadre provided the soap, encouraged its use. Several days ago the peasants used the last slivers (Palmolive and Dial), so they smelled like themselves again. Now Tuyen inched backwards, her broom raised. "Not a calf," she said. "Not a dog." The observed form wavered, rose from a crouch, achieved human height. The sweepers, brooms in hand, hurried to inform the grandfathers, Ong Quan and Ong Troung.

The elders rode in the lead cart pulled by Qui's buffalo. "Where?" said Ong Quan. "How many?"

"One," said Nhi, "sixty meters behind. Maybe a soldier."

"A Viet Cong," said Quan. "An American is rarely alone."

He briefed Hai and Nam, two of the boys entrusted with rifles. "Make sure he's friendly," said Quan. "Capture him if he isn't. Do not open fire and disclose our position unless he leaves you no choice."

Ong Truong pointed to a knot of shadows on the verge of the path. "We'll be under those trees," he said. "Report to me and Ong Quan upon your return."

Nhi and Tuyen circulated among the peasants to inform them of the grandfathers' decision. Hai, before following orders, walked full-circle around the elephant and her cart, and he took a deep breath of pleasure when Thien whispered, *"Can than, can than"* (Careful). Cousin Nam, two steps behind, shadowed Hai, but the latter assumed the girl's concern was for him alone. *"Khong sao,"* said Hai, "it's all right. The one following us is most likely a Viet Cong."

Nam muttered, "I'm scared, cousin. I'm scared."

"Then stay behind me," said Hai, too alive to imagine his life might end.

They made their way to a nest of bushes on the north side of the path. While Hai knelt on one knee, his weapon ready, Nam lay on his belly, the barrel of his rifle slanting between branches. For what seemed a long time, Hai didn't hear or see anyone walking along the path. "Whoever's out there is VC," he said. "Quiet as a grass snake." A split second later he saw someone who appeared VC, someone walking bent over, his steps careful, his head shifting as he studied the contours of the land.

When the man turned, glanced behind him, Hai saw a soldier's pack strapped to his shoulders. The Viet Cong rarely carried packs. At most, a soldier would carry a rifle, several clips of ammunition, a bit of rice, a mosquito net, an extra pair of black pajamas. The man, though he moved quietly, carried a large pack, and was taller and broader than any father or Viet Cong Hai had ever been close to. If this was an American, a GI, where were his comrades? Why was he walking on the path alone?

Hai lifted his left arm and signaled to Nam, *Hold still, don't shoot.* The boys scanned the bombed fields, the craters that devoured the rice, three tombstones near a hut, a distant tree line. Hai listened for helicopters, the dragonflies that normally accompanied American probes, infiltration. He heard the croaking of swamp frogs, the whine of locusts, a lone cricket. The stranger came within ten meters before Hai verified he had no weapon. He glided like a monkey, arms curled, swinging back and forth as though he propelled himself forward by pulling on branches. He wore boots rather than rubber thongs, a helmet tipped back on his forehead. He paused, glanced behind him, then gazed at the sky. In profile, his nose was stubby and flat, quite different from the long, pointed noses of most Americans. *A VC in a stolen uniform?* thought Hai. *A tall VC admiring the sky? A stranger wandering in moonlight, dreaming of his girl, his home, his village?* The man arched his neck, made a humming sound. Knees bent, hands near his ankles, he resumed his monkey-walk, and soon he came abreast.

Hai darted up the path and nudged the barrel of his rifle into the stranger's ribs. Nam, his shoulders quaking, said, "Halt, halt!" but the man already stood motionless, arms raised, shoulders firm and steady. A quick breath lodged in the prisoner's throat. A soft choking sound, a sigh; and then chaotic mumbling, maybe sounds of despair or surprise, or distinct words in an incomprehensible language. Hai stripped him of his pack. He expected to find a pistol, three or four grenades, but except for a small shovel the one who walked like a monkey carried the supplies of a medic. Bandages, rolls of gauze, an IV, morphine, a packet of metal clamps that looked like things a doctor would use in surgery. Hai said, "*Bac si?*" (Doctor), but the man did not understand. Cousin Nam used the few words of English he had learned: "GI soldier? GI?" Arms still raised, the man looked at the sky and snickered. He made soft sounds, yelps, a range of sounds neither boy could interpret. Had Hai been alone, eyes closed, if there were no human being before him, he would have thought he was hearing monkeys or birds, a warble of sounds—high and then low—a creature calling for its mate or trying to communicate an important message. He heard a man who missed something, yearned for something, and he had to remind himself: *This is an American, he could kill you. Maybe the moment you turn away you'll feel his knife in your back.*

Hai fanned his rifle over either side of the road. "*Bao nhieu* GI? How many GI?"

Conchola made a circle with his raised left forefinger and thumb: zero GI. He began to lower his arms until both boys pointed their rifles at his chest.

"GI?" said Nam. "GI soldier?"

Conchola chuckled and wagged his head. "*Indio*," he whispered, "Geronimo." He coughed, blubbered, then held his breath to stifle a shriek. "Apache," he said, "Chiricahua. On my way home."

They led him to a gnarl of trees where he heard the breathing of animals before he saw them. The elephant, the buffalo, the snorting and belching, the air being thrummed and suckled. When he saw the elephant, the dome of her spine, her wide head and ears, he said, "*Puta madre*, you'll never kill me." The beast was as tall as the tallest tree of the shelter. Someone small was feeding it leaves, whispering things in a coddling voice, a mother comforting her child. *Pues*, he thought, *there's the trickster. The one who led the elephant away from the well and from me and Billie. Yeah, blew Billie to bits, blew him to kingdom come or wherever.* The animal was innocent, he knew this. But it obeyed this little runt of a thing who probably set the trap and led the elephant away.

Hai bound the man's hands behind him. Nam looped a section of rope around his waist, tied a knot, and secured the end of the rope to a metal rung on the cart of the elephant. The peasants, who had never captured a prisoner, spoke in confused whispers. Some wanted him shot or knifed (less noise with a knife), but Ong Quan and Ong Truong agreed he might be useful in an ambush. "He'll call to his comrades," said Ong Quan, "and everyone will stop shooting. Not even the Americans are so evil they will shoot their own comrade."

"And he's a doctor," said Ong Truong, "or a medic, who could be forced at gun-point to help us." He perused the supplies, held up the IV and the metal clamps. "Would he carry these things if he didn't know how to use them? We might need his skills if someone is badly hurt."

The elders used every resource at their disposal. Once, nearly three years ago, the grandfathers persuaded a captain ghost that a wounded Viet Cong was a civilian, a farm girl, a dying peasant. A day ghost helicopter ferried her out, carried her to the American base at Cu Chi, to equipment and facilities the Viet Cong could access only through cunning. Six weeks after the surgeons saved Cadre Tu's life, she left their hospital, and made her way back to the tunnels north of the village. Cadre Duc praised the grandfathers' decision. "A more formal commendation is pending," he said. "There was no other way to save our comrade's life."

Clouds in the east, the scent of rain. Thien unshackled the elephant's hind legs, Qui led his buffalo onto the path, and the caravan moved west toward Black Virgin Mountain. Conchola had to keep pace with the elephant. He walked quickly when she walked quickly, slowed when she slowed, his five feet of rope tightening and slackening, putting him at the mercy of the animal. Once, when she lurched forward, he fell face-down and she briefly dragged him. For the most part the elephant ambled, her steps nearly as silent as a tiger's. He prayed to the Virgin of Guadalupe and Saint Francis that this menagerie lead him to Cambodia, lost jungle, *Madre Oscura*. A dark home where they would find little use for him, see no harm in him. A place where they would cut free his bindings and leave him in the shade.

A buffalo on point, an elephant behind a buffalo. He longed to touch the scars on his left forearm, the claw marks, but his hands were bound so tight he could barely wriggle his wrists. He grinned, wagged his head, heard a familiar voice inside him: *If the girls back home could see me.* "Hey Bimbos," he whispered. "What's on the tube, babes? How's things in the 'hood?" He remembered a trippy song the grunts used to play on stand-down in Cu Chi, a song about being far from home, light years from home. *Vaya, this'll work to my advantage*, he thought, *una ventaja importante. Light years from home, light years from almost everything. Tan lejos, tan cerca, where's the nearest tiger? Mundo*, he thought, *fiera. If I'm lucky as sin, this menagerie of animals and peasants will lead me closer to your den.*

The elephant pulled him toward a mountain.

24
Wounds

Before midnight they passed the Renegade Woods, the land they had hoped to settle. The stands of tamarind and banyan, recent targets, were no longer habitable, and the peasants found no shelter in the spray of fallen trunks, vines, branches. Forced to halt several times, they retrieved shovels and hoes from carts, carved detours around bomb craters that had made the trail impassable. Once, as they edged by a crater, the prisoner giggled and would not stop until Hai, who walked near him, raised his rifle as though to strike. The man seemed to be straining to see the east face of the *Nui Ba Den*, Black Virgin Mountain. A rack of clouds covered the moon.

Lightning in the east, the smell of ash. They came to an abandoned hamlet, several huts still standing, the surrounding area pocked with craters. The air had an odd smell, a waft of chemicals, and the wide leaves of coconut palms bowed like the branches of willows. A well near the path, its earthen walls mostly destroyed, exuded a dead fish smell. Lightning flashed, clouds roiled; the elephant lunged forward. Thien said, "*Di cham, di cham*" (Go slow), but the animal spurred the buffalo in front of her into a trot.

Conchola accelerated to a pace between a jog and a sprint. He reeled over the uneven path behind the elephant and the cart, the belongings that shifted as the wheels jounced and jangled over ruts, pot holes. A broom spun through the air, thunked his chest. He leaped, stutter-stepped, avoided tripping on a basket. Sweat rivered his face, his chest. *Payback*, he thought. *Animals'll trip a wire, hit a mine. I get the grease, Billie. Payback*. But he stayed on his feet, surprised himself with his new-found agility, his cat-like responses to the rope around his waist that slackened, pulled, adjusted his speed—animal trot, race, amble. He high-stepped a pot, another basket, ran better than he ever had as a second-string halfback in high school. His concentration was flawless until he imagined a crowd, an audience. White girls, brown girls, checkered skirts, white blouses. On a playing field he saw cheerleaders in blue and gold, amazing kicks and jumps, legs the color of milk, unbound hair like ropes flung skyward. He sprinted, knocked his knees against the back of the cart, but somehow maintained his balance. As he weaved, jitter-stepped, he heard the rumble of animals, the rattling and rolling carts, the alarmed calls of peasants that resembled the roar of an appreciative crowd.

The animals slowed only when they left the unfathomable smells behind them. The elephant smelled the grass again, the mosses and weeds of the canal, the girl beside her who smelled mostly of tamarind and lemon. Thien said, "*Di cham, di cham,*" and the beast trudged forward, drawn not by the command but the scent of the girl's body. Tamarind leaves, the sharpness of lemon and salt, the unwashed skin. The bitterness of a small, lush tree.

A late night storm washed over the land in waves. Heavy rain smothered the lumbering sounds of animals and carts, and lightning—in stuttered flashes—revealed the path as a straight orange line through broken paddies. Conchola, as if he might control the elephant, said, "Slower, slower." The sky darkened and flared. Coconuts and jackfruit, piled high in the elephant's cart, seemed to tilt toward him with each bolt of light. Between the piles, a gaunt elder perched on a stack of sugarcane. Drooling, mouth open—red tongue, black teeth—she stared at him. "*Bruja,*" he said, "stay put or you'll see fangs, claws. *Cuidado.*" In the next stuttered flash he bared his teeth, popped his eyes. Snarled. One of his captors pushed him and said, "*Im mieng, im mieng*" (Shut up).

Conchola understood the language, the severity of the tone. He told himself, *Calla, calla. Before they tear out your heart and feed it to a black-toothed witch.*

The wind littered the path with leaves, twigs, small branches. Hai saw the foreigner's face flash into focus, darken, reappear. He expected the skin to be pale, or to have the pinched redness that blotched the faces of most day ghosts who had patrolled the rice fields and the former village. The man's skin was brown, the brown of coconut husks and dry grass. Hai wondered how this soldier or medic lost his way, wandered off in the night, moved west on the cattle path that led to Black Virgin Mountain. A last bolt of light flickered, snaked west, but Hai saw no planes or helicopters, no sign of Americans on the way to rescue their comrade. Soon the rain slowed to a drizzle, the sky loured. Hai heard the prisoner mumbling, sloshing through mud, but he could barely see him. He groped, found the man's elbow, and said, *"Di-di, di-di."* The stranger muttered something, snarled. *"Nhanh,"* said Hai, *"nhanh"* (faster), and shoved him toward the elephant and the cart.

For a split second they each heard the same succession of sounds. A sharp click, a root pulled with a fist, a high ringing. Hai dove, his arms thrown over his head. Conchola—bound to the elephant—fell on his knees as the path shifted and rose, a small wave that crested beside the cart of the lead buffalo. The elephant's roar shook the prisoner's body more than the explosion. It was as though a canyon breathed, as though it became furious and released the air in its lungs, a wind that buffeted the trees at its rim, that shrieked over stone walls to hurl an insult at the sky, or a challenge. Three times the beast wailed and roared, then hauled the cart and Conchola and the black-toothed grandma off the path and into a ditch. Baskets tumbled. Chickens and ducks, tied together by their feet, flopped on the ground. The elephant swashed forward till the back wheels of the cart mired in a mud hole. Shivering, half-buried in the soup of the ditch,

Conchola swore, "*Puta*! Whore mother! Voice of a canyon!" He heard peasants stumbling in the dark. Heard the breaths and snorts of buffalo, the elephant sweeping long snakes of air into its trunk. A woman picked up a weeping child and began to sing. A lullaby, a one-beat voice, maybe one syllable for each word, each note of reassurance. On the path ahead two old men, side-by-side, seemed to be giving orders. When they quieted, when the animals momentarily stilled, Conchola heard someone straining to breathe. He made a medic's guess: a sucking chest wound, or throat wounds, possibly both. A child called to the elephant, then made sharp clicking sounds. The beast began pulling, swaying, unearthing the cart, and Conchola rose from his knees and followed. A human plow, two tines, two feet furrowing the center of the ditch.

Peasants bent over the back wheel of a buffalo cart. He couldn't see distinct forms, only dark humps, silhouettes. It seemed a wheel had been damaged by the explosion. Peasants were apparently repairing the rim, rounding the bent edges with hammers, refitting the wheel to the hub.

The elephant hauled its cart and Conchola up out of the ditch and onto the path. A boy uttered harsh, quick cries, untied the prisoner's wrists. Pointed a rifle at his chest. A girl untied the rope that fastened the prisoner to the cart. She spoke to the boy, then stepped aside as he motioned Conchola forward with thrusts of his rifle. The elephant leaned toward the prisoner, probably smelled him. The beast was swaying, shuffling, and someone beside it was talking, whispering the same sounds over and over. Maybe the whispery gook was the one who led the elephant away from the well seconds before Conchola darted ahead, tripped the wire, killed Billie Jasper. *A sly one*, he thought, *a trickster. Seems I was fooled by a little girl.*

Someone had lit a candle. Conchola looked down at a woman, an almond-shaped hole on the left side of her chest, several holes in her abdomen, and he saw his aid bag on the ground beside her. The peasants had gone through his supplies. The *bruja*, the black-toothed witch, now scissored away a strip of plastic, the wrapper of a bandage. She placed it over the chest wound, sealed it with tape, then carefully applied the bandage. She snipped away with scissors. Cut away swaths of cloth from the woman's shirt, spidered her fingers, searched for more wounds. The medic saw mother breasts, saggy and small, mostly nipple. Flaccid stubs once stretched and suckled. "*Madre*," he muttered, "*Guadalupe*. Please ease this mother's pain."

The boy with the rifle gave commands in such a way that Conchola did not have to guess at meanings. *Do something, help her. Be useful or we'll shoot you.* The medic knew the woman was almost dead. Maybe she would last the night, maybe even struggle through one more day, but she would not survive without surgery and antibiotics. "Has to go to a triage center," he said. "You understand? Triage? Hospital? Surgeon?" A moment after he spoke, he knew these words were gibberish. Even if his captors understood him, there was no hospital, no triage center, no doctor unless one ascended from the earth, from the labyrinths of tunnels. Conchola had heard rumors of Viet Cong hospitals underground near Cu Chi village, but he had never seen signs of them. "Need a miracle," he whispered. "Need a surgeon to rise from the dead."

He fumbled through the mostly useless supplies in his aid bag. "*Milagro*," he said, "*milagro*," his frayed nerves inspiring more gibberish. He had an IV, a packet of saline solution, so he used it. Found a thick vein in her left arm, inserted the needle, not to save her but to prove to his audience that he meant well, that he would use every tool available. He felt their heat, their bodies pressing forward, crowding him and the woman. Eyes wild, she glared at him, moved her lips. Blinked as the rain spattered her face. A girl whispered something as she placed a towel over the woman's chest and abdomen. Four boys lifted the woman in a hammock, carried her to the cart of the elephant, and lay her inside.

To shield her from rain, they made an open-sided tent with bamboo poles and strips of canvas. "Turn her," said Conchola, "lay her on her side. Help her to breathe." A rifle boy nudged him. The medic crawled into the cart and turned the woman on her left side. "Breathe easier," said Conchola, and took a long breath to illustrate. He held the IV bag a few feet over her body. Maybe this would be his job now, itinerant nurse. Maybe they wouldn't lash him to the cart again, at least not until Mama-san croaked. He spoke with confidence, tried to boost her spirits: "You're goin' home, Mama, whatever this means to you. Green rice fields and buffalo, a slow-moving river. Whatever." He began to sing, his voice soft and soothing: "Summertime, Mama, and the war's over…Fish in the river, rice in the fields, and all the people and animals without a worry in the world." He shook his head. "Yeah, summertime is a happy time, a peaceful time." He paused to conjure more words, a brighter melody, but a boy, one of those who captured him, said "*Du roi*," grabbed the IV bag, and motioned him off the cart.

Two others, waiting, roped Conchola's waist and wrists, again put him at the mercy of the elephant. Someone he couldn't see issued a command, a quick series of grunts, and the beast began pulling. Conchola snarled until the boy on his left waved a fist near his mouth. The medic stuck his neck out, blew on the fist, then bowed his head in feigned obeisance. He was surprised the boy didn't rough him up, shove him or punch him. *But somebody'll shoot me*, he thought, *if I don't find a way to keep Mama-san alive.*

She began to moan. The black-toothed grandma bent over the wounded woman and wiped her face with a cloth. The boy who held the IV bag said, "Ma, Ma," and sang what sounded like a love song. A girl ran up and crawled inside the cart. The wounded one shifted, raised her head, found the strength for language. Her voice was calm, matter-of-fact, and Conchola imagined she was providing her children and the old woman with final instructions. *A brief listing*, he thought, *un resumen*. Because others would have to complete for her the things she could not finish in the span of her life.

Ma Xuan spoke to Hai and to Nhi: "You must always remember the way to honor our ancestors. Tomorrow I may not be here to guide your offerings and prayers."

25
New Home

Later, the sky clearing, they again saw the mountain. The darkness darker than the sky, the horizon of trees and stones, the place maybe still wild enough to shelter a few more animals, a few humans. Nhi, in the elephant cart with her mother and Luu Hai and Ba Ly, pointed to the mountain and whispered, "*Nui Ba Den*, Ma, we'll rest here, and no one will harm us. In a few weeks, you'll be strong enough to walk."

Ma Xuan, attentive, watched the east face of the mountain. To survive, the villagers always had to press themselves to shadows, burrow beneath trees, take refuge in spider holes, bunkers, threads of darkness. She beheld the mountain, the widest dark she had ever seen, and in her prayers to the ancestors she informed them that the needs of the living remained the same: fields of rice, groves of trees, a few caves or tunnels for protection against planes, helicopters, the fires hurled from heaven. She whispered to her son and daughter, "Do you remember how to prepare the altar for your ancestors? Do you remember how to pray?"

"I remember," said Nhi.

"And you," she asked Hai. "You remember?"

"Yes, Ma."

"You must know what to do and what not to do. You and Nhi will be responsible for tending the altar, the family graves, and for consulting the ancestors before making important decisions."

"We know, Ma."

"I may not be here to lead you in prayer," she said. "You may need to listen for guidance and follow what you are given."

"We already do."

"Yes, we have prayed as a family and I have led you. But soon you may have to do what is needed without any help from Ma."

As the cart bounded over clumps of earth, each vibration sent a shiver of pain through her body. She groaned, asked for water, but her children could not let her drink because of her stomach wounds. The sliver of hope was to find a doctor, a surgeon, someone who had the instruments and knowledge to operate, cleanse the wounds, remove the shrapnel, and give the correct medicines to prevent infection. Maybe if they circled the mountain, searched for the place where the Truong Son Trail ended, they would find a small hospital or clinic, a doctor, a Viet Cong base camp. Neither child could imagine Ma Xuan dead, her gravesite bright with candles, incense, altar money, fresh flowers. Hai cupped his hands over his mother's bare shoulder. "Are you cold?" he whispered. "You need a blanket?" She did not speak, but he could feel her body convulsing. Nhi lay beside her mother to warm her. "I'll get a blanket," said Hai, "or two blankets." The boy stepped over a sack or rice and leaped from the cart.

A brief urge to use his fists on the prisoner. The American, slumped with fatigue, his steps heavy, shuffled behind the cart of the elephant. Hai wondered if the friends of this man planted the booby trap that wounded Ma Xuan. Maybe the prisoner knew the culprits, or maybe he assisted them, set the firing device with his own hands. But Hai knew the Viet Cong might have planted the trap, knew the wounds inflicted on his mother might have been intended for Americans. He said to the prisoner, "*Ve nha, ve nha*" (Go home). He used the phrase Cadre Duc taught every villager: "*My nguy, de quoc my cut di*" (Fake American, imperialist, go away). Hai ran ahead to Qui's buffalo, tugged the reins, and ordered the animal to halt. Two blankets tucked in a reed mat were strapped to the beast's spine. Hai grabbed them, patted the rump, and the lead buffalo, snorting quick breaths through his nostrils, resumed his pace.

No grief yet. The moments when Hai felt anything he felt helplessness or rage, a rage that was huge, that longed for a sky to reside in, or a black mountain, a pyramid that altered the horizon. Starlight blurred through openings of clouds. He saw *Nui Ba Den*, the conical shape that once reminded him of a breast, but now the shape meant little, and he pictured the mountainside marred by craters, giant rocks and trees split open, deep hollows strewn with arms, legs, paws—animal and human. He asked himself if only the Vietnamese and their beasts would die here, or would the enemy also bleed, surrender last breaths? Hai had never seen a woman or girl day ghost. Maybe the mothers and sisters and grandmas of American soldiers remained at home, in their ancestral villages. If Ma Xuan died far from Cu Chi, Hai might persuade the grandfathers to kill the prisoner, bury his body far from his village. *Bury him in Viet Nam*, thought the boy, *bury him near a mountain. Bury him so deeply none of his comrades will find his bones.*

He barely noticed Thien as he passed within two meters of her and the elephant. He whispered to the prisoner, "*Co le anh chet som*" (Maybe you'll die soon), then climbed into the cart with Ba Ly and Ma Xuan and his sister. Mother and daughter lay on their sides, face-to-face, and Nhi stroked her mother's hair. Hai draped them with the thickest blanket. He reached for the other blanket, but the prisoner hissed and snarled and repeated a word the boy understood: "No, no, no."

"One blanket's enough," said Ma Xuan. "But I need water."

Hai touched his mother's arm and said, "Not now, Ma, I'm sorry. Maybe you can get some sleep."

Sleep would come soon enough. She coughed, swallowed, tasted blood on her tongue. "You can marry Le Minh Thien," she said. "You already have permission."

"Ma?"

"I spoke with Ba Ly and Ong Quan several months ago, but we kept our meeting a secret."

Hai's mouth opened.

"You were impatient," she said, "and Thien was not ready for a husband. We decided that you should wait at least one year, that it was best not to tell you." She coughed, again tasted her blood. "But to wait three years would be wrong and I cannot let this happen." She glanced at Ba Ly. "You will agree," she said, "that the wedding must happen soon."

Hai leaned over her. He wanted to say, "You'll live, Ma, you'll survive this and much more," but she'd made her decision. She believed she would die, and if she breathed her last before Hai took a wife, tradition required that he wait three years before he married. Ma Xuan's last wish was for her son to marry, to welcome a daughter-in-law into her family. Hai rubbed his eyes as though to clear them. *Le Minh Thien his wife, his mother dying?* The juxtaposition, the cause and effect, stunned him. He could not believe his mother was almost dead.

Before first light the caravan reached five abandoned huts and a functional well on the northeast side of Black Virgin Mountain. The two villagers who had watches reported the same time—4:55 a.m. Ba Ly, eighty-three-years old, spoke to Ong Quan and Ong Truong: "Let us stop here, let us catch our breath. We can make this our home until we are driven somewhere else."

The old men conferred briefly and agreed. "But be careful where you walk," said Ong Truong. "We must check that the area is safe."

As peasants led their animals to a shelter of tall bamboo, Hai and Nam reconnoitered huts. Lighting their way with candles, the boys passed through one-room homes where they found rancid sacks of rice and corn, hammocks strung from beams, a few rusty tools. In one hut there was a low shelf, an altar, the seed and shriveled skin of a mango—no fruit. Hai and Nam looked at framed photographs, the ancestors of the family that once lived here. "Dead," said Hai, "or in prison. They wouldn't move to a new home without taking their pictures." A photograph of a man—his jaw-line stiff and strained, his eyes narrow—reminded Hai of his father. He said, "Wish *cha* were here for the wedding," and Nam said, "Wedding?" Hai held up the picture of the father. "*My* wedding," he said, "*my* wedding." He nudged his cousin's arm. "Le Minh Thien is about to be my wife."

Nam crowed like a rooster. "Sing a song," he said. "Sing a wedding song."

"I don't know one."

"You can make one up. Come on."

Hai shook his head.

"Thien's very pretty," said Nam. "Do you love her?"

Hai struggled to breathe. *Yes*, he thought, *too much, but you don't need to know.* "I remember a wedding song," he said. "I remember a song I learned from Ong Quan."

"Sing it."

"Can you sing with me?" said Hai. "Can you help me?"

"Cousin, I don't know the song."

Hai's lips quivered. "Ong Quan sings in a deep voice. I can't sing this way."

"Then sing like a happy rooster. Sing like a groom."

Hai, in the light of candles, leaned toward his cousin, lifted his face, and sang loud to quell his fear.

Rain on a wedding day brings good luck.
The bride walks in a rice field, her hair black as crows.
The groom follows for nine paces, then stoops and digs with
                    his hands.
Beneath her last footprint—treasure!
Roots, seedlings, bones, the blood of rain.
The bride and the groom have ripened the field.

Nam whistled and swooned. "You're in love, Luu Hai's in love." He patted his cousin's shoulder. "That is a beautiful song."

Hai, because he was shy, because Thien was too much now, said, "Follow me," and the search continued. They found more photographs of ancestors on dusty altars. They found baskets, bowls, pots, pans, rancid cooking oil. In three of the huts they discovered openings in the earth, mouths of tunnels. Two of them were hidden beneath straw mats; the third reminded Hai of the tunnel opening of his ancestral home, the slit in the earth that he and his father had dug behind the fire pit and cookstove. The entrance was narrow, barely wide enough for a child's body. Kneeling, exploring with his hands the circumference of the opening, he wondered if Thien would be able to squeeze her hips through. *I may need to widen it*, he thought proudly. *I may need to bend down and scratch out two hundred more handfuls of earth.*

The boys burrowed through tunnels and discovered passages that intersected. In one place, the tunnel complex widened into a long room ample enough to shelter the peasants and small animals. No tunnel could withstand the direct hit of a bomb that weighed three hundred kilos, but the A-shaped beams—if reinforced—might withstand whatever the enemy dropped near the edges of the new village. "We might get lucky," Hai whispered. "The Americans might not know anyone lives here." He assumed those who constructed the tunnels, the thatch huts, had been murdered. Or else placed in an American compound, a pen of concrete and barbed wire. Trucked away and imprisoned before they could gather their photographs and keep them from harm.

The boys crawled up through the tunnels and reported their discoveries to Ong Quan and Ong Truong. "No food," said Hai, "nothing. But there's a large room that will shelter us if the Americans send their war planes." He explained that one of the tunnel openings might need to be widened to accommodate certain peasants. "And I wonder about a shelter for the large animals," he said, "a shelter built over a crater." He moved his hands. "A bamboo roof," he said, "a layer of thatch. Sandbags." With spurts of language, with quick hands that suggested shapes, he tried to transform an idea into a shared image. "Yes," said Ong Quan, "all the animals need protection. The only question is what kind of shelter would be easiest to build."

A crater near one of the huts spanned thirty meters across. Circling around it, Hai began constructing in his mind a shelter of bamboo poles, palm fronds, a small mountain of sandbags. *The animals will be safe*, he thought. *They will have a place in the earth when the enemy begins bombing.* He widened his circle, walked clockwise around the crater and the five huts, and he prayed in silence the first prayer he learned from his mother: *May our ancestors be happy, our village protected.* He passed Thien and the elephant, smiled to the girl, glared at the prisoner, and climbed into the cart to be near Ma Xuan and his sister. In the first strong light, Hai saw his mother's death color, her paleness, the blood smeared on her lower lip. He began to tell her about the shelter for the animals, but she shushed him. "Today," Ma whispered. "You will get married today."

26
Prison

His captors gave him water, then tied him to a tree. Leaves the size of large hands shaded Antonio Lucio. He strained against the trunk, no give. Thick strands of rope hugged his waist, chafed his wrists. He recognized one of his captors, the buffalo boy he first saw before the Cambodian invasion. It seemed centuries had passed, millenniums. "Hey," he said, "where's your buffalo? What happened to your buffalo?" He remembered a boy who petted a great bull, who let the beast slobber on his hands. A boy who smelled his hands as though to glean information. From his tree prison Conchola saw three average-sized buffalo, but the bull he'd seen before the Cambodian invasion was enormous, a close cousin to the elephant. "Hey," he said, "go find your buffalo. Give me a ride on your buffalo."

The boy, his voice quick as sparks, said something incomprehensible.

"Yeah, sounds good," said Conchola. "Go get your buffalo and give me a ride."

Hai brooded. The American prisoner was familiar. Nearly a month ago, he had walked along the riverbank near Hai's ancestral home and tossed stones in the water. After his child's play, he smiled at Hai and Great Joy, but what did he want? A day ghost, an invader, could only destroy things. It seemed that an American loved nothing more than to bomb and blaze every last inch of earth.

Conchola said, "That buffalo was beautiful, man, a prize-winner. I crown him King of the County Fair."

The boy walked to the nearest cart to help with the unloading. Conchola felt a dull knot of pain at the base of his skull. The small cuts on his left hand throbbed slightly; the bandage needed changing. He thought of the tiger, the dignity with which he carried his wounds, and he thought of Billie, his body torn, his eyes blown away, the sockets empty. He pictured Sara Peters, her white fingers loosening the rope that bound him to a tree. For a short time he slumped against the trunk, eyes closed. He heard the voices of old men, authoritative, precise. He heard peasants unloading carts, whispering to each other, a single groan from the dying woman. He opened his eyes and watched three boys and a girl carry the wounded Mama-san to one of the huts. *Pobrecita*, he thought, *dead by noon. Never see the light of another day*.

Once the bull buffalo's cart was unloaded except for the rice plants, a dozen villagers climbed into the cart and a buffalo boy steered the animal to a small shade tree near a field. The rains had drenched the field thoroughly. Peasants piled out of the cart, squatted side-by-side, pulled weeds, placed the unwanted plants in gunnysacks strapped to their shoulders. *Campesinos*, thought Conchola, *migrant workers. Turn weeds into compost*. After clearing a small section, preparing it for planting, they unloaded baskets of rice from the cart. In silence they arranged themselves in a row. Each farmer took one plant at a time, settled the roots in the earth, reached for another. Stooped over in the field, they resembled insects, a swarm of insects planting instead of chewing. A wave of locusts moving in unison, one smooth line, dotting this field with a band of green.

The adjacent field was useless. A few strips of grass seared by sun, cratered. Two boys began repairing a dike, shoveling dirt into an opening. Fifty meters away, in a clearing, peasants worked with hoes and shovels, plied the earth into small mounds, seedbeds. A few meters from their plot, three women chopped down stalks of bamboo at the verge of a forest. Near Conchola's tree prison, boys shinnied up coconut palms, severed broad leaves with whacks of machetes. Girls carried fallen palm leaves to a sunlit bund, spread them out, apparently so the leaves would dry. Two buffalo boys led the smallest adult buffalo to the edge of the forest. They filled the animal's cart with the bamboo the women had cut, then guided the beast to a bomb crater near one of the huts. Two old men stood side-by-side, occasionally gesturing, giving instructions. The buffalo boys unloaded the cart, piled the bamboo beside the crater. *Maybe the peasants would build a shelter*, thought Conchola, *a wide roof over the crater*. The buffalo boys began digging a slope on one edge of the hole, maybe so the peasants—old and young— could ease their way in, walk down a sort of ramp and into the shelter the moment they heard planes.

Rice birds alighted on the planted field, then flew off squawking when boys tossed stones in their direction. Everyone had a job, it seemed, everyone but Conchola and the dying woman. *But dying's a job*, he thought, *trabajo duro, and maybe I too am dying*. He wished the peasants would bring him something to eat. He closed his eyes, daydreamed, and after a time he smelled fresh food, wood smoke. A wisp of cloud rose from the hut that sheltered the dying woman. Conchola smelled rice, fish sauce, and other foods that were indefinable. "*Oye*," he said, "*ayúdame*." Maybe a peasant girl would bring him something to eat.

He pulled at his restraints, still no give. A bird perched on the branch straight above him. Bright yellow feathers, white face. Work crews began to gather in the shade near one of the huts. A few minutes later they were squatting with bowls and chopsticks, the boys and old men shoving rice and greens in their mouths, the girls eating delicately, as though they might offend the food with sharp teeth, wet tongues. Conchola bobbed his head and grinned. "Hey," he called, "VC number one. *Número uno*." He was surprised they hadn't gagged him, decided he shouldn't talk too much or maybe they would. In the shade of tall trees, the peasants appeared relaxed, almost festive. Conchola opened his mouth, made chewing motions. "Hungry," he said, "*hambre*. VC number one."

His back against the tree, his head slumped, he dozed and dreamed of food. Burritos, steak burritos, his Mama's *enchiladas y tapas y chile rellenos*. The taste of blood in his mouth, the flesh of a cow. *Un tigre, un fiera* might refuse this for it was soft, might weaken the body. The medic dreamed, his head throbbed, and he felt his hunger as a clawed thing, an animal that moved inside him and begged to be fed. It seemed that his body sheltered claws, tentacles, fangs, feelers. And they would protest, use their weapons against their host, until they were given their share of food.

He woke to the smells of smoke, fish sauce. The old woman, the black-toothed elder, stood before him with a small bowl and a spoon heaped with rice. "*An*," she said, and raised the spoon to his gaping mouth. Children gathered to watch the foreigner eat. They giggled, mixed their few words of English with Vietnamese: "You, you! GI *di dau*? GI *buon qua*. Sad GI? *Tai sao*? Why alone?" The black-toothed elder said something and two girls scampered to the nearest hut. A few minutes later the elder was serving Conchola tea, lifting a chipped cup to his lips. He sucked noisily, stared at Grandma-san's open mouth. Three front teeth looked like they'd been lacquered, painted black. Her tongue—like a small red snake moist with blood—lopped over her lower lip. He let her feed him more tea, then leaned back and swallowed. Her rucked face resembled a crumbling wall, the paint cracked and splintered, the surface bunched in places, a scrabble of grooves and ridges, small rises and valleys. Spokes of sun cut between branches, lit her open mouth and one side of her forehead. Sunlight. Wound. Red tongue. Her mouth seemed to be chewing itself, bleeding. As she leaned forward, fed him the last of the tea, sunlight drenched her face.

She drew back and the children scattered. She approached two old men who squatted in front of the hut that sheltered the dying woman. Black Teeth pointed to the prisoner, then to a field beyond the huts, a small path that snaked farther west. She made a sweeping gesture with her arms that Conchola translated as, "Take him away, take him away." She was obviously the matriarch, but she needed the approval of old men to determine his fate. "*Soy inocente*," said Conchola, "*de veras*. Innocent as the bombed fields."

The oldest man said something and two boys came forward. The first, a soldier boy about four-feet tall, carried a rifle; the other, the Cu Chi buffalo boy, carried a coil of rope and an unsheathed knife. Soldier boy stopped ten meters from Conchola's tree, squatted in the shade, the butt of his rifle on the ground, the barrel angled between his thighs, taller than his hunched body. Buffalo boy kept coming, lips jerking, maybe smiling, maybe twitching with tension. "Yeah, *chingate*," said Conchola. "You piss me off...I kick your nuts in." The prisoner aped and showed his teeth and wagged his head for buffalo boy and soldier boy and Black Teeth and the old men and the passel of peasants who watched from a distance. Buffalo boy inched closer with his rope, his knife. Then another, a third boy, skirted past soldier boy, took the coil of rope from buffalo boy's hands, looped one end around the tree trunk, the other end around Conchola. The boy was smiling, glancing at the prisoner and smiling. *Yeah, I get it*, thought Conchola, *soy peligroso. Dangerous. Two ropes 'round my waist serve better than one. But why not three ropes? Why not nail me to the tree? I won't escape if the nails are long.*

He felt a stream of urine soaking his pants, his crotch, trickling down his thighs. He thought of Mundo, the way the tiger would spray a tree, claim territory, but Conchola claimed nothing substantial, only fear. The buffalo boy stepped behind him and he heard the whine of a knife blade severe a length of rope. Then two boys, one at each elbow, led him to a patch of shade.

He looked down at the new rope around his waist. They'd

kept his hands tied but they'd lengthened his leash, given him slack, slung a new rope around his middle, cut away the old rope that had pressed his back to the tree. One of the boys giggled and pointed at his piss-soaked pants. "Yeah, beautiful," said Conchola, "real funny. How much shit do you pile in your pants when bombs are falling on your head?"

Stooped over, the black-toothed elder moved her hands in front of her as though to smooth the air. Buffalo boy said, "*Ngu, ngu*," tilted his head, and placed his hands beneath one side of his face. Conchola was too dazed to decipher simple gestures. No message communicated until the boy lay in the grass, turned onto his side, and used his hands as a pillow. "Mercy," said Conchola, "let me sleep awhile. Jesus mercy." He sank to his knees, swayed, then toppled on his side. He hadn't anticipated how clumsy it would be to go from standing to lying down with his hands behind him, his arms useless. He moaned, curled reflexively in a ball, his knees near his chest. *Dios mío* he was tired, so tired he could barely breathe, pull the air into his body. He wondered if the animals, after being bombed or pursued, sometimes experienced this level of tiredness. His limbs ached; he could feel the wiring, the nerves, the reluctant movement of blood. *Lupe*, he prayed, *Virgen de Guadalupe*. The black-toothed elder came to him and covered his hips and chest with a blanket. A long, thin rag the color of ash.

27
Prayers

Ma Xuan watched her daughter arrange the altar. Before pictures of her grandparents, Nhi placed a candle, three joss sticks, warm tea in white cups, cooked rice, and a large bowl of mangos and bananas. Ba Ly squatted near the reed mat on which Ma Xuan rested. The wounded woman listened to Ba's talk, first about the wedding that would happen at nine o'clock, two hours earlier than usual, and then about the plan—the only possibility—to save Ma Xuan from dying. "We'll carry you some distance from here and leave you in a field with the prisoner. He'll stay with you, we'll tie him, and soon the pilot of a plane or helicopter will see his uniform." She held Ma's hands. "With luck, a helicopter will take both of you to Cu Chi where there are doctors, medicine." She rubbed the hands to bring warmth. "You must live long enough to see your grandchild, yes? You know where to find us once the doctors heal your wounds."

Ma Xuan shook her head.

"You must cooperate," said Ba. "Remember when the Cu Chi doctors saved Cadre Tu?"

"I don't care."

"You *will* care," said Ba. "After the wedding, after you accept my granddaughter into your family, you will go away."

Nhi lit the joss sticks and the candle. Hai came into the hut and bowed three times before the altar. The boy had not yet been told of the plan to save his mother. Ba Ly, the initiator, let him pray for a minute, then called him aside and spoke to him in whispers. His eyes bulged; he questioned her judgment in silence. Hai had no right to protest the decision of an elder. Ba must have already discussed the plan with the grandfathers and received their approval. "We may fail," she said, "but this is your mother's only chance."

And maybe it was. Left to lie in this hut, Ma Xuan would not see another morning. "I wonder," said Hai, "if the grandfathers have any other ideas. Has Ma been told?"

"Yes, she's been told," said Ba. "But her pain makes it difficult for her to know what is best."

Hai went to his mother. He bowed, leaned over her, and wiped the blood from the edges of her lips. In the far corner, Nam's mother and Hai's Aunt Hoa prepared a wedding feast. A small fire burned; the hut smelled of grilled corn, sticky rice, coconut milk, boiled peanuts. The feast would be simple, and Ma Xuan—since she could not be given food—would be taken away as soon as her son married. She said to Hai: "Do you know what to do? Do you remember your responsibilities before the wedding?"

The boy nodded, though his mind was on death rather than marriage.

"Before our family receives a daughter-in-law," said Ma, "we must compensate Thien's family with gifts."

Hai wondered what could be given. Perhaps a rooster, a few hens, a mother duck and her ducklings, a small sack of rice. Since the villagers shared their belongings, the gifts would be symbolic. "I'll give the duck and the ducklings," he said. "Maybe a few hens."

"And the rooster," said Ma Xuan. "And some money."

Hai brushed a hand over her forearm. *Money?* he thought. *Whose?*

"Look for a vase," she said. "A small vase wrapped in brown cloth, the money rolled inside it."

He nodded.

"We don't have much," she added. "Put it in a clean box and present it to Ba Ly."

The boy bowed to her and left.

Village girls searched for wedding flowers. They wanted red ones, but they picked what was available: yellow flowers with wilted petals, cup-shaped blue flowers, pink flowers that hung upside-down from desiccated branches. They stayed beneath trees, avoided the fields and clearings where they might be spotted by the enemy. Helicopters flew over the summit of Black Virgin Mountain. They heard artillery, shells falling to the west, and two spotter planes flew over nearby fields and hedgerows. Tuyen found a small red flower and whispered to the other girls, "Over here, come!" The girls combed through the grass and brush beneath a teak tree, but found only two other red flowers—hibiscus. Ba Ly had instructed them to gather wedding flowers, red ones. Now they bunched together their scavenged flowers to form an inauspicious bouquet. "Not enough," said Tuyen. "We need to find more red."

Conchola watched them. They looked like kids on a picnic, kids with nothing better to do than flick their shadow-like bodies under the trees to search for flowers. One girl, as she lifted a red flower near her eyes, surprised him with her beauty. She had come to within ten meters of where he lay. She glided, made little noise, her eyes as bright and pure as her red flower. At first she seemed out of place, a hint of light in tree shade, a light that might still be seen in the middle of the night, no moon or stars for guidance. Conchola, remembering, muttered to himself, *"Mundo, el tigre."* He smelled peanuts and corn; his mouth watered. *Guadalupe,* he thought, *life is simple.* His own mother would be content to build a fire, cook food, make gardens, and search the dark for flowers.

He wanted the flower girl to notice him. *"Oye,"* he said, *"chiquita.* You have the eyes of a beast."

The pretty one glided through shade, receded, disappeared.

A three-person work party softened the soil near a mango tree. A woman about the age of Conchola's mother set down her hoe, squatted, and scooped handfuls of soil into her palms. Head bent, she sniffed her findings, cackled as she sprinkled soil on bare feet. The other laborers, maybe her son and daughter, kept slicing the earth with hoes. She spoke to them in a singsong whisper, sniffed the soil again. Picked up her hoe and plied the earth.

Conchola rolled over when he heard something approaching from behind. A giant pig chewing on a root, snuffling her snout in wet earth. Her litter of piglets, whining and snorting, groped for her breasts. Mother pig jerked her head, tore another root. Still chewing, she thumped on her side, let her piglets topple over her, clamber their way to her milk-swollen breasts.

Soon she slept in a rain-soaked patch of earth. She seemed oblivious both to the flies buzzing her open maw and to her *cerditos*, her piglets bunkered beside her nipples, most of them asleep, a few still suckling her body. Conchola wished he could root his way among them, sip pig milk. Feel the press of other bodies against his own. For too long he had not touched another being except to touch wounds. *La soledad, el anhelo.* The tiger would never feel this sort of angst.

The Cu Chi buffalo boy, arms cradled in his lap, squatted in the grass near a hut. Eyes closed, lips moving, he seemed to be repeating prayers. Conchola's Mama prayed this way, her mouth full and dark, her lips parting and closing over names: "*San Jude, Virgen de Guadalupe, María La Madre de Jesús, bendíganos.*" The boy probably prayed for the soul of the dying woman, or prayed that his people and animals be spared a day of bombing. Peasant prayers would be dark, *primitivo*. Tooth and claw prayers, buffalo prayers. Rain prayers for the newly planted rice. Storm prayers to send American planes back to their bases, postpone American air strikes. Conchola had never been this tired without being able to sleep. He watched the boy bow, lift his hands, then shake them three times. The movement reminded him of a baptism, of hands that hold grace. A priest's hands that anoint, bless, invite a new being into a circle. *Yeah, keep it up*, thought Conchola, *continua. And put in a word for me, baby-san. If you know a prayer with claws.*

The bull buffalo cropped the grass beneath a shade tree. The girl who cared for the elephant, the one who might have set the trap that killed Billie, walked out of a hut in a white dress. A simple thing, immaculate, a dress that covered her from neck to ankle. She looked toward the hut where the Cu Chi buffalo boy still prayed. Lips moving, he bowed again, made that quick motion with his hands that reminded the prisoner of a baptism. *Prisa*, thought Conchola, *baptize me with rain prayers, buffalo prayers. A tigrito prayer if you have one.* He imagined showing off scars and tattoos, claw marks and rosary beads, somehow explaining their origins. But who would believe him? Who would listen well enough to find meanings beyond the words? *Only Billie*, he thought, *if he's lucky now, knows the truth is more than what happens. The tiger clawed me, or in some way touched me. A powerful wound always remains a mystery. Teeth. Claws. Tree light. Many things other than metal rip the surface of the skin.*

Then day stars, black-armed stars east of *Nui Ba Den*. As they angled down the mountainside, Luu Hai opened his eyes and called, "*May bay, may bay chuon choun*" (helicopters). Children ducked into huts or into the shade of trees. Peasants came in from the plot of *ma* rice, and Hai's cousin Nam scuttled down a tamarind tree where he'd failed his task of surveillance. The helicopters fanned out over the fields several kilometers to the east. Ong Quan said, "They're gone now, come on. Let's have our wedding while we can."

Thien stood in the doorway of her hut in her white dress. Hai spotted her, gaped, grabbed clean clothes from a basket, and hurried to the canal to bathe. *Wedding*, he told himself, *wedding*. The girls and elders had bathed in the early morning before the sun rose.

Hai set his clean clothes on a log, stripped naked, and waded in waist-deep. No soap, no shampoo, he dug up handfuls of dirt from the bottom. He smeared dirt over his armpits, his crotch, and then rubbed himself clean. Other village boys bathed in the soupy mush. Nam and Qui, armed with rifles, patrolled a fifty-meter path between the huts and the canal. Hai scanned the near and far sky for planes, helicopters, rain clouds. The sky was a brilliant blue with stacks of white clouds. His wedding would not be blessed by rain, but it would be blessed if the enemy bombed elsewhere. He saw that Nam and Qui also watched the sky. *Yes*, he thought, *keep watching, keep listening. Don't rest for a minute. Please keep our village safe.*

Hai ducked down and swam underwater. He came up near the bank, stood and walked ashore, dried himself, and slipped into clean pants. His friends were before him, the boys he loved most: Nam, his dear cousin, and Qui, taller and wider than Nam, as stout as a young buffalo. Boys with rifles, who could they save? Hai ran wet hands through his hair and thought, *My friends are on guard; Ma is dying; Miss Thien is dressed for a wedding.* He bit his lower lip and glared at the sun. The boy was aware for the first time that he had little or no control over anything in the world.

Soon everyone donned fresh clothes and awaited the wedding. The peasants joined Hai and the grandfathers in the shade of the tamarind, the lookout tree. The children stared at the prisoner sitting on the ground with his legs stretched in front of him. He was tied to a small tree some twenty paces from the hut that housed Ma Xuan.

Qui, who would miss the processions and ceremony, climbed to the high branches of the tamarind, and Nam, his rifle ready, walked back and forth between the huts and the canal. The two would watch and listen for signs of intrusion:

day ghost patrols, the sound of a jeep or a truck, the low roar of a tank, the thup-thup of choppers, the higher-pitched whine of planes, the clatter of machinery. Nam, dizzy with fatigue, rubbed his eyes and then opened them. North of the canal, abandoned farmland lay between bombed forests, but many trees had survived, mostly tamarind and coconut palm, and thick stands of bamboo and mango grew near the paddy where the peasants had planted *ma* rice. Nam had to watch the open land and the fringes of forests, and he also had to watch the prisoner, make sure he didn't somehow free himself. As the peasants filed into the hut of Ma Xuan, the American started jabbering. Nam said, "*Im mieng*" (Shut up), but the prisoner's voice grew louder. After Nam raised his rifle and repeated, "*Im mieng, im mieng*," the stranger quieted, head tilted slightly, mouth open in a grin.

Conchola peered through the window and doorway of the hut. It seemed the peasants had gathered to decide his fate, and maybe he would inspire their sympathy by facing them directly. He would not ask to be saved, but he would sit with dignity on the earth, smile and bow, sometimes nod, assume an attitude of harmless innocence. By now they knew he could do nothing as a medic. The wounded one would die, but he had not set the trap or triggered the device, had not brought on her slow and terrible suffering. They'd found him unarmed, alone, equipped with medical supplies, and most likely assumed he was lost. He did not believe they would free him, but maybe they would let him live long enough to find some means of escape. Light filled their window: a lone candle, red flowers, spots of pink, blue, yellow. He heard the voice of an old man, the voice of a child, then silence. He rose to his knees, but couldn't see much. Only the backs of heads and shoulders, grayish clothes, a single flame, the light of flowers.

The buffalo boy came out of the hut followed by five boys and a girl. Each boy carried a chicken or duck, wrapped a hand around its feet. A hen squawked, tried to flap her wings, then settled in the claw-like grip that held her. The girl-child carried a small red box near her chest. Except for the dying woman, it seemed the entire village now filed from the hut and formed a procession. They moved past two huts, paused under a tree, then stopped before a third where the black-toothed elder stood in the doorway. The buffalo boy said something that sounded like a question. The elder nodded, stepped back from the entryway, and the villagers crammed their way inside.

A rooster shrieked. The elephant, under a tree near the canal, tore at twigs, leaves, branches. Conchola looked at the sky, no planes or choppers. *Nada.* If the Americans roared in with planes, the peasants would scatter, have no time to kill him. He lay on the ground again, exhausted. The bombs might kill him first, might kill no one else. Or a single ray of shrapnel might cut through the rope that bound him to a tree.

Curled on his side, he saw the buffalo boy and the girl in the white dress leave the hut. The black-toothed elder followed, caught up with the girl, and the hut emptied of people. They walked back to the first hut and again pushed their way inside. For a time Conchola looked at the flowers in the window, the lighted candle. Groaning, he stretched his legs, rolled onto his back and observed the sky. Lots of blue, a few mountains of white cloud. A good day for bombing. He heard Black Teeth giving a speech, a drone that went on for nearly a minute. Then an old man, a briefer speech, his tone congratulatory, cheerful. Eyes closed, Conchola strained against his bindings. The rope that secured his hands cut into him, burned his wrists. Small welts, *sin gravedad*. The sad markings a teenage boy might give himself by holding a burning cigarette to the inner sides of his wrists.

Ma Xuan held her daughter-in-law's hand. She reminded Thien to be loyal, to dedicate herself to her husband and her husband's family. She wouldn't let herself cry, but her eyes moistened when she squeezed Thien's hand and prayed silently: "May you live a long life, may you survive and have children." She reminded Thien of the importance of veneration, the need to honor the ancestors and receive their guidance. "My son and daughter are tired of hearing this," she said, "but it is my duty to remind them." She attempted a smile. "Ba Ly has taught you well, you already know. I have faith that you will be the best daughter-in-law my family could have."

The peasants munched rice and corn seasoned with fish sauce and lemon. Ba Ly had Nhi prepare a bowl of food for the prisoner, and she herself brought him the offering. Ba found the American on his back, eyes glazed, staring at nothing. She whacked the chopsticks on the rim of the bowl. Gasping, twitching, he gaped at her with the stunned eyes of a small animal caught in a beam of light.

"*Xin moi an,*" she said, and he rose shakily to his knees. She chopsticked rice into his wide mouth, then bits of corn. He chomped, chewed, his warm wet mouth slurping and smacking. The Americans always made noise, so most likely even their girl-children ate without manners. When the bowl was empty, Ba Ly fetched another. "Mai," she said to one of the village girls, "bring a hot glass of tea once he finishes his meal."

Their eyes were not unkind. After the elder fed him a second bowl of rice and corn, a girl held a glass of tea to his lips. He drank greedily, drained the offering in seconds, and she hurried back toward the hut where the peasants gathered. Soon a younger girl brought a pot of tea, a tall glass, and Conchola sipped this tea politely. The girl was beautiful. She looked up at him, studied his face, almost touched him. Kneeling, Conchola was still several inches taller. "*Bella,*" he whispered, "baby-san pretty." The sound of his voice must have amazed her. She blinked, her mouth opened, and for several moments she seemed to stop breathing. "Relax," said Conchola, "I'm tied to a tree. *Prisionero.*" He shrugged, grinned; her mouth opened wider. She leaned forward, then back, and gave him a lovely open-mouthed smile before she handed the pot and glass to the old woman and ran laughing toward the huts.

The elder bowed to Conchola and spoke quietly for what seemed a long time. He only understood her tone— supplication, dignified begging. He had no idea what he could offer. Maybe she was so desperate she believed he could save the dying woman, and maybe her delusion was his chance for freedom. If the peasants untied him, freed his limbs, he might scamper away before they killed him. He'd spotted four rifles, a few knives. No other weapons. He nodded and said, "Yeah, Grandma-san, all we need is a miracle." She bowed to him three times and he bowed back. "Whatever you say," he whispered, "as soon as you cut me loose."

The Grandma-san called out and three boys came to her. One of them was the buffalo boy; the other two had rifles. The buffalo boy untied the rope from the tree trunk. "Yeah, keep it up," said Conchola. "Next you can free my hands."

Four boys came out of the hut carrying the wounded woman in a hammock. "Over here," said Conchola. "Lay her down where I can help her." He glimpsed her pained face, twisted mouth, squinched eyes. If they freed him he wouldn't relieve her pain because morphine might finish her, slow her breathing. Mama was beyond help, nearly dead. But he needed her to live long enough to allow his chance of escape.

Grandma-san, the buffalo boy, and two rifle boys surrounded him. The old woman had his aid bag strapped over her shoulder; the buffalo boy carried the medic's rucksack. Conchola wasn't anchored to the tree now, but his hands were still tied, they kept the rope around his waist, and now Grandma-san pulled the rope, jerked him like a puppet. The prisoner was led along the edge of a newly planted paddy, then over a weed-infested field. Grandma-san walked point, the rifle boys flanked Conchola, and the buffalo boy and hammock bearers came last. He forced himself not to plead for his life. They wouldn't understand whatever truth he could tell, and the pleading tone might annoy them, put the last nails in his coffin. The sun beat down, blinded him; he couldn't wipe the sweat from his eyes. They passed through hedgerows, fields, small forests. When they stopped in a dry paddy he said, "Yeah, you can cut me loose here," but the buffalo boy dropped the rucksack and tied him to another tree.

A sapling six-feet tall, heart-shaped leaves. Maybe small enough so he could out-muscle it, wrench it up by its roots. The hammock bearers lay the wounded woman in the bowl of shade beneath the tree. Grandma-san whispered to Conchola, bowed to him, left him his aid bag (the zippers open), and a few ounces of water. The boys followed her over the dry paddy and disappeared in a tree line. Conchola could feel them watching him, but why? Was this a test of his strength, his will? Should he break the tree in half? Wrench it up by its roots? Deserve his life? He strained against the trunk, slight give. Even if he tore the tree from the earth, then what? He'd still be bound to it, would have to move with it, drag it over the fields, leave a trail behind him the width of a broken tree.

Heat. A sliver of shade. He lay down beside Mama, closed his eyes till he heard choppers. For a moment he looked at the sky. He rose and lurched toward light, screamed in Spanish and English, stood and screamed and pulled at his leash, bent the tree but couldn't break it. The choppers continued their flight, a smooth glide several kilometers to the west. As he watched them grow smaller and smaller, finally vanish, he knew why he was tied to a tree near the dying woman. Pray for a pilot to see an American, a soldier in uniform. And pray for the pilot to land his ship, rescue his stranded comrade. Maybe Black Teeth had fed him and bowed to him and given him tea so the wounded Mama might be taken aboard, flown to Cu Chi where someone might help her. *Desesperado*, he thought, *one last chance. La última.* The medic kept vigil as Mama's face began to soften, lose its edges. The dead usually wore an expression of release, the body finally free of tension. He thought she'd breathed her last, left him behind, but then he saw the slight rise and fall of her chest.

28
Rescue

His captors had left water in a white bowl. Conchola lowered himself, dipped his head, slurped like an animal. He understood the plea of the dying woman: "*Nuoc, nuoc*" (water). He slurped another mouthful, leaned over her, trickled water into a mouth that gaped like a young bird's. He gave her enough to wet her palate, no more. She might make it to surgery, might live that long. He left her and stood in the sunlight where he might be seen by those who patrolled the sky.

In the late morning, the American was still standing. A helicopter strafed a tree line to the east. Several others flew forward, and one of them touched down near Ma Xuan and the prisoner. Hidden amid trees, Qui and Hai and Ba Ly watched three day ghosts leap from the dragonfly, roll in the grass, run hunched over to their comrade. The roar of the fly's wings smothered the sounds of enemy voices. One man untied the prisoner's hands while another used a knife to severe the rope fastened around the sapling. Hai aimed his rifle as the third ghost, a red-faced knife-ghost, approached his mother from behind. The freed prisoner, trailing a strand of rope, came between the knife-ghost and Ma Xuan, whirled his arms, then pointed east, the opposite direction from the newly settled hamlet. In one swoop he lifted the hammock that held Hai's mother. Cradling her, he hurried to the dragonfly, lay her in its shell, and crawled in beside her. He raised his bandaged hand, again pointed east, shouted something to his comrades. The red-faced ghost tossed the prisoner's rucksack and aid bag on the floor of the chopper.

All the ghosts boarded, the chopper rose, and soon a stand of mangos to the east buckled with flames. Three dragonflies hovered, dipped their noses to fire rockets. It was all over in less than a minute. They left the earth burning and flew toward the sea.

In the chopper, shouting over the whir of the blades, Conchola told stories. "*Mala suerte, perdido.* Got separated from my squad; can't even remember how it happened." He held up his bandaged hand. "Barely a scratch," he said, "treat it myself. The problem's getting back to my unit." He leaned toward the red-faced gunner who had a mike, communications. "My squad got pinned down, then lifted out. A dozen gooks tracked me like bloodhounds, tied me to a tree. Don't know why they didn't shoot me." A quick breath, a pause. "Weird gooks, man, headed east. Running. Maybe we blew them away when we blew away those trees."

The gunner motioned with his head toward the dying woman.

"Yeah, don't worry," said Conchola. "Friendly as my own Mama."

"Yeah?"

"I swear to Jesus," he said. "Gooks leave me to fry and she sneaks out in that field with a bowl of water." He grinned, shook his head. "Tried to untie me, too, before she collapsed. She's near death's door, hit a trap or something. But she comes out in that field like she's on a mission to save my life."

The door-gunner looked at him for two or three seconds. "The bandage on your hand, man, it's been there a while."

"Yeah, an hour's a while," said Conchola. "A thing looks old when it's dirty."

The gunner bunched his lips. "Yeah, okay. Whatever. We got to call this in, make it official. What's your name, your rank?"

"PFC Manny Meléndez."

"And the gook here, she tried to help you?"

"That's a rog'."

"Can't just fly a gook to surgery. Not in our SOP."

"Ain't a gook," said Conchola. "Been through this."

"We can't—"

"Brought me water," he said, "tried to free me. Suck the wind out of your ears, man. How many times I got to tell you the same simple fucking facts?"

The gunner glared at him as he rearranged his mouthpiece, communicated the information to the crew chief. "Meléndez," he said, "PFC Manny Meléndez. Claims the gook's a friendly, tried to untie him, brought him water." His mouth twisted. "Affirmative, one messed up gook, barely breathing. Meléndez is in love or something. Seems to think we should fly her straight in for surgery in Cu Chi."

Meléndez. Conchola figured it would take a while before some clerk combed through the files and found no one named Manny Meléndez. Then again, if there was a Manny Meléndez, a name common enough, Conchola would be misidentified. He had thrown away his dog tags, his ID, so he could claim to be anyone to anyone who didn't know him. For the next few minutes or hours, he could be PFC Manny Meléndez. Later, at the chopper pad, searching for a bird going west, he could be Gertrudis Villanueva, one of his humdrum *compañeros* who probably still put in his shift as a security guard at the Beech Nut Baby Food Factory. For Conchola, it felt natural to switch names, take whatever name suited him. Geronimo was his jungle name. But he would never mention this to people too ignorant to have a clue.

Ma Xuan began inching her way toward the edge of the chopper. Conchola, at ease, had closed his eyes, but the doorgunner and two other grunts monitored her movements. One grunt nudged his friend and said, "Watch her fly. She's a jumper, hard-core airborne. I've seen this before."

The other grunt shook his head. "Negative," he said. "She just takin' in the view."

Ma Xuan used most of her remaining strength to raise her head. The paddies were mostly gone, riven with holes; few farmers remained to farm them. Three peasants worked a strip of *lua* rice, harvested a section of crops the bombs had spared. On the horizon one field remained, small and bright, the green of newly transplanted *ma* rice. She saw gravestones near a bund, four of them flanked by craters. She imagined what could not be seen: the graves that had been destroyed, the gravestones dispersed, strewn over the earth like handfuls of worthless pebbles. She thought of bodies torn in death and then torn again, the remains too fragmented to be recognized, reburied. Two buffalo grazed a dry paddy; a yellow dog walked a path that led to a village. The land was mostly destroyed, but there were three huts and a buffalo shed near a bamboo grove. She didn't know how her ancestral village would look from up this high. Maybe Ma Xuan was looking down on her birthplace, her home, the place where she spent her childhood, where she married and raised her children. She couldn't see anyone in or near the village, only the yellow dog walking the narrow pathway. The animal probably had no one to feed it, but would scavenge to stay alive. Ma Xuan rested, then raised her head higher. Six more gravestones in a field, a bomb crater filled with water. Maybe the bones of her ancestors lay beneath polished stones, in graves still unharmed.

Conchola crawled over the floor of the chopper and pulled at her waist. She moaned with pain as he turned her, dragged her back from the door and repositioned her on her side. "A long way down," he whispered. "You almost home, Mama, another few minutes." He glanced at two grunts who were watching. "A friendly," he said. "Tried to save my life. She makes it to surgery, she'll live to tell it." He paused, gave himself time to think. It was best to communicate with as few people as possible, avoid authorities altogether. "When we land," he said, "you can carry her in. I need to haul ass to the chopper pad. Okay?" He had to speak up, nearly shout, tell lies about the urgency of rejoining his unit. "Bad times," he said, "can't leave my buddies without a medic. Make my way back to them on the first ship west."

The two grunts were nudging each other, saying things he couldn't hear.

"You read me?" said Conchola. "My platoon's missing a medic, wandering around looking for PFC Manny Meléndez." He shrugged. "'Meléndez,' they'll say, 'where the fuck's Meléndez?' Nobody saw me get captured, all happened too fast." He rubbed his left forearm. "Mean little firefight," he said, "one of the worst. My buddies got choppered out, headed west." He licked his lips. "They'll join up with this other unit that's probably leaving Cu Chi in the next half hour."

One of the grunts cupped his hands and said something.

"Louder," said Conchola. "Can't hear you."

"I said, Good luck, man. You look like you seen some shit."

Conchola grinned.

A minute later he saw Mama-san wasn't breathing. She lay motionless, her face slack, her eyes empty. He turned her on her back, bent down, and breathed into her mouth three times. Five seconds, five long seconds feeling for a pulse at her neck. He pushed firmly on her chest, drummed her sternum. A few minutes later one of the grunts said, "She's gone, man, give her a rest." For fifteen counts Conchola worked her chest, her sternum, then breathed into her mouth. She wasn't with him, he could sense her indifference, the emptiness of the body. He should've stayed by her side, kept her from seeing what had happened to the fields. *Demasiado*, he thought, *too much at once. Lo siento*. He pumped her chest fifteen more times, breathed into her, felt her shape. Mama-san bones, frail sticks. Lengths of muscle that felt more like tendons. Crouched on all fours, he breathed into her fully. The softest thing inside her was his breath, his long exhale that stretched and widened, rounded her rib cage. He kept filling her, breathing deeply, and one of the grunts said, "Kissin' a gook, man, ruin your luck forever." Conchola looked into her eyes, warm and clear, shiny as flint. For a moment he thought he'd saved her, felt for a pulse at her neck. "Hang on," he whispered, "you're almost home, Mama. Almost." But she could not hear.

In Cu Chi two grunts carried her from the chopper. They set her down and one of them bent over and closed her eyes.

"Tell them she's friendly," said Conchola. "Deserves a decent burial. Okay?"

"Whatever."

"Promise," said Conchola. "Can you promise?"

One of the grunts tilted his head, seemed to be thinking.

"Fuck it," said Conchola, "fuck you guys." He tossed down his pack and his aid bag and went into the receiving room himself.

He explained the woman's death to an orderly who kept turning away, probably disturbed by the smell of sweat, urine. "Tried to save my life," said Conchola. "We can at least give her a decent burial."

"I'll pass the word."

"Promise," said Conchola. "I got to hear it."

"Well—"

Conchola stepped closer.

"Yeah, all right," said the orderly, "I promise. I'll take her to Graves and make sure they do their best."

Conchola heard one of the grunts behind him: "Should've closed her eyes first thing; bad luck when a dead dink sees you." The medic would have played with him, clawed his face, his throat, but a skirmish would draw attention, distract him from a more essential mission. He hurried out the door and toward the chopper strip, the grunt pad. The sun was almost straight up, something would be flying. He'd create a story, some bullshit about joining a new unit, needing to hitch a ride on a westbound chopper. Every day there was so much chaos, so much trouble, units being sent in every direction. With patience, feigned innocence, he would find out which unit was going where, board a chopper a few seconds before take-off. Cambodia. He wondered if there were still units in the jungles. Conchola was unarmed, but he had some medical supplies, and units always needed medics. He would shy away from platoon leaders, company commanders, glean his information from common grunts. Conchola could convince any grunt in the army he was a new member of their unit. If he said, "Hey, need another medic?" the grunt would reply, "Well's, a bear shit in the woods? Is the pope Catholic?" Conchola could ditch his new platoon as soon as they entered a hedgerow, a forest. Grasslands. Even in open paddies, broken fields, it was easy to disappear.

29
Field Animals

In the early morning, the sky still dark, Ong Quan walked near an unplanted field. Before the bull buffalo and the female buffalo dragged plows over the earth, there had to be water, a confined flood between rice bunds. He watched villagers dip buckets into a nearby irrigation ditch, shoulder the yokes, and move toward the dry paddy. This wedge of soil, once flooded and plowed, would be as pliant as a bowl of porridge. It would yield to hooves, human feet, rain, the first fingers of roots, the first seedlings. By harvest time the rice would be strong, the grains hard as wood chips. But in the beginning the land had to be coddled, nursed like an infant. Once water softened the soil, the bull buffalo and the female buffalo would plow and keep plowing until they dredged their way through warm slush that rose to their bellies. If rains did not come, the paddy had to be fed, suckled with water. A field ready for planting was no less strong and delicate than a human womb.

Ong Quan brought Hai to this field shortly after sunrise. Facing east, he said, "Where should we plant our rice? In this paddy and where else?"

The sun flared gold on puddles. Hai, his face happy and bright, said, "We can plant rice all the way across the fields, Ong. We can plant rice for as far as we can see."

Ong grunted. Tamarind trees edged the horizon some three hundred meters to the east. "A wide paddy land?" he said. "A wide glade of green? Is this what we need?"

Hai glanced at him. The old man's eyes, half closed, divulged nothing. "I don't know," said the boy. "Maybe we need to be more patient. Maybe we need to look around until we find the best soil."

Ong nodded toward the fields in front of them. "This is good soil," he said, "nothing wrong with it. The question is whether we want to plant all our rice in one large space."

Why not? thought Hai, but to answer grandfather's question with a question would be rude. "I'm not sure," he said. "Maybe we need to be more careful about where we plant."

Ong glared at him. "When will you wake up?" he said. "You're married now. You're a leader of this village."

"Yes, Ong."

"Why do we need each planted area to be small, separate from the others?"

Hai hesitated. "To hide?"

"Yes," said Ong. "If we plant all our paddies together, the day ghosts will bomb us as they did in Cu Chi."

Ong, eighty-one years old, bent over, still had strength in his bearing. Hai was taller, but beside the old man he felt feeble, awkward. "We'll have many small plots," said the boy. "Many rice paddies in different places."

"Do we have a choice?"

"No, Ong."

"The Americans have one fatal flaw," said the old man. "What is it?"

Hai was afraid to guess.

"They don't know us," said Ong. "They don't know our ancestors. They cannot defeat us any more than they can defeat the sun."

Ba Ly, squatting beneath a *sau* tree, removed dry threads from the outer husks of coconuts. She began braiding the threads, creating a spool of rope that would be strong enough to secure packages, lids of baskets, or to restrain a prisoner or small animal. For buffalo rope, more was needed, someone would find the rope tree—*cay may*. A rope made of *cay may* would restrain a bull buffalo, a wild animal. The rope that joined the buffalo to their carts and plows came from the fiber of this tree.

Hai and Qui caught frogs and snails near the canal. The frogs made choking sounds, tried to leap from nets, tangled their feet in netting. The clear brightness and darkness of their eyes reminded Hai of Nam's buffalo. He had little feeling for the snails, but the frogs saddened him. He silently apologized as he set each one in a sack that he fastened with a string made of coconut husk.

Ong Quan distracted them. "Over here," he said. "Let the girls catch frogs. You need to cut bamboo."

The grandfathers organized work parties. The tunnels beneath the settlement had to be lengthened, improved. New escape routes had to be dug, and the largest cavern where the peasants would hide from B-52s had to be strengthened to prevent collapse. A nearby bomb crater would be transformed into an emergency home for animals. The crater—30 meters wide—would accommodate the elephant and the remaining buffalo. The mother pig and her piglets would also be sheltered here during air strikes, and the peasants would take with them into the tunnels only the ducks and chickens. Under the guidance of Ong Quan and Ong Truong, several boys dug post-holes around the crater. A work party of girls cut away the low limbs of palms and lay them on the earth to dry.

The construction would take at least five days, during which the large animals would be especially vulnerable. Vast quantities of bamboo and palm had to be cut, the palm leaves dried in the sun before they could be woven into a roof. Ong Quan told three woodcutters what they already knew: "Take a little from each stand of bamboo, each stand of palms; never cut an entire section." In part, the work proceeded without supervision. Children as young as five years old swept and cleaned huts, carried supplies. Seeds were planted in small plots: pumpkin, lettuce, corn, tomato, pepper. While three girls hacked out a drainage furrow around the crater, two others worked on a ten-inch-wide water-path from the crater to the nearest paddy. Once the roof was in place, the layers of bamboo sandbagged and covered with palm leaves, studded with beams, the crater would stay dry during rainstorms. The shelter was a priority, for the peasants could not afford to lose more animals. They could not farm the land without the bull buffalo and the female buffalo. And the elephant, if they should have to move again, would be essential in carrying whatever supplies remained.

At noon, Hai and his cousin Nam and his friend Qui took a short break at the edge of a bamboo grove. Hai sang for his audience, his voice quieter than the wind in the leaves.

> *The crickets fold their black wings, asleep now.*
> *The sun, high and hot, presses water into steam.*

Nam said, "Who's high and hot?"

"What?"

"Who married Miss Thien?" said Nam. "Who's shooting steam? My cousin or the sun?"

Qui, after he and Nam stopped laughing, said, "Both."

Hai shuddered in the heat.

"Sing another one," said Nam. "A newlywed song."

Hai blushed.

Qui, consistently practical, said, "Rest now, save your energy. You can sing to your wife all night long."

Nam disagreed. "No, you need to practice your song. Sing to us in the day, your wife at night."

"Sing your own song."

"I don't know any," said Nam. "You're the one with the songs, you and Ong Quan."

Hai sucked a breath. His throat felt hot and swollen. "I know field songs," he said, "buffalo songs." His voice rose, shrill as a cricket's. "Ong Quan knows every song in the world."

"Ong would want us to work," said Qui.

"We've rested enough," said Hai.

"Come on," said Qui, "what are we doing? We can't cut bamboo with gossip and song."

Hai breathed a bit easier as he reached for an axe.

The grandfathers spotted minnows in a bomb crater filled with water. Ong Truong ordered one of the youngest boys to dig for worms. A half-hour later, the boy brought a small basket of night crawlers to his elders. The grandfathers had bamboo poles, fishing line made of green worms, and various-sized hooks made of sewing needles. Ong Truong and the boy fished the canal for catfish and carp. They caught a few small ones, but these would not be eaten any time soon. They dropped them in a bucket, and Ong Truong carried them to the crater, the fishpond. If grandfather had hooked something large in the canal, the villagers would have enjoyed fish for dinner. These immature ones could have been eaten today, added to soup or rice, but they would be more useful once they multiplied and grew.

Thien and other village girls carried basins and dirty clothes to the south bank of the canal. Watching the sky, heads dipping and rising like those of birds, they filled the basins with water, squatted, and added pinches of powdered soap. *Noi chuyen*, they chattered, cleaned, and Ba Ly—more an overseer than a worker—sang a patriotic song:

> *Each night the snake emerges from his hole,*
> *the spider spins a new web.*
> *The moon rises, the owl cries.*
> *The enemy sees and hears nothing;*
> *we live safely by his side.*

The smallest girl thought she heard helicopters and planes. She hid herself in the shadow of a bush until Ba Ly held her and talked to her and convinced her the sky was clear.

Hai and Nhi remembered their mother as they worked. Struggling to concentrate on their tasks, they rarely spoke, and paused only for occasional sips of water. They wondered if Ma Xuan was alive. Hai, cutting bamboo for the animal shelter, told himself they should make their way to Cu Chi, sneak onto the American base, and find out if the day ghost surgeons had saved her. Since the base was fifty kilometers away, the grandfathers were unlikely to grant permission. As one of the oldest boys, Hai was needed as much as anyone to make this village a place where they could live, or attempt to live. He was expected to provide guidance, leadership, and to be a model for every boy younger than himself.

He whispered to Nhi, who was sprinkling lettuce seeds on a patch of orange earth: "Maybe we should go to Cu Chi, try and find Ma."

Nhi did not pause in her task. "Ma will find us when she recovers." She glanced at him, then looked toward the huts, the fields, the mountain. "This is our home now. Ma would be very angry with us if we failed to do our part."

But in the late afternoon Hai asked Ong Quan for permission.

"You already know the answer," said Ong. "I cannot allow you or anyone to leave until this settlement is established."

Hai looked at the ground.

"You have a wife here, many people to protect. Do you understand?"

"Yes, Ong."

"Soon you will be a father, your wife will give birth. You will make your contribution and help all of us survive."

They squatted side-by-side in a grove of bamboo. The

tall stalks, fence-like, cast slats of shadow on the ground. *A father?* thought Hai. *A birth? How could this be?* Last night eight villagers slept in Hai's hut, and no one had time to arrange curtains, partitions. His wife's five-year-old cousin had nestled his way onto the reed mat between Hai and Thien. Once, Hai reached over the sleeping boy to touch his wife's hair, her forehead. *Dep, dep qua*, too lovely. He pulled back, his hands tucked under his head as a pillow. Hai spent much of the night sucking at the soft flesh of his gums, the tender spot where his tooth was missing. He wanted to touch his wife's hips, her breasts, but how could he? For a long time he forgot his mother. A child lay between him and his wife, but Hai did not hate this child because he did not yet know how much beauty he could take.

Presently, waiting for Ong to dismiss him, he thought more of Ma than of Thien. He had watched the prisoner carry his mother to a helicopter, but he could not conceive of a Vietnamese person other than a puppet soldier flying off in a machine—*may bay chuong chuong*. The dragonflies looked identical, swarmed the sky like oversized insects, and one of them had killed Hai's father. How could Ma have flown off this way? Was she still alive? Did someone save her? She had survived long enough to see his wedding, to welcome a daughter-in-law, but now Hai doubted he would see her again, his living mother. The spine, the bones in the center of the body, are called *xuong song*, river of life, and his had grown strong in her presence. Partly through Ma he knew the dignity of animals, the strength and beauty of the land: banyan tree, buffalo and bird, tall bamboo. Hai had difficulty absorbing the contradictions. His mother was near; he could feel her steadiness, her gift of strength. But he knew in the firm center of his body Ma Xuan no longer breathed.

"Come on," said Ong Quan. "I'll show you how to cut bamboo." He gestured to the adjacent bamboo grove. "Follow me," he said. "We'll cut the tallest bamboo we can find."

Hai carried the double-handled saw that had to be worked

by two people. Ong selected a bamboo trunk, took one of the handles, and they began sawing. Hai was surprised by the old man's strength and agility. Rocking forward and back, Ong set the pace, and the boy struggled to match him. When Ong leaned back Hai leaned forward, and when Ong leaned forward Hai felt himself being pushed as though a small but concentrated wind entered the center of his sternum. Ong, still working, said, "You can look for your mother and tend ancestral graves once our village is established. I don't want to wake one morning and discover you are gone."

Hai looked away, let go of the saw.

"What's this?" said Ong. "What are you doing?"

"Ma's dead," said the boy. "Already gone."

Ong glared at him. "You would not know this."

I would, he said silently, for he could not openly confront his elder.

"Back to work," said Ong. "You have much to work for. You have a wife, you are married, and soon you will have a son."

A few minutes later the teeth of the saw severed the long trunk of the bamboo. "Come," said Ong Quan, "we'll tie it to Qui's buffalo cart. Tonight I give you permission to take your wife to the fields."

At dusk, women lit lanterns under trees. Jungle moths flew toward the light and women and children caught them with cupped hands. They removed the wings, placed the bodies in jars, fastened the jars with lids. After they captured many moths, the women brought the jars inside the huts and killed the moths by jabbing pointed sticks through their abdomens. Each hut had a small fire pit, a few stones topped by a grate. The girl-children helped their mothers barbecue jungle moths over flames.

After dinner, Luu Hai held his wife's hand, led her along a rice bund, and past a small grove of coconut palms. Ong Quan had ordered Hai to stay within sixty meters of the new village. "Just go far enough away," he grinned, "that we won't hear you and your wife thrashing in the grass."

Wife? The boy did not know how to behave, how to be a husband. By instinct he knew what he wanted: the bowl of Le Minh Thien's hips, the darkness he was allowed to touch now, the swellings in her chest that startled him, that might fit his two hands. Each part of Thien confused him. Even her fingers, her arm, the flared bones of her shoulder. How could he hold shapes that were more complicated? His wife's breasts, for instance. Or her hips, the widest hips of any girl in the village. Hai did not know what commands to give his body. Holding her hand, he limped, dragged his left leg for no physical reason. "Are you hurt?" said Thien. "Is something wrong?" The boy straightened, cleared his throat, and said, "*Khong sao*" (No problem). But a few moments later he was limping again, aware that he did not know how to behave.

Hai led her to a fallow field adjacent the newly transplanted *ma* rice. Thien knew what a wife was supposed to do: take off her clothes, lie down on her back, open her legs, wait for the baby to come and hope for a boy to please her husband and her village. She was supposed to lie still tonight and every night, invite her husband's pleasure. But what if the weight and thrashing of his body tired her? What if he hurt her? Ba Ly had whispered to Thien on the morning of her wedding: "Just lie still, don't fight him. After he rolls over and starts snoring, you'll have the rest of the night to nurse your wound."

But she was curious. She felt a subtle warmth circle outward from the center of her body. Her belly ached slightly, the inner sides of her thighs tingled. Had her grandma ever felt this way? *No*, thought Thien, *never*. She pictured Ba Ly chewing betel nut, half-smiling, spitting the red juice onto a clump of dry grass.

Hai wondered what to do with his hands. In the unplanted field, he turned to his wife and began rubbing her shoulders.

The girl with the widest hips in the village surprised him: in some places she was bony, angular, as smooth and hard as plaited bamboo. They glanced at each other, their faces dark, and then Thien looked at the mountain. When she asked Hai if he knew the story of how Black Virgin Mountain got its name, he said, "Twice my mother told me." A dark woman, a virgin, was raped and killed, and for many years her spirit did not allow any man to come near *Nui Ba Den*, this mountain that rose from paddies. "Now men come near her," said Hai. "She no longer twists their heads until they turn away from her body." The summit was at least four kilometers away, but rose high enough to be seen from a far greater distance. Hai rubbed his wife's shoulders until Thien whispered, "*Chong lam gi?*" (What is husband doing?) Stretching, arching forward, she let his hands slip down her shoulders to the tops of her breasts.

His middle part pressed against her stomach. She felt the heat of him, the line of tension, the tremor in his thighs. She stooped and spread a reed mat over the grass. She didn't know if the field or her body still held the sun's warmth, and as Luu Hai glanced away, his arms limp at his sides, she understood his fear. Who would they be, how much would they change, before sunrise? Thien lay on her side, slid a hand under the mat, and removed a small stone.

Still standing, Hai looked at the fallow field, the sky, the pyramid shape of *Nui Ba Den*, the woman who stayed black, pure black, who did not soften in starlight. *Day la nha toi*, he thought, *my wife is my home*. One could introduce a spouse this way: *Day la nha toi* (She is my home, my refuge). Presently, he did not look at Thien because it was easier to watch the sky, the field, the great mountain that frightened him less than the body of his wife.

"Buffalo have worked here," he blurted.

"Hai?"

"In this field," he said. "And they will work here again once we pull the weeds and make a flood."

He lay near her, but he could not look at her directly. He rubbed her left elbow and began to memorize the various angles, the bones that reminded him of field rocks. River rocks were worn smooth, but the bones of Thien's elbow had irregular edges. He rubbed them until he felt their warmth through the cloth of her shirt. On his side, head tilted, he counted the bright stars over her body. *Mot, hai, ba, bon, nam...* "Hai," she whispered, "*chong.*" She leaned forward and kissed his left cheek.

He watched the sky as Thien unbuttoned her shirt. Planes flew over far to the north. They heard bombs, muffled explosions, but the earth around them lay silent. Hai glanced at his wife's breasts. "Run," he said weakly, "if a plane or helicopter comes close. We may have to split up if a helicopter shines a light."

Half naked, Thien lifted her legs and began to remove her pants. "Hai," she said, "please. While there's time."

Undressed, they lay side-by-side. Hai again touched her elbow, the bones he had begun to study, the contours partly memorized. She rested a hand on his abdomen, the hollow beneath his rib cage. She knew she was supposed to lie on her back, wait for him, but she didn't. "*Chong?*" she said. "May I?" Her husband seemed mute, so she grabbed the shank of his middle part in her left hand.

She could not touch him here for long. This strange growth, tree-shaped, mushroom-shaped, that extended like a second body. *A brother*, thought Thien, *a new brother. Smooth hard muscle.* The muscle stood firm in a sheath of skin so soft she could not believe it. She pulled her hand away, then touched him once more to feel what was true. At birth, her own cheek could not have been much softer. But here there was softness and something else—a tree shape, a mushroom strong and smooth that she would have explored further had she forgotten Ba Ly's instructions. The new wife did as her grandma told her: she lay on her back, legs open. Hai was making odd sounds, groping for breasts and pressing his tongue into the place where his tooth was missing. He rubbed his face against his wife's neck, her cheeks, her breasts. He wanted to memorize her, every softness, every bone, but he knew as he kissed her that she was larger than the field, larger than the mountain, that he could not touch the edges of this one body. A breath caught in her throat as he clumsily entered her. Hai filled her, burst with seed, but his middle part stayed swollen. Thien had not expected him to pause a few puzzled moments before he relaxed, continued. She felt his fear leave him as he rubbed against her more gently. Rocking, thrusting her hips, she gripped the small of his back. All his days and nights near animals, all his days spent in fields, he gave to his wife who let her hips flare, her legs rise high, the earth warm and moist beneath her, her feet pointed toward mountain and stars.

30
Sound and Light

Maybe he was religious. He believed in his wounds, his scars, his ability to survive, *demonios y santos*. More than once Mama told him if he did what was right, what the Virgin of Guadalupe approved of, he would receive divine assistance. At the chopper pad he saw grunts who resembled waifs, boys with no scars, no powerful wounds, no meaningful support. They sat on rucksacks, smoked cigarettes, read comic books and dime-store novels, or they lay flat on their backs in hot sun, their forearms over their eyes, poor grunts with nothing better to hope for than a few moments of amnesia. For where they were headed they needed saints, scars, claw marks, but most would receive the opposite. Mines, booby traps, Billie Jasper's fate, unspeakable pain and misery. They had no lucky charms, nothing to assist them. Simple grunts, they probably knew they were unlikely to survive the war.

He avoided the lieutenants, the platoon leaders with sergeant stripes, anyone who would ask questions. He chose a boy he could trust: *un vato*, a home boy, a lit cigarette in his mouth, dark shades, a crucifix and a tarantula etched in blue ink on his left forearm. Vato had the look of an urban warrior, a real smooth *soldero*, somebody who would be dangerous and respected if he ever made it back to his *barrio*. Head tilted, sitting on his rucksack, breathing smoke, he seemed to fix his eyes at some point in the distant sky.

"Hey," said Conchola, "where's the war today? *Adónde vamos?*" He licked his lips, stepped closer. "Some bad shit all around," he said. "But I hear this unit is heading west."

"*Oeste*," said Vato. "East, west. Who gives a fuck?"

"I do," said Conchola. "Like to know where I might die."

Vato peered at him over the top of his shades.

"Serious," said Conchola. "East or west, man? Just give me a direction."

"Who the fuck are you?"

"Gertrudis Villanueva, your new medic." He squatted, hunched over. "Got transferred, man. Had this captain who pissed me off, finally lost my patience." He held up his bandaged hand. "*Pelea*," he said, "but you should see the captain. I doubt his own wife, *pobrecita*, will recognize the poor motherfucker's face."

Vato smiled and offered Conchola a cigarette.

"How far west?" said Conchola. "They tell you?"

Vato shrugged, drew on his cigarette. "West of Tan Ninh, they say. Do or die. Cambodian border."

Conchola smiled and nodded. "Pretty scenery. I've been there."

"Do or die," said Vato. "*Qué más puedo decir?*"

Conchola couldn't stop smiling. The Virgin intercedes, she does. You step on the right path *y la gracia viene*, lifts you with wings. Being captured was an advantage, being picked up by a chopper another advantage. He wished he could thank the Mama-san and say he was sorry for how she died, how it ended. Like the Cu Chi grunts, she lacked charms, scars, basic protection. Without claw marks, grace marks, one entered a jungle or forest or even a simple field with little chance to survive.

Vato was crinkling his nose, scowling. "I got to tell you, man, I'm sorry, but you smell like you pissed your pants."

"Yeah," said Conchola, "I need a shower. Some food, too. Where can I scrounge some Cs?"

He gathered his rations, loaded them in his rucksack, then sidled away and sat near a sandbagged hooch till the choppers arrived. Head down, he fought the wind of the blades, hurried to the last chopper with Vato and five other grunts, and he was smiling, restraining laughter, thanking the Virgin of

Guadalupe and Saint Francis and Saint Jude as he made his way on board.

Paisaje. The Cu Chi countryside, seen from the sky, was a maze of tree bones, skeletons of branches, black stumps, charred hedgerows. And there were bomb craters, some filled with water, most empty and dry, their edges almost touching. The fields were now ghost fields. Conchola saw few peasants in black pajamas, few Mama-sans and Papa-sans, few buffalo boys and buffalo. "Best to leave all this shit behind," he said, but Vato wasn't listening. "Go farther out," said Conchola, "*lejos.* It's not so bad once you make your way farther out."

In the sky over Tay Ninh, the sky near Black Virgin Mountain, the medic looked down on fields and trees. The peasants, those who unwittingly helped him, were hidden somewhere below, in the few corners of land that hadn't been ravaged. The fields, where they were green, shone so brightly Conchola shaded his eyes. He wanted this light for Billie, for the dead Mama-san, for whoever still needed it. To the west he could see jungle, or what appeared as jungle. Thick domes of trees, a mass of foliage. Most likely the area had been bombed repeatedly, but some places fought back, became nearly un-killable. *Can't bury every gook*, he thought, *every root and claw. The most determined animals always find a way to survive.*

Vato nudged him and said, "Where's your weapon? I don't see no weapon."

"I'm a medic. Already told you."

"Yeah, *estúpido. Loco.* Titties on a bull."

The choppers came down in an auspicious place, elephant grass perfect to disappear in. Any grunt but Conchola hated it, its sharp edges, the way it sliced skin, razored clothes, the way it fought the passage of any human or animal that wasn't blessed with skin thick as leather. Conchola got cut, his arms bled, but he didn't mind. Coming in, he saw the tree line to the west, and now as the grunts in front of him began moving in the opposite direction, he lay still in eight-foot-high grass. In a few seconds the platoon vanished. He pictured soldiers bunching up, moving as a team, wiping the sweat from their eyes and following each other's tail to whatever sorry place their commanders had sent them. He heard Vato cursing, fighting the terrain, heard the choppers as they rose and receded. Then he was alone, no sound in the air but the drone of insects. He rose and began walking west through the ocean of grass.

At dusk he reached a river. On a muddy bank he studied hoof marks, probably deer. He heard frogs croaking and hopping; he searched for them in shadows. He imagined catching one, building a small fire, roasting frog-meat on a stick. He bent low and saw a beetle, a spider the size of his palm, but he didn't see any frogs, only heard them. He opened a can of ham and limas, a can of chicken, and ate with his fingers. The water darkened, almost black now. No trace of light under the trees on the far shore.

He couldn't swim the river with his rucksack. He took out his Cs, his peaches and pound cake, fruit cocktail, cans of chicken. He would toss all this good stuff to the other side, his medical supplies too, then paddle with one arm while holding his rucksack above water. Maybe the other side was Cambodia, *tierra salvaje*. He wished he had something that only a human being needed—a map. He would bury it once he arrived, once he found the tiger's pugmarks along a stream or in a clearing. After he reentered Cambodia he would change course, move north toward the jungles of Parrot's Beak, one of the insertion points of the Cambodian invasion. At present he was maybe fifty kilometers from the stream where he and Billie first saw the tiger, where he first longed for something he could not fathom. A wild animal, the light of tree shade, the glare of eyes, the wounds that became blessings. Some wounds blessed, others killed, so you had to pay attention. *Lo siento, Billie, fooled by a tame elephant. The most dangerous things are things that can be controlled.*

He held a can of pound cake like a baseball, drew back his arm, but had to hit the ground before he could throw. A shot rang out, then three more. He heard someone behind him slithering through a swale of grass. "Lupe," said Conchola, "Geronimo," his voice tender, amazed. Within seconds he had shed his boots and belly-crawled down the bank and into the river. He heard voices, Vietnamese, and then the firing came from several directions. Bullets ripped through water, blazed through trees and brush on the far shore. Conchola, trying to give the impression that he had comrades, men on his flanks, called, "*Compañeros, compañeros*! *Vengan*!" He sucked a deep breath, went under, plunged through darkness. Unencumbered—no rations or supplies—he moved with powerful thrusts, with the sweep of arms, the surge of currents. He rose to breathe, shots rang out, but they were off target. The VC must have been afraid of coming too close, afraid he had comrades in hidden places. Again he dove, thrust his arms and legs, but the river did most of the work, carried him where it was going. He passed to the other side and belly-crawled up a steep bank. There were stars above the water now, a few stars above the trees.

He lay on his back and rested in marsh grass. If he was in Cambodia, he would have to move north now, keep moving until he entered a vast jungle, and maybe move farther until he found a place not yet bombed, a place where his *maestro*, the tiger, might have found refuge. He was not sure which star was the North Star. The sky seemed too uniform, the stars too much alike, and maybe the one in the north was hidden from view by the trees along the river. Conchola wanted to know the patterns of the sky. He wanted to know everything beyond his skin, and now he knew just enough to know he knew nothing. *Mysterio*, he thought, *that's all I have. What else is there*? He carried the essentials: his wounds, his longing, his hunger that was not for food. His senses were alert, he had no fatigue. He almost spoke aloud, "This is beautiful, *enorme*. The world beyond the skin."

He got up, swatted at mosquitoes, removed the bandage from his left hand. He remembered Billie's wounds, pictured them, and wondered why his friend didn't have better luck, why he himself was graced with nine lives, maybe more, whereas Billie died without warning. He pictured the elephant and the girl who led it along the path beside the canal. His captors had a new ville, a few shacks, but he doubted they would live there for long before being discovered, bombed, forced to flee. Like him they would move west, cross the border, search for a place that hadn't been ravaged. Dignified animals, they wouldn't stop, wouldn't give in, wouldn't say, "No, this is too hard, we are better off dying." He remembered their bull buffalo carried part of a field, wedges of rice planted in baskets, and though their buffalo might be killed, though some of the buffalo boys and peasants might be killed, others would survive and have the strength to move themselves and their field—some fragment of earth that sustained them. Maybe they'd capture him again, tie him to the elephant's cart, drag him westward. Without trying, they already helped him, and the chopper going west with Vato gave him a free lift, carried him farther than he had hoped for. His Uncle Mundo would be proud, Billie too, but his Mama would worry. Conchola wished she could hear his voice: *Escúchame, no te preocupas. Estoy vivo.* He knelt on the shore, dipped his hands in water. *Alive, Mama. More than you will ever know.*

The sky darkened and more stars appeared. He stood, again tried to orient himself by the North Star, but he wasn't sure which one assisted a traveler without a compass. That's what he was now, a traveler, an explorer, not a medic, not a soldier. He had no bandages, no rifle, no supplies. *Nada.* His hand tingled, throbbed, but he had no medicine. Amazing how much pain from a sliver of metal, a knife the size of a gnat. He thought of Billie's wounds, the wounds of his *maestro*, and they in no way seemed bearable. His throat and then his chest softened, ached—a signal to pray. He held his wounded hand palm up to the sky.

Prayers came partly in silence, partly in whispers, and maybe the world was intimate enough that all beings listened. Antonio Lucio had faith. He believed in *La Virgen de Guadalupe*, in *Jesús y María*, in Saint Francis and Saint Jude, and he believed in ghosts, *fantasmas*, in presences that lingered when bodies were abruptly broken. Human ghosts, animal ghosts, tree ghosts, water ghosts—they might listen. He looked up past the crowns of trees to the sky, the stars. The only truth he could tell was stripped to a few utterable words, words he prayed to his Mama and the Virgin, and the unknown sky above them. "*Sencillo*," he said, "more simple than we imagine. The world is mostly made of wounds, more than can be counted. Beauty is what surprises us. A tooth, a claw. A body of sound and light."

He searched the heavens for the North Star. "*Maestro*," he said, and walked in beauty toward tall trees.

ACKNOWLEDGEMENTS

I am deeply grateful for Maxine Hong Kingston and the Veterans' Writing Group, and for Marg Starbuck and Bill Boykin who have offered their home as a place for us to write. Many thanks to Therese Fitzgerald, Carole Melkonian, and Sherdyl (Charlie) Motz for their work in founding this group, and to Thich Nhat Hanh, a Vietnamese monk, for his support of American veterans of the Viet Nam War.

The generosity and friendship of Scoby Beer and Vicki Dern added much to this book. Mil gracias to Jeremiah Calvillo who helped me to better understand Antonio Conchola and myself. I also wish to thank Paola Dovholuk, Eraca, Reiko Fujii, Ellen Garms, Daphne Hardesty, Tom Janko and family, Jackie Karp, Mary, Michael Job, Eddie S. Kasik II, Pat Mayo, the Miura-Raffa family, Robin Rose, Joan Siebert and family, Brian Sheppard, Michele McDonald-Smith, and Steven Smith.

A big thanks to Victoria Shoemaker, my agent, to Jim Coleman, Sandy Taylor and Judith Doyle, and to the staff at Curbstone Press. *Mil gracias* to Maria Proser for her help with the Spanish phrases.

The Vietnamese chapters of this book could not have been written without the help of many. A bow of gratitude to Xuan N. Evans, to Le Minh Quan, rice farmer and *xich lo* driver, and to the family of Huyun Thieu Qui and Chi Long, especially Chau Gai Minh. I thank Nong Trieu for twice taking the time to tell me how he made fishing line from green worms. I thank two former Viet Cong soldiers, combatants in the Cu Chi tunnels, for trusting me enough to tell me of their experience, and for introducing me to the present-day Cu Chi countryside. I also wish to thank Anh Lam San, Trang My Duyen, Minh Hoa Ta, and Trang Luong for taking the time to answer my many questions.

The following books about Viet Nam were helpful in my research: *After Sorrow: An American Among the Vietnamese* by Lady Borton; *Monkey Bridge* by Lan Cao;

When Heaven and Earth Changed Places by Le Ly Hayslip; *The Other Side of Heaven: Post-War Fiction by Vietnamese and American Writers*, edited by Wayne Karlin, Le M. Khue, and Truong Vu; *A Viet Cong Memoir* by Truong Nhu Tang (with David Chanoff and Doan Van Toai); *Ca Doa Viet Nam: A Bilingual Anthology of Vietnamese Folk Poetry* edited by John Balaban; *Viet Nam: A Traveler's Literary Companion* edited by John Balaban; *Kim Van Kieu* by Nguyen Du (with translation and commentaries by Le Xuan Thuy); *Catfish and Mandala* by Andrew X. Pham; *Understanding Viet Nam* by Neil L. Jamieson; *Southwind Changing* by Jade Ngoc Quang Huynh; *Paradise of the Blind* by Doung Thu Huong; *The Stars, The Earth, The River* by Le Minh Khue.

Kristen Pelzer's essay, *On Defining Vietnamese Religions: Reflections on Bruce Matthew's Article*, helped me to gain a clearer understanding of the role of ancestors in Vietnamese religions.

Any shortcomings in representing certain Vietnamese peasants in the Cu Chi countryside in 1970 are my own.

Long ago, my teachers in the College of Natural Resources at UC Berkeley inspired in me a great respect for the natural world. I am especially thankful for Alan Miller and Arnold Schultz.

A U.S. Department of Agriculture publication, *The Seen and Unseen World of the Fallen Tree*, edited by Chris Maser and James M. Trappe, investigates arboreal ecosystems. The main implication of this study—the union of life and death—rooted its way into *Buffalo Boy and Geronimo*.

The following books on animals aided my research: *Elephants, Majestic Creatures of the Wild*, consulting editor Jeheskel Shoshani Ph. D.; *When Elephants Weep* by Jeffrey Moussaieff Masson and Susan McCarthy; *Tigers* by Jean Pierre Zwaenepoel; *Tigers in the Snow* by Peter Matthiessen (which provides an overview of eight tiger subspecies, including the species once abundant in Southeast Asia); *The Animals of Southeast Asia* by

Margaret Ayer; *Lizards of the World* by Chris Mattison.

Although I studied with great interest the animals portrayed in this book, I am by no means a zoologist or wildlife biologist. My purpose is to communicate something of the beauty and mystery of the beasts.

For places to write I thank Punya, Rick, and Sidney Droz of Phnom Penh, Ellen Minotti of Phnom Penh, Kate Beckwith of San Francisco, Elliot Roth of San Francisco, Lisa Wagner and Brian Pilipavicius of San Francisco, Lillian Hoika of the Ukiah mountains of California, and my parents of La Salle, Illinois.

A bow to you, Chanpidor, my sweet wife, and to *Mak* and my Cambodian family.

ABOUT THE AUTHOR

In the Viet Nam War, James Janko was a medic for the 25th Infantry (2nd of the 27th Battalion, Company C) in 1970. His platoon operated primarily in the Cu Chi and Tay Ninh areas, including Nui Ba Den, Black Virgin Mountain. In May of 1970, his platoon was part of the Cambodian invasion.

His post-war experience has been varied. He has been a taxi-driver, a flower vender, and a strawberry picker. For more than thirteen years (1979-1993), he worked alone as a night watchman on Alcatraz Island. Solitude suited his post-war temperament.

He studied Conservation of Natural Resources at UC-Berkeley and graduated in 1979. He notes that his love of the natural world and his wish for peace are the forces behind his writing *Buffalo Boy and Geronimo*. He has long been interested in the natural landscapes of Southeast Asia and its once abundant wild animal populations—elephants, tigers, monkeys.

James Janko comments that it took him nearly thirty years to discover the beauty and dignity of the people that he and his country once defined as the enemy.

He began writing *Buffalo Boy and Geronimo* in Maxine Hong Kingston's celebrated Veteran Writers' Workshop, in which he has participated since June of 1993.

Currently he teaches at City College of San Francisco and lives with his wife, Uong Chanpidor, in Oakland, California. His stories have appeared in numerous literary journals.

CURBSTONE PRESS, INC.

is a non-profit publishing house dedicated to literature that reflects a commitment to social change, with an emphasis on contemporary writing from Latino, Latin American and Vietnamese cultures. Curbstone presents writers who give voice to the unheard in a language that goes beyond denunciation to celebrate, honor and teach. Curbstone builds bridges between its writers and the public – from inner-city to rural areas, colleges to community centers, children to adults. Curbstone seeks out the highest aesthetic expression of the dedication to human rights and intercultural understanding: poetry, testimonies, novels, stories, and children's books.

This mission requires more than just producing books. It requires ensuring that as many people as possible learn about these books and read them. To achieve this, a large portion of Curbstone's schedule is dedicated to arranging tours and programs for its authors, working with public school and university teachers to enrich curricula, reaching out to underserved audiences by donating books and conducting readings and community programs, and promoting discussion in the media. It is only through these combined efforts that literature can truly make a difference.

Curbstone Press, like all non-profit presses, depends on the support of individuals, foundations, and government agencies to bring you, the reader, works of literary merit and social significance which might not find a place in profit-driven publishing channels, and to bring the authors and their books into communities across the country. Our sincere thanks to the many individuals, foundations, and government agencies who have recently supported this endeavor: Community Foundation of Northeast Connecticut, Connecticut Commission on Culture & Tourism, Connecticut Humanities Council, Greater Hartford Arts Council, Hartford Courant Foundation, Lannan Foundation, National Endowment for the Arts, and the United Way of the Capital Area.

Please help to support Curbstone's efforts to present the diverse voices and views that make our culture richer. Tax-deductible donations can be made by check or credit card to:
Curbstone Press, 321 Jackson Street, Willimantic, CT 06226
phone: (860) 423-5110   fax: (860) 423-9242
www.curbstone.org

IF YOU WOULD LIKE TO BE A MAJOR SPONSOR OF A CURBSTONE BOOK, PLEASE CONTACT US.